3-91

Note by Note

A Guide to Concert Production

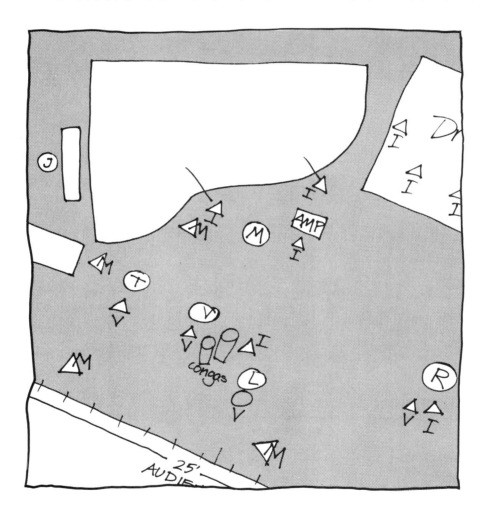

Written by Redwood Cultural Work, Community Music, and Friends

Edited by Joanie Shoemaker

Book design by Pamela Wilson Design Studio

Published and distributed by

Redwood Cultural Work

P.O. Box 10408

Oakland, CA 94610

(415) 428-9191

FAX Number (415) 652-5012

ACKNOWLEDGEMENTS

It is hard to know where to begin to acknowledge the hard work of all the people who have contributed to this concert production guide over a period of years. This book has passed through many stages and many hands; it has been a labor of love for the individuals who cared enough to donate their time and energy to make sure it happened.

The book began in the mid-seventies when Holly Near and Amy Horowitz wrote a few pages called *How to Produce a Concert* to mail to new producers who were working with Holly. Several years later, Redwood Records received a grant to hire someone to write an expanded guide to concert production. This became Ginny Z. Berson's much-loved and well-used book *Making a Show of It*, which went out of print in 1985.

At that point, Redwood Cultural Work (RCW), formerly Redwood Records Cultural and Educational Fund, decided to create an updated concert production guide. Si Kahn and Cathy Fink's tour to benefit the National Campaign against Toxic Waste in 1985 was helped by using their personalized addenda to the older book. This experience was the inspiration for Cathy Fink and Sheila Kahn of Community Music to join forces with RCW in the research, writing, development, and publicizing of the book.

Although many people are identified as contributors by each chapter, there were several whose contributions are seen throughout. Their help was invaluable to the book's formation. Amy Bank wrote the first drafts of most chapters for us. The writing, community involvement, and logistics were guided by several dedicated individuals: Amy Bank, Marti Mogensen, Carrie Koeturius, Jo Durand, and Joelle Yuna. Jeanne Bradshaw of Great American Music Hall and Jo-Lynne Worley of Redwood Records were instrumental to this project through their contributions of knowledge and forms, and their work on the development of this book. Caryn Dickman and Peggy Kiss contributed hundreds of hours of development work by computerizing the drafts.

We especially want to thank Joelle Yuna for the exceptional amount of time and energy she put into the final stretch, bringing the book to publication. Without her work, this book would not have been completed. Thank you also to Martha Ley, who did a great deal of editorial work in the final stages, and to Pam Wilson, who designed the cover and final format for the book.

Many thanks are due to those who critiqued the whole book when it was finally assembled: Torie Osborn, Katie Schlageter, Virginia Giordano, Nona Gandelman, Brynna Fish, Jo Durand, Dulce Arguelles, Cathy Fink, and Sheila Kahn.

Acknowledgements

The book would not have been possible without the much-needed financial assistance we received. We gratefully thank and acknowledge the contributions of: Maya Miller, Joelle Yuna, Susan Anderson, Bette Shulman, Jeanette Paroly, Robbie Osman, Jo Durand, Casey Kasem, Virginia Fine, Paul C. Butler, Chris Pereira, Carrie Koeturius, and Christine Padesky. Danielle Green and Holly Near presented fundraising events in Berkeley, California and Kansas City, Missouri, to benefit the production.

Many thanks to the volunteers and staff of Redwood Records and RCW who have had a big hand in the book's development and completion through the years. They will now have a new role in being instrumental in its distribution and promotion.

Finally, we want to acknowledge the motivation provided by Holly Near's constant encouragement for us to finish this new version. For the many producers who kept asking *"When will the book be ready?"*, this book is dedicated to you!

PREFACE

Twelve years ago I was a fledgling producer in Kansas City, Missouri, trying to learn quickly how to produce my first concert with Jo-Lynne Worley. We received a packet from Amy Horowitz, giving us some brief notes on how to "do outreach" and what color gels to use for the concert with Holly Near and Jeff Langley. They were great notes, and the concert was quite a success. In the tradition of those notes, and of *Making a Show of It*, by Ginny Z. Berson (which Redwood Records published in 1980 with the help of a grant), this book is dedicated to the producers, organizations, artists, and students who need it.

If you are a new producer, an organization considering a benefit concert, an artist who wants to perform for non-profit organizations or special audiences, or a curious onlooker who may want to dabble, please let the book be your guide -- and don't be intimidated. We have tried to pack lots of information into what we hope is a readable format. (We would like your feedback on how this book works for you; please fill out the last form in the back of the book and send it to us.)

This book is also for the experienced producer who wants a brush-up, a fresh idea, or who wants to use some of the forms.

And we hope it will be useful as a text for workshops, seminars, and college courses.

A production is the weaving of dozens of elements and people creating a finely patterned fabric. Just as it is hard to find a single thread in the fabric, so it has been difficult to isolate the elements of this guide. Thumb through the Table of Contents -- the titles of each chapter describe the chapter's main element. The resource section lists books and other sources for further information. And the glossary defines many of the more technical terms that are scattered throughout the chapters.

The chapters are treated chronologically, beginning with what you as the producer need to consider first as you begin the thoughtful, creative planning stages of concert production. With time and experience you will recognize when and how to combine steps, extend the timeline, or manipulate the pieces so they work best for each event.

The forms are referenced in each chapter and numbered with the chapter number first, but they are placed together in the back of the guide along with a complete listing for convenience.

We think this is a book you'll want to use as a reference guide -- feel free to make copies of the forms and use them *as is* or adapt them to fit your needs better. You may want to cut the binding off, punch holes in the book, and put it in a ring binder for easier use as a manual.

Some information is subject to change, and you'll need to check for revised data (like visa regulations) or local/regional prices instead of using the *national ballparks* we have provided.

This book is a guide, a tool for you to use and make relevant to your particular circumstances. We have tried to make it informal, readable, flexible, and, above all, practical. We truly welcome your feedback and plan that future editions will incorporate reader suggestions.

We have written from our experiences, and we've involved many writers and readers to broaden that experience as much as possible. However, our biases come through -- as artists, artists representatives, record labels, non-profit presenters, community-based organizations, fundraisers. We hope you can apply the correct cultural and professional screens you need to present your event your way.

It is tremendously satisfying to produce successful events, and gravely disappointing to fall short of your expectations. We hope this production guide can assist you as you weave together the fabric of many fine events.

Joanie Shoemaker
Editor

INTRODUCTION

by Holly Near

The phone rings. My manager interrupts our meeting to take the call.

"Would Holly be interested in doing a concert for an environmental issue? We feel that a concert would allow us to bring our issue to public attention as well as provide a wonderful energy boost for the community."

Jo-Lynne Worley answers, "Holly is very interested in doing such an event. Have you ever produced a concert before?"

I can tell by her face the answer is no. Her head leans heavily on her hand. Some callers do not realize what they are asking. They do not know what it means to produce a concert. They are not just asking if I will arrive and offer my voice and spirit to the event -- they are asking to be trained in the complex field of concert production. Of course, we could let them discover this for themselves, but such a lesson will cost them a lot of time and money and could possibly result in an event that disappoints the community rather than inspiring the audience to get involved in environmental issues.

Daily Redwood Cultural Work gets calls from students, community organizers, women's movement leaders, artists, managers, agents, and peace activists asking for consultation and help as they pursue their commitment to present conscientious culture. They are in search of well-worn paths. And they are right; why repeat the mistakes those of us who have been doing this for years have learned from long ago?

And so, after four years of writing by many organizers and producers . . . the book I've been waiting for! I want it to be mandatory reading for all the producers I work with so I'll know we are meeting on common ground.

The presentation of music (as well as the other arts) deserves to be handled with tender love and care. I try to bring that respect to my work every time I walk on stage, appear on a rally platform, or stand before a class. Music, dance, film all have the power to affect our lives . . . for better or for worse . . . and we have a magnificent opportunity as we do this work to offer our communities cultural experiences dedicated "for the better."

I want to trust that the promoters/producers/organizers will plan the event with the same care and respect with which we approach our responsibilities for the presentation. We find, in most cases, that that is their desire. The missing link has often been the step-by-step pragmatic information.

Here, we have joined together the years and years of experience of many fine cultural workers to create a guide to concert production. I hope it can be a friend to you, a book you can read in the middle of the night when you dream and scheme about the events you would like to present in your community, your town, your city, your school. I especially hope you will choose to work with music as a major part of your commitment to world peace and social justice. If we can become fascinated by each other's differences rather than afraid of our rich diversity, we will have made a great contribution to creating a world based on understanding and co-existence rather than a nightmare based on war.

I look forward to being one of the lucky artists you present with the skill and grace you will obtain from working with this book.

TABLE OF CONTENTS

Acknowledgements

Preface

Introduction *by Holly Near*

CHAPTER ONE

Setting the Stage for Success

Contributors Amy Bank, Cathy Fink, Sheila Kahn, Torie Osborn

Producing a concert can be a challenging, delightful, and sometimes, even lucrative experience. Or, it can be a time-consuming, expensive, and emotionally draining nightmare. This book is written by many skilled and experienced people who know how to produce good concerts and see dreams fulfilled. So if you are a community organizer who wants to put on educational or fundraising events, a music lover who wants to bring your favorite artist to town, or a professional producer who wants to improve your skills or expand your audience, this book is for you. Use it as a guide; it will serve you well.

Setting Goals
Think for a few moments before you commit yourself to producing a concert. Why are you producing a concert? Establish some goals right from the start. This will enable you to chart a clear course of action as well as evaluate your work. Remember, once you begin, there is no way to recover the time and money spent if you change your mind midstream and decide to cancel the event. You also will lose credibility with your potential audience and the artists. You may even be legally liable for many fees. That is why this first step is so important.

There are many reasons to want to produce a concert. To help you get you started thinking about your goals, we have listed a few:

- To make money as a producer or for a cause.
- To present an artist in a unique way in your city — for example, as part of a national tour.
- To gain media attention for your organization.
- To focus other fundraising activities around the event.
- To build membership, whether you are a music club or an issue-oriented public interest group.

- To promote coalition-building among organizations in your community.
- To provide a community service for a specific group or population in your area.
- To offer a consistent number of concerts per month or year.
- To move into a larger class of production -- for example, going from house concerts and small coffeehouses to a 300- to 500-seat hall, with tickets sold in advance to the general public instead of relying on club members or regular customers.

You may have other goals. Write them down, and keep them close at hand. In the heat of concert production, it is often helpful to be reminded why you decided to produce a concert. The important thing is to identify your goals at the outset and build your strategies and budget around them.

As you use this book, create a complete plan for your unique event. Depend on your goals and your plans to help you analyze what you have to offer in terms of time, energy, skills, and money. You should begin with a realistic vision of the task, including liabilities and opportunities.

Remember, once you begin, there is no way to recover the time and money spent if you change your mind midstream and cancel the event.

Fewer than 20 Questions
Here are some more questions you might want to consider.

1. What kind of community is this? What resources in the community might help/hinder in accomplishing your goals? Resources include organizations, media, other local promoters, schools, church groups, political allies, special people in your community, money available through grants, etc. Identify which parts of the community can help most, and see if your goals are consistent with what you realistically think is possible.
2. What already has been done in the area of concert production in your community? What experiences do other groups/promoters have to share? Do you need to re-invent the wheel or can you use someone else's blueprint? And are you stepping on anyone's toes?
3. How much staff time (including volunteers) will you need to put into the project?
4. How much money can willingly, or ably, be paid in advance? What will happen to you or the organization if you lose money or don't make as much as intended?
5. What limits are there because of weather, economic conditions, halls in the area?

Feeling overwhelmed? That's okay. Better now than in six months as you wait at the airport to meet the arriving artists. These questions are not meant to discourage you. They are here to save you time and energy later. If they have raised some doubts, however, rethink your goals. Perhaps there is another type of event you can produce that is more within your reach. Maybe a concert is not your best option. However, if you still feel certain a concert is right for you, then read on. We have more things for you to consider before you commit yourself to the art of fine concert production.

The Professional Concert Promoter
Let's look at your image as a concert promoter. We suggest you build a good reputation by being competent, trustworthy, and efficient. Professionalism is an honored trait and will serve you well in the work of concert production. It is important to establish a good relationship with artists, audiences, and the community. Even without experience or full-time involvement in concert production, you can behave in a professional manner.

Be sure that everything the public sees or hears about your concert gives the impression that you know what you are doing and care about doing it well — from neatly-typed press releases to well-distributed posters and flyers (with a unified and attractive graphic theme) to highly-skilled technicians hired to enhance the performance. When the show looks good, you look good. If you have a confident, detail-oriented approach combined with the ability to work calmly and persuasively with others (your staff, concert hall technicians, media contacts, and community groups), you will gain a reputation for being a professional.

Although solid planning offsets most of the difficulties of production, professionalism also requires *crisis management* skills. Develop the ability to anticipate snags, make accom-modations to unexpected situations, and improvise good solutions under pressure.

Being a professional doesn't mean being a fast-talking, rip-off business person with a reputation for untimely exits — although certainly there are such types in concert promotion circles. Rather, professionalism should enable you to be more effective and visible in your community.

The benefits can include better press coverage, higher attendance, and successful fundraising. If word gets out you are a professional, you will find artists more willing to work with you, which is essential if you want to be a concert producer.

Let's move on to an overview of concert planning so you can get a sense of the scope of your task.

CHAPTER TWO

Planning

Contributors Amy Bank, Cathy Fink, Sheila Kahn, Torie Osborn

We are now in the planning stages of concert production. Look over all of the chapters briefly. Pay particular attention to the timelines to get a feel for the tasks and potential snags that await you. After you have a sense of the whole picture, you can go back and reread all the chapters that are relevant to your production.

You will need to contact the artists, agree on a date, acquire a hall/space, plan a publicity campaign, and construct an estimated budget. No matter what the size or nature of the event, this work is going to take time, money, and energy. Careful planning helps you save on all counts. In this chapter, we lay out an overview.

The Date
Consider your organization's and your personal calendar. If you plan an event for the second week after the entire staff is going on a one-week retreat, who will be around to make press calls and last-minute decisions? Is the event being planned for the day you are flying out to be in your younger brother's wedding? Perhaps you aren't producing this event alone, so your partner(s) can pull off the day of the show without you, if you just make sure you don't leave with essential information and experience in your head.

Is the concert date in conflict with a holiday, the world series, spring break, an annual harvest festival? Is there another competitive event already planned for that date?

Alone/Together
Working as a concert producer alone can be wonderful. You are in charge, you don't have to make collective decisions, you can work at your own pace. It also means the responsibility rests completely on your shoulders. You will need to learn to delegate, then follow up to see that the work you have delegated is done to your satisfaction — because the buck stops with you. Keep in mind that

personal crises or commitments do crop up. You must have a back-up plan.

If you are working with a group, a collective, or in a partnership, you have the benefit of numbers. From an organizational standpoint, it is often desirable to have two or more people working closely on production, to cover personal contingencies and to create a stronger production company capable of doing more than one task or more than one event at the same time.

Timelines

In the forms section in the back of the book you will find a Timelines form (Form 2:1). Use it to plan and accomplish your coordinating activities. The form can help you manage the weeks before the concert date. It is important to learn that there are stages and steps to production and, if you are well organized, it can all get done on time. This form also will allow you to look back at your timelines and revise them for future events.

Contacting Performers

Some artists have a manager and/or booking agent. Some arrange their own concert dates. Find out whom to call, and establish contact with the appropriate person. You need to find out the availability, interest, and fees of the artists. If there is interest, you can ask artists to hold a selection of available dates for a week or two. This will allow you to check out the hall, estimate your budget, and review other details before confirming a final date. Arrange for the artists' representative to call you if any of the dates being held for you are requested by another producer. That way, when you check back, you will not find that the dates that had been available are all booked.

The Hall

Next, get possible dates and cost estimates from several halls. Find out exactly what the price includes, when a deposit is required, and how long the hall can be held before it's given to another producer who offers a deposit. When you ask about the price, make sure it includes the "hidden" costs, e.g., piano tuner, hall refurbishing charges, security people, marquee advertising, or expensive add-on fee requirements for overtime.

Publicity

Good publicity is a fine art — one to be mastered because this is how the public learns there is going to be a concert. Unless the group you are presenting is very well known and all you need to do is whisper its name to the wind, publicity must transmit a lot of information in a simple and direct manner.

> *Is the concert date in conflict with a holiday, the world series, spring break, an annual harvest festival?*

You will have to estimate the time and costs of getting the word out. Are you good at writing press releases, or do you need to hire a publicist? Can you write copy quickly, or does it take up your whole day, time better spent elsewhere? Leave enough time in your timeline for doing it well. Develop a list of people in the press you will contact. It takes time to find out how many papers there are and to familiarize yourself with their deadlines and requirements. Does such a press list already exist? What papers does your audience read? What are the ad rate costs for one to three ads?

Without finalizing it completely, design a publicity campaign. Will it require a phone call, a mailing, a follow-up call? Is a second follow-up mailing necessary? How many press contacts can use photos? How many may want to review the artists' record albums? Do the artists have a press kit you can send with your press release? Who will pay for the artists' press material, complimentary records, and press photos? (Often artists can supply a few copies of photos, etc., but you'll have to pay to reproduce more.) Envelopes, paper, photocopying, and printing of photographs are costs to consider in addition to postage and time. If you are in a rural location or producing out of your city, phone calls to the press might be long distance. This expense should be accounted for in your budget.

Budget

The area of budgeting is the most essential part of successful concert planning and production. Constructing a budget of projected expenses and income is the only way to know realistically if you will make money, break even, or lose money. Many people are intimidated by having to be specific and commit themselves to dollar figures on paper. However, there is nothing to be afraid of in putting together a projected budget. In fact, because preparing the budget requires researching every aspect of the production, you can eliminate most of the guesswork and anxiety. By completing the projected budget, you will have done most of the legwork of planning your concert. You won't have to just hope that the production will work out; you will know that it will.

Every item in the budget needs to be researched every time you put on a production. Almost all costs vary from production to production, especially if your events differ greatly in size, halls, and complexity. Previous budgets can be used as guides but are no substitute for current research.

Remember, there are more ways to make money on a concert than just through ticket sales. Related fundraising activities are discussed in a separate chapter. However, it's important to keep these budgets separate, since the expenses and the income from those other activities are exclusively yours and separate from the production budget you negotiate with the artists. An exception to this may be the arrangements around record sales in the lobby. By looking at both budgets you will have a sense of the whole picture. You may discover, for example, that although you will only break even on the concert, you can raise extra money by selling ads in your program or selling tee shirts.

In the forms section at the back of this book is a Budget form (Form 2:2) for you to use in researching your projected concert budget and recording actual expenses and income. Keep a separate budget for optional fundraising activities. Estimate income minus expenses to see what a reasonable net income from the concert or fundraising activities would make for you. Later in this chapter we will refer you to a more complex Contract/Budget Settlement form for producing larger events in halls with more than 500 seats.

Cash Flow

For many producers, coming up with the *front money* — the money you'll need to spend before you've received income to cover those costs — can be the biggest obstacle to producing a concert, especially a large one. So, in addition to preparing the projected budget of expenses and income, you need to prepare a set of Cash Flow Projections (Form 2:3). By charting when bills will be due and when income is expected, you will see what you need to cover early expenses.

The amount of front money needed will vary from concert to concert. Again, research every item in advance and find out when payment is due. Major advance expenses include hall fees (sometimes a deposit is required, sometimes the full fee), printing and promotional expenses, and often a deposit to the artists. It's helpful to establish credit with printers, graphic artists, advertising departments of local papers, etc., so you can defer those payments — even though some of the bills will be due before you've received much income. For example, you may not be able to collect ticket money from the box office until after the concert, but costs for postage, posters, and programs probably will have to be met before the concert takes place.

Your organization's budget may include

funds that can be used for front money, or you may have to take out a short-term loan or find one or more people who will advance the money. Other options are to co-produce the concert, which means sharing the work, expenses, and proceeds; or to get a financial sponsor, obtaining advance money from a person or organization in exchange for mentioning them on all your publicity or providing them with some other form of acknowledgement.

The Cash Flow Projections form roughly outlines when you will have to spend money.

> *Previous budgets can be used as guides but are no substitute for current research.*

Plot each expense on your Cash Flow Projections Budget form week by week, so you will be prepared for the few weeks before the show when demands on your cash will be greatest.

Budget Settlement
Contract/Budget Settlement Statement (Form 2:4) is designed to help you put together as complete and accurate a projected budget as possible. It is more complex than the Budget form but contains essentially the same information in a more specific format.

For any event of more than 500 seats you should use the Contract/Budget Settlement form. Fill in actual expenses as bills come in. On the day of the show you will have filled in all (or almost all) of your actual expenses and income, and you'll use this form to settle with the hall and/or artists' representative. It also shows where you under- or over-estimated expenses or income. It will help you plan more accurately for future concerts. If you are working on a percentage basis with artists, any overage on the budget may require advance agreement from them.

Contract/Budget Settlement forms are set up with back-up worksheets (Form 2:5) that will facilitate your budget research. The work-

sheets correspond to the budget forms, following the same order. They are designed to make sure you all ask the necessary questions and don't get stuck with unexpected expenses because you didn't know what to ask. Some of the items on the worksheets may require explanation; refer to the glossary for definitions.

The Contract/Budget Settlement forms and worksheets are designed for large and relatively complicated productions; however, some of the items will be applicable to smaller productions. Even if you are planning your first small production, take advantage of these forms. Look them over. The more familiar you are with everything on these forms, the more knowledgeable and professional you will be.

The Contract/Budget Settlement form and worksheets are divided into three sections: Show Information, Facility Expenses, and Producer Expenses. Facility Expenses and Producer Expenses are separated to make settling with the hall and artists' representative easier and more efficient.

Working Vocabulary
A few terms and definitions will be helpful, both for your own planning and for negotiating with artists and/or halls.

Gross Potential. Theoretically, this is the total amount of money you take in. It is calculated by adding up the sale value of all tickets and subtracting the value of complimentary, unsalable, and discounted tickets and city taxes (if any). For example:

Add:	500	tickets	@ $10 =	$5,000
	+300	tickets	@ 9 =	2,700
	+200	tickets	@ 8 =	1,600
	1,000	tickets		9,300
Add:	+ 40	comp.	@ 10 =	$ 400
	+ 8	unsalable @ 10 =		80
	+ 50	discounts @ 2 =		100
	98	tickets unsold	=	$ 580
Gross Potential	$9,300 - 580		=	$8,720

However, in concert planning, never plan on a sell-out. Your budget should be estimated on a lesser gross potential: 65 to 75 percent, normally.

Artists' Guarantee. This is the minimum guaranteed amount you agree to pay the artists. It is the producer's obligation and must be paid even if you lose money.

Producer's Fee. The producer's fee is often figured at 15 percent of Total Show Expenses including Artists' Guarantee. Other options are:

- A percentage of net or gross revenues (for high-risk productions).
- A 50/50 percent split of net revenues with the artists.
- A flat fee plus a lower percentage of net revenues.

No matter how you arrive at the amount or percentage, it is not a *guaranteed* figure. If you do not create enough income to pay yourself, it is your loss.

Working on a Percentage. A usual arrangement is to pay the artists a guarantee plus a percentage of the net. That means the artists are paid an extra percentage if there is net income after all your expenses are paid. This is one of the reasons why the artists' representative will want you to estimate accurately figures in each category during the budget negotiations. If you are working on a percentage, the expenses obviously affect how much net income will be left to divide. You will need to provide the representative with copies of all receipts and expenses during settlement.

Net Income. Net income is the concert gross potential minus total show costs, which may be divided by producer and artists.

Split Point. The split point is the point where the net income is divided by the producer and

artists. Percentage splits are likely to be 70/30 percent (artists/producer), but they can be anything from 50/50 to 90/10.

Refer to Form 2:4 and follow along to see how this form will work for you as you plan your concert. Put in each expense item line by line (no matter how rough your figures are initially). The following equations will help you understand the relationship between the important terms.

- Expenses + Artists' Guarantee x 0.15 = Projected Producer's Fee.
- Expenses + Artists' Guarantee + Projected Producer's Fee = Total Show Costs.
- Gross Potential - Total Show Costs = Net Income (also called Split Point).
- Artists' Guarantee + Artists' Percentage of Net = Potential Total to Artists.
- Producer's Fee + Producer's Percentage of Net = Potential Total to Producer.

Projecting Income
These potential amounts are based on obtaining the highest expected sales. You can scale that down by multiplying your gross potential by various percentages of tickets sold, i.e., 90 percent, 80 percent, 70 percent, to give you a realistic range of future income.

Using the guidelines and the information provided in this book, you can construct your budget. But your budget will vary from our figures depending on your local circumstances.

For instance, you may find that you need to spend more money on advertising than suggested. If you can find a hall that's free and people who want to donate their services as ushers in exchange for complimentary tickets, you will save money. In that case, you could increase the advertising budget.

Planning the Budget
The important thing is to estimate your budget *before* you begin, not halfway through the production process. The best surprise is no surprise at all.

After working out your first draft of the budget, you can predict a range of how much money you'll be able to make on the concert. Once again, normally you should not plan on a sell out. Estimate the income based on past experience — 70 percent of gross potential is a good starting point. This gives you a chance to rethink strategies, to consider other fundraising alternatives, or to realize that the bases are covered and the event could do quite well.

Problems in Production
The planning stage is the time for anticipating potential problems so you don't waste time, money, and energy. Most events pose conflicts that require careful thinking. These are a few of the types of dilemmas you can expect.

You want to have a fundraiser in time to finance a campaign on a local issue. The hall is available on the date of your choice but the artist is not available until eight weeks later, when the hall is not free.

Consider: Is the hall the place you want because everyone knows its location? Is its size the next step up for the kind of productions you are producing? Is it the only free hall in town with good acoustics and accessibility for disabled attendees?

These considerations may be important enough for you to decide either to change the place of your event or to select another artist.

You can reach a compromise that does not sacrifice your main goal. In this case, since the main *event* is really your campaign, the selection of the artist may be less critical than the timing of the concert. However, what a particular artist stands for may make it worth re-evaluating the timing of the event.

Your group has wanted to produce a certain artist for years, and she/he has got a new album coming out in six weeks, so you may be ready to choose a larger hall than the group's usual one. This event will not be part of a regular series, but a special event in an out-of-the-ordinary place or at a different time or day than people expect. Such a change requires extra attention to publicity, since the people who normally attend your events are accustomed to a different schedule.

Another problem might arise in this way: you want to have flyers ready early to distribute at a special event that attracts the same people who may be interested in your concert — but ticket outlets are not yet firmly booked. Balance the cost of running two smaller printings (and money spent in adjusting the layout) with the opportunity of reaching new people. The difference between a single larger printing and the two smaller jobs may increase the printing cost by $50 or more.

If you realistically can expect to reach 100 people at the event you don't normally reach in the course of your other advertising, and if eight of those 100 buy a $7 ticket, you could break even. Of course, managing the shortage of information has to be considered, too -- a central information number instead of ticket outlet information will mean extra person-hours for phone answering in your budget and time plan. And because things are still in flux, remember to advertise only those services, such as an interpreter for the hearing-impaired, senior discounts, or child care availability which you are sure you can deliver.

The decisions you make should be checked against budget, cash-flow projections, and the calendar. Staff shortage during a critical time period -- say, grant deadline time -- could result in a waste of money if you've printed flyers but no one can get away to deliver them.

Planning the time, money, and energy for an event does not happen in a vacuum; it has to fit into the entire agenda of your organization. If you plan your concert carefully as this chapter suggests, the basic steps will be in place for a successful event.

CHAPTER THREE

Working with Artists

Contributors Cathy Fink, Brynna Fish, Holly Near, Jo-Lynne Worley

The starting point for producers, artists, and managers to work cooperatively toward a successful show is to communicate clearly about what each party requires. This can be done by including specific needs in the performance contract or letter of agreement, covering the needs both of the producer and of the artists. The contract should be detailed and clear enough for each party to understand fully the expectations of others.

Continue to stay in touch with the artists' representative. It is better to ask than to assume. And it's critical to accommodate artists' personal needs regarding housing, food, privacy, and health, as well as their performance needs. Feel free to try out a creative idea but always keep the artists' specific requirements in mind. When the artists are happy the show will run better.

The Producer's Requirements

As a producer, you need photos, biographical material, and any other press material the artists' representative can provide. You need technical specifications (sound and lighting requirements, etc.), a stage diagram, and a list of stage props (stool, table, etc.). This information may be described in the contract. You may even wish to indicate a date by which you need all materials and information.

You will want travel information in advance, as well as hospitality/accommodation requirements. If you are responsible for the expenses incurred for travel and accommodations, it is not unreasonable to have an indication of the extent of your responsibility spelled out in the contract. Find out the artists' expectations and negotiate the details, then follow through on delivering them. Continue to stay in touch with the artists' representative. However, it's not necessary to make daily phone calls; group your questions and ask several at once. Everyone is busy, and there is no need to run up big phone bills or play phone tag. Plan ahead so all your questions are answered at least two weeks before the concert.

If you and the artists have agreed to have the concert interpreted for the hearing-impaired, you will need one tape of the music being performed and one set of lyrics. As covered in Chapter Fifteen on accessibility, be sure you request this in advance so your interpreter can be prepared.

The sound and light people also may want tapes or special instructions and cues in advance. On the day of the show you will need several copies of the set list for the lighting and sound technicians, stage manager, interpreter, and record distributor. You can get this from the artists or road manager at your scheduled sound/light check.

> *Do not give out the artists' accommodations or itinerary.*

Artists' Needs

Artists have differing needs and expectations, and they should let you know what they are well in advance. A thorough artists' contract is helpful in defining their needs. Some prefer staying in a hotel, for privacy or to ensure better accommodations. Some may ask for community housing with specifics: a private bedroom, a house where smoking is or is not permitted, no parties or meetings in the house, a separate bed or room for each person traveling, no pets, etc.

Some may accept clean, *vacated for the duration of the artists' stay*, community housing so that expenses are kept down and there is some connection with the community while respecting the artists' need for privacy. Unfortunately, artists sometimes encounter producers who are not considerate of the rigors of travelling and offer lodging on a lumpy couch or expect the artists to entertain *after* they've entertained. Artists are hardworking people who travel a great deal, rarely spending more than two nights in the same city. They often

have played 20 cities in 40 days. Their requests should be treated with respect and consideration.

If you feel that their requests are unreasonable, or your budget simply can't afford a hotel, let them know early in negotiations so alternate, mutually agreeable, arrangements can be made. Although styles and personalities of artists vary, the goal of the artists, as well as the producer, is to present a great show. **You must provide whatever accommodations you agreed to furnish in the contract.**

Often you will deal solely with the artists' representative before the concert and will not have talked to the artists until the day of the show. When they arrive, the car(s) used to pick them up must be big enough for them and all their luggage and equipment. It is sometimes helpful to have an extra person available to carry equipment. Allow the artists to take the lead in conversation, rather than barraging them with information and questions. You will find out quickly enough if they feel like socializing or need some time to reflect and acclimate. Give them a **written** schedule for their visit in your city, including times and places of any media commitments, sound check, their address and phone number while in town, and yours (Form 3:1). Give them phone numbers of people to call in case of problems. If you loan them a car and expect them to get to all these events on their own, provide clear directions and maps.

Do not give out or make available any information about the artists' accommodations or itinerary. This can create a security problem or invite invasion of privacy.

Also, a no-drugs policy should be enforced. Never have drugs in the artists' house, car, or backstage.

It is important to communicate with the artists' representative *before* the arrival of the artists about any hospitality plans, such as parties or meals you would like the performers to attend. Some artists don't eat at all before a concert; some have specific food preferences (vegetarian, religious dietary needs, etc.); some want privacy the minute the concert is over, and some want company or to party; some need several hours of quiet/private time before the concert. Many artists thrive on involvement in the producer's organization and enjoy meeting community members; others are protective of their personal privacy and need to conserve their energy for the event.

Many artists appreciate the familiarity of working with someone they know from other productions or festival work who lives in your city. This person may be a good friend or liaison for the day of show.

Artists may want to bring some friends to the concert, and you should set aside the number of complimentary tickets agreed to in the contract. Notify the artists if there is a minimum age limit at the venue.

When artists and their tour party arrive for the sound check, introduce them to the key people: the stage manager, the sound and lighting crews, the interpreter, and any other members of your production company. Artists or their road people may want to use some pre-concert time to meet with the security staff about backstage security. They may want to restrict access to the backstage area; if so, they should supply a list of those authorized so the producer can provide appropriate safeguards.

If there is to be an emcee, the artists and/or road manager may want to review introductions and announcements. They also may want to work out time warning signals with the stage manager or technical details with lights or sound, or they may simply want to unwind and prepare quietly.

Find out how the artists want to be introduced. Occasionally, they prefer no introduction at all. If you are doing a fundraiser for a special cause you may want the artists to plug your cause from the stage. If the artists agree, give them material in writing (a typed 3 by 5 inch card is convenient) several hours before the show, perhaps at sound check, so they can think about how to integrate it into the show.

Producers face a complicated and sometimes unbalanced interpersonal situation in working with artists: famous performers are coming to town to work with you. You know a lot more about them than they know about you, and you may feel that some of their requirements are extravagant, but they may feel they're necessary for survival on the road.

Helping the artists with laundry, ironing of stage clothes, running errands, etc., is necessary. Remember, the artists have probably been travelling heavily, are tired, have a suitcase of wrinkled clothes, and a last minute request for a jar of juice or bag of M&M's , although not specified in the contract, could make the artists' day. A little kindness is never wasted. Try to have dinner catered at venue or at a restaurant within walking distance. Include amount of money per musician covered by producer.

Although styles and personalities of artists vary, the goal of the artists, as well as the producer, is to present a great show.

Be sure to clarify who is expected to pay for any special food or beverage requests not listed in the contract. Again, reasonable communications between artists or the artists' road manager and producer will help foster a smooth collaboration. It is good to assign someone (again — that familiar person is sometimes best) to be the *performers' friend* — to pick the artists up at the airport, iron, run errands, introduce them to the key production staff and make sure their needs are met.

Post-Concert Evaluation
Once the concert is over, many producers find it helpful to formally evaluate the entire production. Sometimes it is also feasible to get the artists' ideas of what to do differently or better next time (for those particular artists or someone else) and to find out what specif-

ics the artists appreciated most about your production. Many artists will be happy to answer brief questions, although they probably won't have the energy to comment extensively.

Those who can invest more time may want to attend a short post-production meeting the morning after the show, or the artists or road manager could complete an evaluation to answer your questions after the event.

The producer and the artists share the same goal — to present the best concert possible. You are members of the same team. You are familiar with your local situation, and the artists are experts about their show. Advance planning, communication, attention to details, and follow-through on agreements will be appreciated by artists and their representatives and will serve to focus your energy on putting on a great show.

CHAPTER FOUR

Booking the Event

Contributors Jill Davey, Cathy Fink

Selecting the artists for your event based on the goals you have set will help ensure that you reach those goals. Through the use of the artists' names in advertising, in the artists' statements during pre-concert interviews and throughout the entire show, the performers become your spokespeople. Coalition building, developing the career of local or new talent, conveying a cultural message, creating a sense of community, fundraising, presenting a *spectacular* event are examples of the goals around which you might be planning your event.

It is important to pick artists with publicity presence and performance styles which contribute positively to your specific goals.

If your goal is *to make money*, select your artists with that goal in mind.

Selecting the Artists
In addition to your own ideas of whom you would like to produce, ask your friends or colleagues whom they'd like to see.

Attending *artist showcases* and festivals (folk, jazz, women's, blues, etc.) is a great way to acquaint yourself with potential artists. Make a list of a few artists whom you would like to contact, in order of priority.

If your event is multi-artist, build a tentative schedule for the show before you contact the artists so you can describe the event accurately and tell them how long you want them to perform. Although the sequence and the lengths of acts won't be final until you confirm all the artists, you can estimate the number of acts or sets and add in time for introductions and announcements, set changes, and intermission.

The program should not be so lengthy that the audience becomes restless by the time your last, and often main, artist appears.

Set-up time between acts can be lessened by scheduling artists according to their technical requirements — for example, saving the band with the most complicated microphone arrangements for after intermission at the opening of the second half of the show. If artistic and technical considerations allow, use the set-up time for a *front of curtain* act or announcements.

Contacting and Contracting Artists
Some artists book themselves; others work through managers and representatives. If you don't know how to reach a particular artist or representative, look on a recent record album to see if it includes booking information. Or call the record company and ask for a current phone number, address, and contact person for that artist. Contact a producer in another town who has worked with the performer, or use one of the good reference books (see Resources section) that catalog this information.

Next, make an introductory phone call or write a letter. Identify yourself, briefly describe your organization and the event, state that you would like to have the artists participate. Note whether you are asking the artists to be part of a concert or to headline it. Ask about the artists' usual fees and availability at the time of your show.

Plan to include reasonable artists' fees even in a fundraising concert budget. Most performers (and especially well-known ones) are approached many times a year by people who want to raise money but have very limited budgets for artists' fees. If your event is well planned and promoted, there should be no need to ask artists to volunteer their services. (Chapter Twenty on fundraising describes many other ways to raise money at an event.) At least offer an honorarium, but come as close to the usual fee as possible. The fee to the artists must stretch to cover many expenses: booking, management, musicians, road manager fees,

Contracts avoid problems that might arise from spoken agreements, even among friends.

and expenses like telephone, office rent and supplies, rehearsal space, travel, *per diems*, etc. Like producers, artists must be successful as business people to continue their work.

The size of your event will help determine whether you can book a new artist or if you need the drawing power of a famous performer. If you want to fill a 1,500-seat hall, *big name* artists will be needed, unless the event itself is so well-known in your city it will draw enough people if you do great publicity and grass roots coordination. If you are booking a community event for 200 people or less, an artist who is not well known may be just fine.

When artists want to tour, they or their booking agent often call producers. Such an unexpected opportunity may be a great concert for you to book. And although the artists initiated the call, your procedures are the same: look at your goals, budget, hall, timetable, and staff resources.

The artists may be on a tight timetable to get confirmations so you'll have to speed up your decision-making process. The more often you present concerts and become established as a good producer, the more calls you'll get. This will be how you will book many of your dates.

If the artists or artists' representative are interested in your event, the next step is negotiating a financial deal that benefits all parties. Fee negotiations can be simple (flat fee) or more complex (fee plus a percentage of the net). Either way there may be plenty of discussion. A flat fee is usually higher than a fee plus percentage and may be a bigger risk for the producer. (This part of budgeting was explained in detail in Chapter Two.)

The basic rule of thumb is to put it into writing as soon as there is agreement on the date, fee, hall, and length of performance time. A written agreement can be anything from a short letter specifying all the details to a multi-page contract. The Simple Contract (Form 4:1) is slanted toward the producer or employer, and the Complex Public Appearance Agreement (Form 4:2) is from the point of view of an established artist who knows exactly what she wants.

Artists often have their own contract, which may include fees, hospitality, sound, and technical requirements, cancellation policy, advertising, terms of payment, and more. If you are writing your own contract, put in as many details as you can to clarify the arrangements.

Contracts avoid misunderstandings arising from spoken agreements, even among friends. Generally, two signed copies of the contract are needed, one for the producer and one for the artists. Any changes to the original agreement must be in writing and be initialed by both parties.

Often, especially when it is a full concert by one artist or group, the contract will be contingent on the approval of the budget, and a percentage of net profit becomes part of the agreement.

Opening Acts
Artists have different feelings about opening acts, so check before you book or in any way obligate yourself and, therefore, the artists. Some producers like to bring local talent to the attention of the large audiences better-known performers can draw, but some performers feel that since they get to a particular

city only once a year they prefer to do a full concert.

The main performers may want to hear a tape of the opening act's material to decide if the quality and content fit with what they have planned for the concert. If the performers approve of having an opening act, choose this person or group carefully. Select a performer who can handle the exposure to a larger audience well and is appropriate to the occasion. For example, if the event is a fundraiser for a domestic abuse shelter, make sure the performer's set does not include songs which may be interpreted as insensitive or offensive to the cause.

The length of set and fee (if any) should be determined and written into the contract. An inexperienced performer may not understand that the time specified includes the total time on stage, not just the music. It is better to have a short set that is well received than one which *feels* long — 15 minutes is usually a good length. The set-change time between the opening set and main performers should be as short as possible, ideally no change at all. Don't make the audience wait long! Opening acts that run over frustrate both the audience and the main performers and may cause overtime charges.

CHAPTER FIVE

Halls

Contributors Mary Conn, Cathy Fink, Sheila Kahn, Jennifer Leith, Penny Rosenwasser

Finding a hall is one of the first tasks of producing a concert. If you are not familiar with the halls in your area, you will need to do some research. Use the Hall Research Data form (Form 5:1) to help ensure you get all the information you need when you contact each hall. Keep a separate sheet on each hall you investigate. Even if you don't use it for this event, save your research for future events. A hall may be unsuitable for a concert, but ideal for some other type of fundraiser you plan for next season.

The best and most popular halls often are booked months in advance, and even secondary halls, such as high school auditoriums, may not be available on short notice. Put halls on hold immediately so you have some options to consider. Putting initial holds on halls usually doesn't cost money, although you may have to pay a deposit at a certain point to keep the reservation. A hold can be challenged or lost if another producer puts

deposit money down first. Make sure to communicate clearly with hall managers about your holds so they will call you if there is a challenge on your date. When you do make the deposit on the hall, follow up with a phone call to verify that they received and cashed your check with no problem. If you decide against a particular hall, let the management know as a courtesy so that they can release the date.

Rent a hall that is in line with your goals for the show. For example, if having the event as part of a campaign is more important than the headliner, secure the hall for that date before doing anything else. However, if you're most interested in a par-

> Make sure to communicate clearly with hall managers about your holds so they will call you if there is a challenge on your date.

19

ticular artist, then contact her or him first, and book the hall on a date that is available for the performer.

You may have to choose between a classy hall that is very expensive and one that is not as nice, but cheaper. By doing your budget and break-even projections you can estimate the value of a higher ticket price and higher hall expenses versus a lower break-even point, but possibly smaller audience and less potential profit. Use your goals, resources, and audience/community knowledge as guidelines in this decision.

Use the Facility Checklist (Form 5:2) for halls under serious consideration in this planning and decision-making stage — then use it and/or the Contract Budget/Settlement Statement (Form 2:4) later on to keep track of confirmed hall information. Again, even if you don't use the hall for this event, save your research for the future.

Every hall is different, so to stay within budget, it's very important to research in detail what the hall rental fee does (and does not) include before you confirm. This is one of the more complicated, demanding aspects of producing, but it's necessary to good planning. Your whole concert will run more smoothly if you do the necessary legwork.

There are many things to consider in choosing a hall. Some affect your budget; others, the production itself. For example, be sure there are adequate electrical outlets and power. You need to visit the hall to get answers to all your questions, so make appointments to see the halls you are considering. The more you know about a facility, the better judgment you can make about its suitability. Be sure to note why you decided to use or not to use that space.

Features of the Hall
Size. Estimate conservative and ideal attendance projections for your concert. Ask the artists' representative for the number of attendees the artists have drawn in your area or areas of similar size, under similar circum-

stances, and ask how many they think you could draw. Ideally, choose a hall that has (as close as possible) the number of seats you anticipate you can fill.

Remember, even if the hall is small, it can help the artists psychologically if it sells out. It also can enhance your reputation as a successful producer. People who wait until it's too late to get tickets will rush to get them the next time the artists come to town. It leaves everyone with a strong sense of the artists' popularity.

If you have to choose a hall that is larger than you expect to fill, provide more tickets as promotional giveaways and be generous with complimentary tickets to reviewers, students, nonprofit agencies, etc. A great crowd of 500 people scattered through a 1,200-seat hall will look dismal and discouraging to artists, audience, and reviewers alike. Talk to the hall management about options such as blocking off rear seats and side and balcony sections.

If the artists could fill a hall five times the size of the one available, the goals of both producer and artists need to be discussed and understood. It may be possible for the artists to make just as much money in a small hall or club by selling all sponsorship tickets or high-priced tickets, but there needs to be an agreement about what adaptations will be made if a hall that is quite out of character for the artists is selected.

For a hall too small you also can consider two shows the same night, a weekend matinee (weekdays usually are not suitable for this option), or two concerts on consecutive nights. Again, consult with the artists before making any alternative arrangements.

Two Shows. The advantage of doing two shows on the same day is that it costs less than two shows on different days. Although most halls, union and other personnel, and the artists will want more money than if they were doing only one concert, it generally is less than twice the one-show rate. The cost of equipment rental should remain the same, and equipment will have to be loaded, unloaded, set up, and returned only once.

The disadvantages of doing two shows in one night are that the artists and crew may be exhausted by the addition of a second show; the artists may not be able to perform as long for each concert as if they had the whole night to perform; and you will have to turn the house over quickly and efficiently — that is, get the people from the first show out and the people for the second show in within an hour or less.

The advantages of doing concerts on successive nights are that all the workers, including the artists, probably will be more relaxed; the artists can do their whole show; and showtime may be at a more attractive hour for the audience. Also, equipment may not have to be moved, and lights should not have to be refocused (unless the hall is being used for another function between your concerts). Key personnel do not have to be paid as though they were doing two entirely separate concerts. The lighting designer, for example, will undoubtedly use the same design for both nights; she or he should receive more than one night's pay, but not twice as much. The disadvantage of two nights is that it costs more than one night.

> The rule of thumb for union halls is $1 per seat including equipment and skeleton crew.

Rent. Some churches or schools do not require a fee, but they will ask for a donation or payment of the custodian's wages. On the other hand, the rule of thumb for union halls is $1 per seat including equipment and skeleton crew. Your costs will often fall between these two.

Hall rental usually is charged in one of three ways: a flat fee; a minimum guaranteed fee versus a percent of the gross, whichever is greater (sometimes there is a maximum, too); or a guaranteed fee plus a percent of the gross. Some halls use the same arrangement for all events; others will negotiate rental based on the kind of event. Some halls give special rates to nonprofit groups or for benefit productions.

If rental is a flat fee, your expense is clear cut. If it's a minimum versus a percentage of the gross, the minimum is the base fee you must pay even if you don't sell a single ticket. To figure the maximum rental fee, multiply the percentage they charge by your net gross potential — the most income you could possibly generate by ticket sales alone.

Until you set your ticket prices you won't know your exact net gross potential. But you can figure out your potential hall expenses based on several scales of ticket prices and find a range of maximum hall fees. If the hall's maximum fee is lower than what you get by multiplying the net gross potential by the percentage, the hall's maximum is your maximum charge. If there is no maximum, or if the hall's maximum is higher than the percentage multiplied by your net gross potential, then your maximum charge is solely determined by the number of tickets you will sell.

Contracts. Almost every hall has a rental contract. An example is included in the back of the book (Form 5:3). Even if you are investigating different halls before making a commitment, get a copy of their contract to see the details of what you are renting.

Check the contract for a cancellation clause. Is there a charge for cancelling after a certain date? Are there exceptions for things like union strikes and natural disasters? What insurance is required?

Save contracts in your files for future reference. After you've confirmed with a hall, use the worksheet to document when you receive the contract and when you send it back signed.

Availability. Find out what hours the hall is

available to you on the day of the show, what hours are included in the basic rent, and any time for which you will be charged extra. Sometimes the hall will charge overtime after a certain hour; that can be very expensive. Make sure the hall is available early enough so you can get everything set up and hold technical and artistic checks in time to open the doors and start the show on time.

Also find out when you need to be out, so that you can set the showtime accordingly, alert the performers in advance to when they have to be off the stage, and allow plenty of time to strike the set after the show is over.

Location. The location of the hall is important for a number of reasons, including safety of the area, how well known it is to concert goers in the community, availability of parking, and access to public transportation. The location will in part determine who will come.

A church basement will definitely draw a different crowd from a posh hotel convention spot. Therefore, it's important for you to clearly identify your primary audience. The hall most appealing or convenient to a rhythm and blues audience may be different from one you would choose to draw a folk audience.

To find the names and locations of halls people are used to patronizing, check newspapers and concert producers. People are often hesitant to go to halls they are unfamiliar with or where transportation or parking is difficult. If there are no regular concert halls in your area, check out churches, school auditoriums (not gymnasiums usually), women's clubs, folklore societies, and recreation centers.

The town business association or chamber of commerce may be a knowledgeable source of what halls are suitable as well as which are the familiar gathering spots for various audiences in your community.

If your choice of hall is not located in a particularly safe area, you may want to hire security people to watch outside the hall when the show is over or to patrol the parking lot.

Legitimacy of Halls. If it is a production goal to reach a new and bigger audience with a performer, you are most likely to be successful in an established hall. People often will go to hear a performer for the first time in a legitimate concert hall. Another reason to hold your concert in a well-known hall is that more people will know how to get to it. If you are using a space that is not well known as a concert site, or if are you using a hall for the first time, it is helpful to give more than a simple address in the publicity. If necessary, print a map on your leaflets.

A well-known hall also helps get press to cover the event, both in advance and in reviews. Some critics will not consider attending a concert if it is not in what they consider a legitimate hall.

Atmosphere. This is a totally subjective appraisal, but if the place looks and feels uninviting or shabby to you, then it probably will feel that way to your audience. The setting should make you feel comfortable and also be compatible with the artists' style. Some performers, especially soloists, prefer a more intimate setting rather than a large hall; others may feel that their music is best heard in a big room.

Be sure you can control the temperature in the hall and dressing area. If it is too hot, people will get restless and uncomfortable. If it's too cold, performers especially will suffer, particularly if they play instruments that require agile fingering.

A cautionary word about holding performances in churches and other religious centers: wooden pews can be very uncomfortable and can make your audience restless. Large crucifixes or other religious paraphernalia hanging behind the performers can create a strange and sometimes alienating atmosphere. Find out if you can remove these items or veil them during the performance. However, some performers lend themselves well to church atmospheres, and the audience members feel closer to each other in pews. Check with the artists' representative for preferences.

Personnel. Are the people who manage the hall easy or difficult to work with? Do they supply you with needed information? Check by visiting personally and by comparing your impressions with other producers who have presented shows there before. If the hall manager never returns your calls you have a clue as to what it will be like to work there.

In your initial hall research, inquire about what personnel the hall requires you to have and what is included with the hall price. Then decide on your needs for personnel.

The hall may come with security guards and a staffed box office. There may be a stage hand or electrician as part of the cost of the hall, or you may need to have a minimum union crew in a union hall. Ask questions until you are satisfied that you have all the answers you need.

Staff, whether part of the hall union or others you provide, must be on hand the day of the show to have a smooth-running performance. This includes a stage manager and crew, a lobby manager, a house manager, a sound technician and crew, an electrician and/or lighting designer, a piano tuner, ushers, ticket takers, box office people, a security coordinator, and others. Chapter 10 provides a more complete discussion of staffing.

Unions. Find out if the hall is a union hall, and if so which jobs are union controlled. In some halls it may be only the stage hands, while in others it can be everyone from the loading crew to the ticket takers. In the more unionized halls you cannot hire any workers who are not union members nor get help from volunteers. Be sure to check all details on union costs with the hall manager.

Find out the minimum crew requirements, and try to use that minimum. Can you supplement the minimum union crew with your own people, or are only union people allowed

to do certain jobs? You also need to know the union regulations. For example, after five hours without a break do you start paying double time? You need to arrange your schedule around when the union people work.

It's often advisable to talk to the union representative about these details in addition to the hall manager. (See the Union Personnel section in Chapter Ten for additional details.) It is important to get started on the right foot and maintain good relationships with the local unions.

> *If the place looks and feels uninviting or shabby to you, then it probably will feel that way to your audience.*

There is always the chance that a union will go on strike at a time that affects your concert. If this happens, you and the artists will have to come to an agreement about how to proceed. Some options include: moving to a different hall (that the union does not oppose), negotiating with the union, changing the date, cancelling the event.

Acoustics. Good acoustics are crucial for the success of the show. Acoustics are affected by features of the house — does it have plush seats with carpeting and curtains or hardwood pews, cement floors, and bare walls? Make notes so you can discuss the hall's acoustical properties with sound technicians. Find out what sound equipment, if any, is available in the hall.

Power. Make sure there is enough power in the hall to run your sound system, lights, and the musicians' equipment at the same time — without creating a buzz in the sound system or blowing a fuse. In addition, there should be enough outlets, conveniently placed. If you do not have enough experience to evaluate power sources, bring along a technician.

Lights. Get specific agreements about what the hall supplies in lighting equipment and what you will have to bring in or rent from the hall. Determine whether union technicians and spot operators are required.

Stage. The stage space must meet the artists' minimum technical requirements (if any) for width, depth, and height (and, for dancers, type of floor). If you are using a church or other space that is not usually used as a concert setting, check the lighting and stage at night. The ambiance is complemented by the stage relationship to the audience — high stages separated by an orchestra pit create a sizeable distance for audience and artists to bridge. Most artists do not like audience members seated on stage or behind them. Moving or rotating stages may not be acceptable to the artists.

Loading Door. Check out the facility for how easily you can get production equipment in and out. If you have much equipment — or a piano — to unload, the most desirable hall will have a loading door at the back or side of the stage to which an equipment truck can drive right up. If the hall has no loading door or it's a long haul from the truck to the stage, let the equipment people know in advance so they can bring dollies as well as extra hands.

Dressing Rooms. Performers need a quiet, private space in which to get ready for the performance. Some halls have mini-motel rooms with showers, couches, cots, etc. The bare necessities are a private toilet, a chair, and a mirror in a room with a locking door. If the hall doesn't have a dressing room, you can improvise. The basic considerations are for it to be a private and relaxed space, secure and clean, close to the stage, and thermostatically controllable so the performer is neither too cold nor too hot. A phone close by is a plus, too.

Seating. Check out the house space, the arrangement of the audience, the comfort of the seats, and audience leg-room. Is the floor raised so everyone looks down to the stage, or is everyone on the same level as the performers or below, looking up? Sometimes it is desirable to build a platform to raise the artists and put them in everyone's view. The stage you build should be high enough so the people in the back row can see the performers clearly while looking over or around the other audience members. If building is necessary, allow additional time in the schedule and money in the budget.

Check for the best locations for wheelchairs and for a hearing-impaired section. If the house is divided into separate sections (orchestra, balcony, loge, side sections), you may decide to block off certain sections and/or scale ticket prices. In many halls there is a map of the house showing each seat. This will not necessarily indicate seats that are blocked by pillars or sound equipment or seats with poor sound. Check this out on the site, walking around through the house while someone speaks or sings to you from the stage.

You probably will have to use some seats to set up the sound board and possibly the light board as well. Figure out the number of seats needed for that purpose and their exact location so you can remove those tickets from those being sold. Allocating seats for the technical crew and equipment affects potential income, particularly if you have reserved seating and different ticket prices according to location.

Accessibility. Is the hall accessible for people in wheelchairs? Ramps should go wherever the steps go, and they need to be wide and sturdy with only gradual inclines. Are bathrooms also accessible? If the hall doors have a ramp but the washrooms are not accessible, the building is not totally accessible. Clearly state partial accessibility in your publicity.

Chapter 15 provides greater detail about accessibility.

Child Care Space. The ideal child care space consists of at least two separate rooms — one for sleeping, one for playing — that can be made safe for children (no sharp objects, loose wires, etc.). There should be space to run and it should be close to the bathrooms. Noise from the area should not be audible in the performance hall. If you are providing this service, the space should meet your needs for size, comfort, and compatibility with the show. Chapter 16 provides more information about child care.

Lobby Space. This area can be important to artists, audience, and producer. Figure out space requirements needed for selling records, holding raffles, bake sales, pamphlet displays, and so on. Ask if there are any restrictions on the use of the lobby and how many tables you can fit in without crowding the audience who will be browsing there before the show and during intermission.

Are tables and chairs available from the hall and at what price? Also find out if the hall takes a percentage of everything sold (is it negotiable?), and let your vendors know in advance so they can set their prices accordingly. Many halls don't allow you to sell food. Does the hall retain the right to sell all beverages? Do they regularly sell alcoholic drinks or would you be allowed to do this? (Regulations and licenses are obtainable for single-night events, but the artists may prefer not to have alcohol sold at the concert.) Are the artists expecting you to sell their records or will the distribution company be there? How much space do they need?

> **Insurance is quite an expense, but it is less expensive than being sued for personal injury.**

Toilets. Find out how many toilets will be available for audience use. There is no real audience-to-toilets ratio, but realizing women take longer than men, if the audience is more than 50 percent women you might convert the bathrooms to *folks*, or another sensitive, creative arrangement. Make sure there is ample toilet paper the night of the show and that the toilets all flush and are clean.

Box Office. Box office operation is part of the package deal in some halls. This can be a major convenience if it is centrally-located and people are used to getting tickets there. Specifically find out when you can pick up advance ticket money. If management of the box office is a non-negotiable part of using the hall, familiarize yourself with the particulars of the hall's financial agreement — and be prepared to go over the reconciliation at the end of the evening. If the hall does not provide this service, you will need to set up a box office on the night of the show and have other centrally-located advance ticket outlets. It is not difficult, but it does require careful accounting. Chapter 6 discusses ticketing in detail.

Insurance. Liability insurance coverage for the day of the show is desirable and often required by the hall. If you do have a choice about whether to purchase insurance consider the following in your evaluation: does the organization you are renting from have insurance that covers you for this evening as part of the fee? Is there a minimum amount of liability insurance you must have before you rent the hall? Can you be covered on the organization's policy for an additional fee? (Find out what that fee is exactly before you agree to it.) Are you willing to take the risk of not being covered?

As an individual producer, are you covered already by some *umbrella* insurance that can include this event? Also, most professional sound and light companies have their own insurance to cover their equipment; check with them to make sure.

Insurance costs more than tripled between 1985 and 1988 so check current costs. If you have to buy a separate policy to cover an event expected to draw about 500 people in a hall regularly used for concerts, the 1986 estimate was $2.65 a seat, approximately $1,325 if you can get it. This is prohibitive, so check the hall and other local resources for a way to extend their coverage to you for one night. You ought to be able to get coverage for less than one half of that amount. Establish good relations with an insurance broker, so when you need insurance, you'll have someone to contact.

Americans very commonly bring suit these days, so consider insurance coverage carefully. If you do decide to get insurance, fill out the line on the budget so it won't be a surprise when the bill arrives six months or even a year later.

Insurance is quite an expense, but it is less expensive than being sued for personal injury or for replacing a vandalized or stolen sound system.

Artists' Approval. After you have completed your hall research, discuss the options in depth with the artists' representative. All the variables mentioned will be important to them in agreeing or disagreeing with you about hall choice. You must have the artists' approval before contracting with the hall. As in all discussions and negotiations with the artists, don't gloss over negative factors to present a rosier picture for your hall preference — it's best to lay everything on the table early on than to have surprises later.

CHAPTER SIX

Tickets: Pricing, Distribution, and Collecting

Contributors Mary Conn, Cathy Fink, Sheila Kahn, Penny Rosenwasser

Setting ticket prices is one of the early concerns of planning. Factors to consider are: your primary goal in producing the event, your financial needs, the cost of the production (including the charges of ticket-selling services and any hall or city tax), the usual charges for entertainment in your area, and the minimum or anticipated audience size.

For a rough estimate price on a low-budget concert, think in terms of the price of a movie. Usually tickets for a live show can cost more than for a film, but check the ticket pricing on similar events in your community.

> *A hall with more than 500 seats should offer reserved seating.*

There are a number of options for choosing ticket prices and sellers. Often you'll need to clear your arrangements and pricing with the artists, and sometimes with the ticket agency or hall box office as well, when it affects their income.

Reserved Seats or General Admission
In a 500-seat hall or smaller, general admission (unreserved) seating is okay and, in fact, sometimes preferable to reserved seating. But a hall with more than 500 seats definitely should offer reserved seating. Otherwise, many people waiting to get in early may rush the doors as soon as they open, run into the hall, throw down sweaters and jackets to save seats for their friends, and generally create a more chaotic scene than if seats were reserved.

Sliding Scale
The sliding scale concept offers a price range for each ticket to encourage people to pay what they can afford, the general principle being *more if you can, less if you can't*. Sliding scales are used most often for general admission fundraising events, in the hopes that people will pay more as a contribution to

the organization or cause. Although some people do pay more, often people pay the bottom of the scale. In planning your gross potential estimate, base it on the bottom of the scale to be safe. A sliding scale also complicates your ticket bookkeeping. After doing it once or twice you can evaluate whether it's a worthwhile approach.

Scaled Ticket Prices
Scaling means setting different ticket prices for different sections when there is reserved seating. Two reasons to scale are if the quality of seats varies significantly according to the location in the hall or if the audience values some seats as more desirable.

Different Scale for Advance and Door Sales
A higher ticket price can be set for buying tickets at the door instead of in advance. Some producers like to do this because it encourages advance ticket sales which provides more ticket money in hand sooner and an early idea of the crowd size. However, charging a higher price at the door makes it hard

The sliding scale concept offers a price range for each ticket to encourage people to pay what they can afford, the general principle being "more if you can, less if you can't."

for people who can't spend the money in advance because of their low income, or for those who might not know if they can afford to come to the concert until the last minute. You can charge more at the door with either general admission or reserved seating, even if you use a computerized ticket agency. Generally, the door price is $2 higher than the advance price. Make sure the ticket agency is willing to print the two prices on the tickets so that when you collect the unsold tickets to sell the day of the show, the door price appears on the ticket.

Advance and door sales also can be the same price(s).

There are many advantages to selling tickets in advance.

1. You have an ongoing idea of how well your concert is selling. Often, a large percentage of sales takes place the last two weeks before the concert, allowing some lead time to make last-minute additions to your ad campaign.
2. Cash coming in can help pay for sound equipment or program printing if the costs must be paid before the concert. However, if a professional ticket agency handles advance sales, you may not be able to take advantage of this cash because agencies often pay the day of or after the event.
3. The box office will be less hectic on the day of the performance, and lines will be shorter.
4. People coming from far away can be assured of seating.
5. You'll have less cash to handle on the night of the concert.

There are disadvantages to selling advance tickets, too.

1. You have to print tickets. (Remember to include this expense as a budget item unless the ticket agency does this.)
2. You will have to research outlets, work out deals, and often pay a ticket commission with individual ticket outlets or with a ticket agency (also a budget item).
3. Time and money will be spent on calls and gas for delivering tickets, keeping track of sales, possibly redistributing them, and picking up money.

If you are working in a hall with 200 seats or less, it is probably not necessary to sell advance tickets. For the 200- to 500-seat hall, it really depends on you and your community. The goal is to make it easy for people to buy the tickets they want, with a minimal additional ticket service charge. If the hall seats more than 500 you should sell advance tickets. For an event over 500, using a computerized ticket agency can provide access to outlets in a broad geographical area and the flexibility of charge-by-phone purchases.

Advance tickets should go on sale to the public at least one month before the show. If you are expecting a sell-out, you probably will sell most of your tickets in advance.

Ticket-buying patterns vary according to the locality, the time of the year, economic and weather conditions, the act you are producing, ad placement, pay periods, the political climate, and many other transitory variables. After producing a few concerts in an area you'll be able to predict local ticket-buying patterns more accurately.

Discounts
You may want to offer discounted prices for senior citizens, students or young people, disabled people, or others on fixed incomes. If you are working with a computerized ticket agency or hall box office for sales, you should discuss your ticket needs with them early on to see if they can accommodate you. Selling discounted tickets requires special information and *education* of the ticket sellers on how to handle those sales. One option is to make discounted tickets available at certain outlets, although that limits accessibility.

Work Exchange
A producer might choose to pay people for preproduction work — putting up posters, addressing envelopes, telephoning potential sponsors, etc. — by giving them tickets instead of cash. This approach benefits those who might not otherwise have been able to attend. This system also alters your (and possibly your ticket agency's) potential income. Every seat given to a volunteer figures into income like a complimentary ticket, and losing the sales from these tickets is especially notable if you are close to a sell-out.

Complimentary Tickets
Offering complimentary tickets can be important to your goals for coalition-building, press coverage, future fundraising, artists' relations, and community service. In general, the complimentary tickets should be held in envelopes, in alphabetical order by last name, at the box office or at will-call along with any paid-in-advance tickets. The tickets should be marked with a *"c"* or by the computer as *comps* for auditing purposes. At the end of the evening pick up any unused *comp* tickets so you'll know who was able to attend, especially from the press.

The crew should receive passes rather than complimentary tickets, since they won't be occupying seats. Again, every comp represents a potential loss of income to you as well as to the hall, but they may be invaluable forms of goodwill and public relations.

Mail and Phone Orders
If you make tickets available through mail order, set a deadline for mail order sales. This guards against tickets not arriving in time or having to return money or get in touch with people in case of a sell-out.

There are pros and cons to mailing tickets out. Occasionally tickets get lost in the mail. More often, people forget to bring them or misplace them at home. To offset such problems, you can print up and send a postcard which says: "We've received your order for (number of tickets) tickets and are holding them for you at the door."

However, if you expect the show to draw a big crowd with a rush of people at the box office, it might be best to mail tickets in advance. Just be prepared with vouchers for those who may have lost their tickets.

The voucher system is viable if your hall has reserved seats. To maintain a workable system of vouchers, keep careful records with the name, address, ticket numbers, seat locations, and check number for each order. Then if people show up and say they didn't get their tickets, you'll know the specifics and can write a voucher for those seats.

Vouchers create a problem only if others who actually have tickets for them are in those seats. This means either the lost tickets were found by people who wanted to go to the show or the people who claimed their tickets were lost were not telling the truth. Both circumstances are very uncommon and usually don't undermine the convenience of using vouchers on the night of the show.

Series and subscription tickets, as well as block ticket sales sold through other organizations, may be handled mostly by mail or by phone. If your organization can arrange to accept MasterCard/Visa charges, this is convenient for a lot of people. Credit card companies do charge for this service, so figure it in your budget or add on a fee. Be sure to put the charge-by-phone number on your publicity.

Refunds

Discuss the ticket refund and show cancellation policy with the hall manager. In addition to clarifying your obligation to the facility, check the policy for ticket refunds to customers. Refunds may be available only at certain outlets or at the main box office. Find out, too, how long after notice has been given of show cancellation people can ask for refunds. Service charges and commissions generally will not be refunded, but check.

Printing Tickets

The tickets themselves should include as much information as possible. They can be printed on plain ticket stock or with graphic elements related to the publicity for the concert, but they must have the vital elements: price, artists, time, date, hall, address, and seat number.

When you work with a ticket agency, they print the tickets for you. There may or may not be a fee for each ticket printed by them. They generate the tickets as needed by the customer or you (such as for comp tickets). Check over the ticket copy with them, as well

as with their graphic artist.

For your vendors' convenience the advance price should be in larger lettering than the door price. On the day of the show, you could block out (with a black marker, for instance) the lower price so people at the door don't see a big $6 on the ticket for which they've just paid $8.

For general admission concerts, you can print extra tickets to sell at the hall if they haven't all sold before then. This way you won't have to run all over town to pick up unsold tickets on that last and busiest day. Every ticket should be numbered for bookkeeping purposes. The printer can number them in one or two places for a nominal charge.

Ticket Distribution

When you decide to sell advance tickets, identify ticket outlets on your publicity whenever possible. Some information should appear on all publicity, even if only to say "Tickets available at area book and music stores" or "Tickets available at all Ticketron outlets." But the more specific the information, the better. Names, addresses, and phone numbers of alternative outlets ideally should be on all posters and flyers advertising the event. If you are using a box office that comes with the facility and/or ticket agency, publicity should state phone number, address, and hours when possible, a charge-by-phone number, and mail order information.

Let your goals help you decide between using a professional ticket agency and alternative outlets, or a combination.

If you are producing a morale-building concert for the progressive community, you might effectively reach most of your supporters with alternative papers and outlets and not need the services of a ticket agency. If you are planning a big media campaign, it would be counterproductive to have tickets available only at local bookstores. If increased audience is one of your goals, a ticket agency or professional ticket seller will reach the broadest number of people. If you are interested in attracting disabled individuals to the concert, you may want to have a local independent living center serve as an outlet. Similarly, look for outlets or alternative ways to serve any special audience you want to reach.

Ticket Control
Ticket control is important whether your event is general admission or reserved seats, and numbering saves a lot of time. For community or alternative outlets, keep a numbered sheet, and every time tickets go out, write down the batch numbers: 1-50 Jane's Bookstore, 51-100 Health Center, 101-110 artists' comps, etc. A Master Ticket Accounting form (Form 6:1) can be used for this purpose. As you distribute tickets to various outlets and organizations, note the ticket information listed on the form. This form will help you identify your best outlets, so you

> *"We've received your order for tickets and are holding them for you at the door."*

can use them again, and unsatisfactory outlets so you can look for others to replace them. This form or one like it should be kept with your final budget sheet for documentation. Accuracy is important. A complete form will let you determine *when* your sales were greatest, *where* your sales were highest, *who* paid promptly, and *who* were conscientious bookkeepers on your behalf.

Alternative Outlets
Choosing your ticket outlets is as important as any other publicity effort. Pay attention to geographic, special interest, and buying pattern needs in choosing your outlets. If you are considering alternative outlets, look for:

1. Places where advance tickets for other similar concerts are generally sold (check flyers for information on other concerts).

2. Bookstores.
3. Record stores -- also request that they stock the artists' records.
4. Folklore centers.
5. Affiliated organizations.

Be creative in selecting outlets, but be conservative, too. Start by giving a select number of outlets a small number of tickets. Then see who's selling what. When you do your second round, give larger batches to those outlets which are selling more. There is nothing more frustrating than having your biggest seller run out of tickets two days before the concert while a store 90 miles away is sitting on 100 tickets. Make it convenient for people to buy tickets, but don't run yourself ragged trying to keep up with 20 different outlets.

Sign a contract with alternative outlets, just as you would with a hall or professional ticket agency (Form 6:2). It serves as a written confirmation that the seller has received the tickets, includes the various ticket prices and the ticket numbers the store is given, the commission the store is taking and how that will be paid, and clarifies who is responsible for missing tickets or money or bad checks. It's very important that you also have an information sheet all ticket sellers can use to answer any questions customers might ask.

In addition, it's sometimes possible to work with other producers in town to sell tickets. If your concerts are well-spaced and pose no conflict, they may allow you to set up a table and sell tickets at their events. Ask the artists if you could arrange a record signing at a store carrying the artists' records. While they are there signing albums, you can sell tickets to the concert. Publicity for this event may be handled by the store, the distributor, or by you. Record signings require a strong publicity effort to ensure good attendance.

Hall Box Offices and Ticket Agencies
If the concert is held in a *legitimate* hall, you may be required to use its box office. It is

usually to your advantage to do so for at least the week before the show. In addition, the hall also may have its own contract with a computerized ticket agency, so you deal with the hall box office and they deal with the ticket agency. The hall box office usually charges the producer a flat fee for having tickets on sale for a certain number of weeks -- usually four. If you want to put your tickets on sale earlier (six weeks is good for a big show), there is often an extra fee. The box office usually does not add a service charge to the customer for buying tickets at the box office.

Using a ticket agency can be convenient for you and the audience. A computerized agency has a centralized computer which stores information about all the tickets available for sale. This means that people can buy unsold seats at any of the branch outlets. Using a computerized agency cuts down on your running around to different outlets and makes it easier for audience members to get the seats they want.

Be creative in selecting outlets, but be conservative, too.

A major consideration in using an agency or hall box office is that you often cannot collect money from advance ticket sales until the day of the show at the earliest, and sometimes not until a week after the event. Obviously, this affects your cash flow, and you will need money other than revenue from advance ticket sales to pay early bills.

Ticket agencies usually charge a service charge to the customer as well as sometimes a commission to you. Service charges to the customer are from $.75 to $1.50 (more on credit card telephone sales). The commission fee to the producer is usually three to seven percent of the ticket price, or it can be a fixed price, such as $.30 per ticket sold. For credit card sales, agencies usually add about

three to four percent commission on top of the base commission. Therefore, the actual ticket price to the customer is higher, and your income is lower than the face value of the ticket.

It's a courtesy to your audience to offer them a way to get tickets without paying a service charge. One way is to offer mail order sales, handling this yourself or through the hall box office. Or it may be important in your community to have tickets available at alternative outlets even when you are using a computerized or commercial service. Both options may be considered out of the ordinary and require negotiation and arrangement with the agency or hall box office. Also, since computerized agencies print out hard tickets only after they have been sold, negotiate with them to pull off their computer and print hard tickets ahead of time if you want to have mail order or alternative outlet sales. Some ticket agencies make you pay in advance for any ticket printed for you. Find this out before signing a contract.

Ask the agency to pull your comp tickets and remove from the computer any seats that should not be sold -- for example, seats for the sound and light boards or seats with an obstructed view. If the hall is clearly bigger than your potential audience, you may want to close off the balcony so the hall will feel as full as possible. Clear this with your facility and ticket agency, and make sure that tickets for the closed-off section are not sold. The hall should provide you with an up-to-date map of the hall, showing every seat. Go to the hall and check each seat's accuracy, then use this to pull tickets for producer and/or mail order sales, complimentary tickets, unsalable seats, alternative outlets, and special-access sections. Form 6:3 is an illustration of a hall's seating map.

If the hall fee is a minimum versus a percentage of the gross receipts, the organization may limit the number of tickets they're willing to pull and print for you since this leaves them with fewer tickets to sell from their system and reduces their percentage income. Halls that work on a fee plus percentage usually have a maximum ceiling, so they won't be as worried about these tickets if they think the show will sell out or at least sell well enough to meet their maximum.

Find out what the procedure is for getting ticket counts from your facility box office and ticket agency. Can they give you an accounting of everything they have on sale (their own box office plus the outlets)? How often and on what days of the week can you get ticket counts? Whom should you call?

As showtime approaches you'll want to get ticket counts more often. In the last week you should get a count every day (the artists' representative may ask for this information as well).

Ticket agencies and hall box offices vary greatly in capabilities and range of flexibility. Anything out of the ordinary complicates the arrangement. Therefore, problems are more likely to arise. If you want to offer special discounts or special seating sections (hearing-impaired or wheelchair accessible, for example), see if the agency can program its computer accordingly.

Provide the personnel at the outlets with specific and clear, written instructions so they can handle requests with respect and accurate information.

Particularly with special arrangements, follow up every phone call or negotiating session with a cordial, brief letter recapping the agreements reached. Keep a copy for yourself in case a misunderstanding arises later and for reference on future productions.

Although not too common, an agency can mistakenly sell a ticket in error. They could double-sell a ticket by not pulling it off the computer after they've sold and printed the hard ticket. Or they could sell unsalable seats if you don't accurately check the hall map. You need to handle errors like this both from a bookkeeping/settlement perspective and on the day of the show at the hall. Ushers will need to seat people in as com-

parable seats as are available, and/or the box office may need to refund a portion of the ticket price. When pulling tickets from the box office or computer for outside sales and comps, hold out a few extra, especially if you're expecting a sell-out or near-capacity crowd. Having a few spare tickets can solve a lot of problems -- last-minute changes in the artists' comp list, a problem with seats the day of the show, additional reviewers showing up (people important to you). Clarify in advance that if you don't use them you can sell these tickets the day of the show at the box office.

Setting Up Your Own Box Office
You will need the following items:

Tickets. The tickets may or may not be *hard* tickets. Each one represents a single seat: for example, for a 200-seat hall there are 200 tickets only.

If tickets have been selling at three outlets around town, you will have to collect all the unsold ones, making sure the comps for press, artists, or friends are set aside. Then, you are free to sell the rest. As mentioned earlier, you may prefer to print up a larger batch of tickets than seats so on the day of the performance you can call your outlets, get an accurate count of sales at that time, tell them to sell no more tickets, and start selling the tickets you have in hand up to the hall's capacity.

Change. Take plenty of small bills and change, a cash box, receipt books, pens. Also, a stamp with your organization's name makes check writing go faster.

Envelopes. These are used to file paid and comp tickets, alphabetized by last name.

Credit Card Equipment. Take a MasterCard/Visa imprinter, forms, and pens, if you offer credit card sales.

Deposit Bags. Bank bags or other secure storage is needed for money you receive. At most concerts a considerable amount of cash is taken in. It should be accounted for and safely handled until deposited in the bank. Many producers do a bank drop off as the last task of the evening. If possible, it's handy to have locking bank bags ready with deposit slips and a *FOR DEPOSIT ONLY* stamp so you don't have to sign checks.

Ticket Sellers. Have people selling tickets who are good at making change and are used to handling money. At least two should be at the table at all times; three are better — allowing one to run an errand and still leaving two at the table.

The box office should open at least one-half hour before the hall opens and should stay open through intermission. After the intermission the tickets should be counted and the number of tickets reconciled immediately with the amount of cash, checks, and charges received. Form 6:4 is a sample Box Office Statement.

Bookkeeping and Settlement

When the concert is over or when you close the box office, make a final ticket register. List each outlet and the number of tickets sold there. If you call outlets regularly, you can record sales information each time. After a few concerts, some patterns will emerge: certain regions or outlets sell more tickets than others; more are sold after a certain date; the percentage of charge-by-phone versus walk-ups is evident; alternative outlets sold heavily in the last week and commercial agencies sold heavily in the first week. All this information reveals who your audience was for the concert and what their buying habits were. It can help you plan your cash flow, ticket outlets, and promotion for the next concert.

Figuring out your gross receipts is very easy when you have a single advance price and a single door price: multiply number of tickets sold by the price. With various priced tickets, it's the same — there are just more combinations to add.

In a hall where the box office is part of the contract package, you may be settling the box office account as part of the overall hall settlement. If so, all hall charges and box office charges will be deducted from the ticket income. The hall may have a sample settlement form that you can get in advance to review. Find out when and with whom you will settle -- the earlier the better, since most of your income will be tied up until then. A good time is the day of the show, after intermission (you might miss part of the show, but among producers it's an occupational hazard).

When you settle, one of the expenses might be a user's fee or hall or city tax. Some halls or cities tack on an additional fee for renovation, etc., to the ticket price. This fee is taken from the gross receipts by the box office before settlement. If a significant amount of money is involved, you may decide to include an explanation in the publicity so the audience knows the price is higher for that reason. For example, if you set your ticket price at $8 and the hall requires a $2 user's fee, you could list the price as "$10 ($8 plus $2 user's fee)."

> *It can help you plan your cash flow, ticket outlets, and promotion for the next concert.*

Ticket fraud by hall management is, unfortunately, an ever-increasing problem in concert production, but it can be hard to prove. The box office can claim to have sold fewer tickets than they actually sold and not pay you for those sales by showing sold tickets as still available for sale in the computer. (This also can happen by mistake, as described previously, but more frequently the box office may be committing fraud.) The way to investigate possible fraud is to take your map of the hall, compare it with where people are sitting before the end of the show, and get the hall management to agree with you. Otherwise, it is impossible to prove how many people were there. This is one of the many reasons to settle on the day of the show before the show is over.

To get more specific, you'll have to match ticket stubs against the hall map. To do so requires making sure in advance that the ticket takers do a *drop count*, meaning they rip the ticket stub (which has the seat number on it) and drop it into a box as they admit people into the hall. Ticket takers are in a different union from the box office workers or are not affiliated with the hall precisely to reduce corruption. If you're going into a major hall for the first time, ask the hall or box office manager if they will do a drop count. Then check that against the map and your unsold hard tickets (called *deadwood*).

The process is very time-consuming and painstaking, so you embark on it only if you're really suspicious about the settlement.

## CHAPTER SEVEN

Promotion and Advertising

Contributors Cathy Fink, Melissa Howden, Sheila Kahn, Torie Osborn, Jo-Lynne Worley

Promotion is all of the activities you engage in to get the word out and sell tickets to your event. The main methods of promoting an event are: articles in newspapers or magazines; press releases to all media; interviews in the broadcast media (radio and TV); paid advertising, both print and broadcast; calendar announcements; public service announcements (PSAs); posters and flyers, including distribution by direct mail; networking — shared mailings, speeches at meetings, monthly organizational newsletters, and personal contact; and promotional tie-ins, such as sponsorship tickets and ticket giveaways (usually via radio).

Effective publicity is essential even if the concert features top performers. Your event will be competing with other attractions, and you must always motivate the audience to leave their comfortable homes and attend your concert! Promotion is even more critical if the artists or their art form are not well-known in your location.

Promotion is a major budget expense; it is very labor-intensive, and it demands good planning. Start planning your promotion campaign as soon as you have confirmed the artists and hall — but at least two to three months in advance.

Getting the word out early to potential concert sponsors and other producers in your area (when you have non-competitive relationships with these producers) is both a courtesy and an important method of protecting against conflicting events on the day of your show (see Form 7:1).

Start by analyzing your own organization's strengths, the character of the community, your budget, the kind of event you are producing, and the kind of audience you want or expect to attract to determine which activities — mailings, telephone work, major media advertising — will give you the greatest return for your money and effort.

As a very general rule (and subject to your own experience and needs), expect to spend $1 on promotion for each ticket that, realistically, you expect to sell. If you want to develop or build your audience beyond your *natural market* — those you think you can easily draw — increase that figure to $1.50. Sometimes promotion is done free or for a discounted rate. For example, if the hall has a regular ad in the Sunday newspaper, it may automatically advertise your event as part of its ad (and as part of your deal with the hall), or it may allow you to use its advertising contract to get a better rate than you could get yourself.

Don't spend your whole promotion budget at one time or in one place. And save some for a possible last-minute blitz — you might not need to spend it, but it's good to have some leeway if you need an extra push at the end.

Planning Promotion
Intuition, analysis, and experience are the best guides in planning your promotion strategy. Ask people who have put on similar events about what has or has not worked, and consider whether their experience is relevant to your city or artists. Think about what kind of event you are putting on and the audience it will attract. Planning is essential. After you identify your markets develop a timeline and plan based on deadlines.

There are three major groups of people your promotion efforts can target: *your natural market* — the people who surely will want to come and just need to know that the event is happening; people who might generally be interested in *the type of event* you're producing but might not automatically buy a ticket; and people quite unfamiliar with your organization, or unaccustomed to participating, whom you would like to *develop as an audience*.

At a minimum, direct the promotion to your natural market; how much time, money, and effort you spend on additional audience development depends on your (and the artists') goals. For example, you could decide to print 500 flyers to distribute at similar or related events attracting your natural market, rather than take out a paid ad in the Sunday paper's entertainment section. But if a good article appeared in the daily paper, running a paid ad that uses a quote from the article might be the best strategy.

Billing
Examine how to bill the event in a way that will attract the most people and further your goals. Usually the artists are the main draw, and they already might have a preferred billing for producers to use. On the other hand, the reason for the event may be more significant than who's playing. For example, deciding to bill a benefit event with the slogan "Festival for Peace in Central America" as the headline and the artists' names below *versus* headlining the artists and adding "Benefit for the People of Central America" underneath will depend on the draw of the artists, the draw of the issue, the audience you're trying to attract, and the kind of image you want to present. Once you have decided how to bill the event, be consistent in all your publicity materials (posters, flyers, press releases, etc.).

> *Don't spend your whole promotion budget at one time or in one place.*

Working with the Artists' Representative, Record Company, and Distributor
The artists' representative may have recommendations or requirements about how the artists should be promoted. Discuss the artists' availability for interviews — both advance phone interviews and in-person interviews on the day of the show. Newspapers, magazines, and radio stations sometimes will do an article or feature only if they can interview the artists. If the artists are willing to do interviews but time is limited, you'll have to

decide which vehicle will provide the most effective exposure.

If the artists have a record out (especially a new one), the record company, local distributor (supplier of records), or local record stores might be willing to help promote the concert. The artists' representative, record companies, distributors, and producers can share the tasks and expenses of promotion in a variety of ways. Each party should know the others' responsibilities to avoid confusion or duplication of effort. Consult the artists' representative on how best to work together so you can allocate your promotion budget and responsibilities.

For example, artists' representatives should be able to supply promotional materials, such as press kits and photos. When artists are touring, artists' representatives sometimes provide posters that have space to print in local concert information, as well as materials you can use in developing your print publicity. You probably can make good use of promotional records to give to radio stations and media people. Do you get records from the artists' representative, the record company, or the local distributor? Is there a limit to how many you can have? Has promotional work already been done in your city so that the radio and media people already have the records? Who is making the follow-up phone calls?

It's clearly in everyone's best interest for the media to receive records and be called by phone, so it would be worth discussing whether it is more effective for the representative or distributor to send the record or to have you deliver it. The distributor may be willing to take concert flyers around to his or her record store accounts; you also may be able to do cooperative advertising with the distributor, in which you split the costs by advertising the concert and tagging the record and/or stores.

It is important for distributors to know that artists whose records they carry are coming to town so they can order records for the stores they supply (and in some cases for sale at the concert). Although the artists' representative usually lets the distributor know, it's a courtesy — as well as a good way to initiate a working relationship — to call the distributor directly to let her or him know you've booked artists whose records she or he distributes.

If the artists' representative doesn't know which distributor covers your area or doesn't know much about working with the record company or distributors, call the record company or distributor directly (let the artists' representative know you'll be calling) to see if you can work with them to promote the concert.

Print Media
Getting stories in the press is a very good way to broaden your audience, create interest, and confirm the legitimacy of the artists and your production company. Most people will not go to a concert by an unknown artist, and even ads won't help convince them. But a well-written story or interview can make people curious enough to want to check out your event for themselves. Some community papers will edit and reprint a short article you send in. Others will run parts of your fact sheet or public service announcement in their calendar of events.

Do not send a feature-length article to a newspaper hoping they will print it for you; their writers do such pieces. You can interest a writer in doing an article, however, by sending a thoughtful, brief press release and following up with phone calls. Don't be afraid to do aggressive follow-up. Often it takes four, five, or more calls to get a return call or to stimulate interest.

The first step is to compile a press list. Do this early. Go to a well-stocked newsstand or library, and make a list of all the relevant papers and periodicals that list community events in a calendar listing arrangement or cover events similar to what you are interested in promoting. The writers may write for a number of sections of the newspaper or for more than one paper. Become familiar with the entertainment, features, or city life editor, as well as individual writers who regularly review music.

Another way to start a press list is to get names from someone else, like another concert promoter in your area who does not consider you *competition* or the local distributor. Concerts are one of the biggest boosts to record sales.

Calendar Listings. From the press list make a second listing of calendar sections. Sending the community calendar listings a short press release (and photo if requested) with who, what, where, when, why and how much is an easy, important, and timely task. Many calendar listings are prepared weeks in advance. Check the paper for deadlines. Refer to later paragraphs on press releases for more information.

Getting Articles and Features
Every newspaper story has a particular *angle*. Try to develop an angle and pitch it in your press release and calls. What's especially unique, exciting, or interesting about your concert or artists?

Identify potential story writers and their editors at papers that cover events like yours. Because newspaper contacts can be hard to reach, begin your efforts early. For most events eight weeks in advance is not too early. Call editors first; it is their job to assign stories. If you attract their interest your event is likely to receive coverage. However, if you get nowhere with a particular editor, try one of the writers. As you gain experience and develop a track record, you'll know when it's appropriate to call a writer directly.

> *When writing a release put all the most important information in the first paragraph.*

Newspaper editors often are harried and focused on production matters, like their own deadlines. If you have trouble getting through, ask when is generally a good time to reach them. If you reach them and they are impatient or distracted, politely ask if there is a better time for you to talk — later in the day or early tomorrow. If they agree to a time, definitely follow through! You will need to make plenty of calls — don't expect the editor to call you.

When you reach the editor or writers, introduce yourself, let them know what the event is, and tell them you will or already have sent more information. On this introductory call, confirm that you are beginning with the right person. If an editor says it's not his or her beat, but belongs to Ms. Q at the next desk, ask to be transferred or ask for her direct phone number so you can try later.

After you've made the initial call, send a press kit. If the artists' record company or representative doesn't supply you with a press kit, make your own. You need a good photo, a one-page biography, a press release, a list of credits (which can be included in the bio), and reviews of the artists or other stories about them. The press kit should look professional, if not totally unique, to get the attention of the media. You also should send an album or tape if the editor is unfamiliar with the artists or if it's an album-release show. Accompany all of these materials with a personal letter, reminding the editor or writer you will call in a few days.

Press Release. The press release which goes out to your media contacts should be brief — one page is adequate (see Form 7:2).

The most important elements are well-known journalistic tools — date; your press contact person; brief description of the event; artists' names and simple description; time and place; where tickets are available and prices.

Additional information might provide background information about the artists, including records released, major performances, and names of other artists' credits on the tour. Be sure there is a phone number for tickets and more information.

When writing a release put all the most important information in the first paragraph, followed by additional information. The important facts must appear first because when space is limited, editors will knock out secondary paragraphs. Include photos if editors use them. Check the papers for deadlines, and mail with a week or more to spare.

If the concert will have an interpreter for the hearing-impaired, or if other organizations will participate in lobby activities, it's an option to include or highlight these special features.

Follow up the mailing with a phone call in a week or so, allowing enough time for the package to have arrived, but not enough time for it to be lost or buried on someone's desk. Keep track of your calling and mailing schedule with whatever system works for you, such as file folders for each media type (newspapers, magazines, radio, etc.), on a computer, or index cards. Sometimes you will need to contact two or more people at the same place for different sections of the paper, different radio or TV shows on the same station. The Media Contact Sheet (Form 7:4) may be a useful format for keeping track of media information.

When you call, ask if your materials were received. Then explain again briefly about your event, and suggest some angles they might use. Offer to set up interviews, provide additional photos, supply more background information. Some writers may be more interested in your organization's work than the event *per se* — so even if the story is different from what you might prefer, encourage their interest. (See Form 7:3 for an issues-oriented press release.) If you doubt their angle's acceptability to the artists, check with the artists' representative. Use good public relations skills to work with the media to get a suitable angle.

Dealing with the Press. Success with the print media comes from persistence and developing good personal contacts. If you say you are going to call, call. For example, an editor might say that he or she hasn't had time to look at the material yet. Respond that you'll call back in a couple of days and do so until you move toward something final.

Take the time to sort out just what you want to say before you call so you can be brief and concise. State clearly what you are offering and what you would like the media person to do. Working with notes in front of you is a good way to keep all your points on hand. In short, the more confident, enthusiastic, and direct you are with media contacts, the more favorably they will respond to your efforts.

When an editor or writer expresses interest in doing an advance piece, you can offer to set up a phone interview (assuming the artists agree to this kind of promotion). Ask the media person to identify the times that are generally convenient, then call the artists' representative and ask for three dates and times (and numbers) when the artists can be reached for a press interview. You will have a better chance of finding a time that can work by getting three possibilities. If they don't work, reschedule as necessary. Non-business hours may work best.

Remind the artists' representative several days before the interview is scheduled. Call the media person the day before, too; leaving a message is good enough to jog a memory. The message should include your name and phone number and a reminder of the artists' names, the time, and the phone number.

An editor may say that she or he can't run a story but could send someone to do a review. Complimentary tickets should be offered in pairs and left at the door. If possible, find out when reviewers are arriving so you can be there to meet and greet them. (Your staffing may include a press relations person whose job is to meet and help the press at the concert.) Make good seats available for the press. If there is no reserved seating, rope off a center section, several rows from the front. Be as generous with the comps as your hall capacity allows. Invite members of the major press to be your guests at the concert; not all will show up, but this is a step in building good media relations.

If anyone does write a story or a review, call and thank the writer or send a card. If they attend the show but nothing appears in print, call them to follow-up. Did the editor delete it? Would the reviewer like to come again in the future? Always build on the relationship.

Broadcast Media. Broadcast media should be approached much like the print media. A Public Service Announcement (PSA) can be sent to radio and TV — including local cable stations which make concert or event announcements (a sample is included as Form 7:5). To get more significant coverage follow up the PSA with contacts similar to those described under print media, except keep in mind that it's more likely the artists must be in town for the interview.

The person who chooses the program content is often the producer rather than the talent or host, so contact producers. On television an interview is most common, with some music interspersed between the talking; occasionally an event is covered as a news story, especially if it's a large outdoor concert or the artists are newsworthy. Entertainment shows (or entertainment spots as part of interview shows) are gaining popularity. Don't overlook the cable and community access channels.

Begin negotiating dates for TV segments as soon as you start work on the print media, and move quickly to reserve acceptable times. For example, even if the show airs every weekday, they may tape only Mondays through Wednesdays or have other studio time restrictions. If the show is done live, the schedule is finalized well in advance.

Radio frequently features interviews with artists — either live or pretaped (often by telephone). It is helpful for the artists to know in advance what kinds of questions the interviewer will ask; you might even be able to suggest some. Preparation gives the artists the opportunity to respond more readily and thoroughly, it also can make the interview more interesting. Be sure the interviewer and artists are thoroughly prepared with press kit and concert information in advance.

In setting up interviews with the broadcast media, keep in mind the artists' preferences. Do they want to do everything in one day or spread out appearances and interviews over a few days? If the artists' time is limited, set priorities for the interviews, and schedule those that give you the most exposure. It is not worth getting the artists into town two days early for a cable TV show that is broadcast at 6 a.m. on Sundays, but for a segment on a National Public Radio affiliate station during the morning and evening rush hours it may be. Some artists' busy schedules will not allow them this in-town time. It often creates extra costs to your budget for food and housing in advance of the concert, but the publicity may make it worthwhile.

> *It is not worth getting the artists into town two days early for a cable TV show that is broadcast at 6 a.m. on Sundays.*

You also may have a good program if the disc jockey just talks about the concert and provides a fair amount of airplay. If the artists have a new album out or one that fits well into the format of a station or particular show, see if the DJ's can play one or two cuts and mention your event several times during the week before your show. The record company or distributor already may have sent the album directly to the DJ's or stations. However, sending a press release along with the record usually will get the best results for a concert.

Another good option for radio promotion, especially if your concert is part of the artists' tour, is to offer local radio stations a prerecorded interview cut with music (either reel-to-reel or cassette). This piece must be of excellent quality and must be recorded so it can be broken easily into segments — ideally a 10-minute spot, a 20-minute spot, or a half-hour show. See if something like this is available from your artists. Or, if the artists have a promotional video, you can offer it to TV stations as part of a talk or news show or it can become part of a PSA spot.

Concert Taping and Broadcasting. People may want to record or videotape the concert for public or commercial purposes, such as a later broadcast on a radio show or university television station. To do this, they must have the artists' permission in writing on a release form. The station or the artists should have a copy of the standard forms (see Forms 7:6 and 7:7). Either or both the producer and the artists can refuse permission to tape, especially on the grounds that extra microphones or lighting will be required, that camera operators will be standing in front of the stage, interfering with the audience's view of the concert, and that extra hall and crew costs may be involved. These are all negotiable points to be considered in advance. However, the public relations benefit may be worth the additional technical set-up on the day of the show, and the station may pay the extra costs.

A radio station may want to broadcast the concert live over the air. This could be a good opportunity for the artists to reach a larger audience and also be good publicity for your production company. Begin by checking with the artists' representative — simultaneous broadcasting requires the artists' permission in writing.

For a weekend event, broadcasting the Friday night concert might bring a larger crowd on Saturday. However, it's possible that advertising simultaneous broadcasting of a single concert in advance will work to keep people from buying tickets since they know they can stay home and listen.

Sometimes news channels are interested in filming a brief piece of the sound check or concert to air on a late afternoon or night time news show. All these angles can be pursued for publicity reasons, but don't ever surprise your artists with an unauthorized media event.

The Clip License Agreement (Form 7:8). This agreement is used when a small promotional piece is desired from a longer TV news or entertainment segment. Normally the artists would control this negotiation in future use, but you, as the producer, may be able to make good promotional use of it, too.

Networking
Direct Mail/Bulk Mail. One of the most effective ways to use print publicity is targeted direct mailing. The term direct mail simply means promotion sent directly to potential consumers, as compared to indirect means for reaching a market (such as media advertising). Any nonprofit — or profit-making person or organization — can obtain a bulk mailing permit for mailing a quantity of pieces at reduced postage rates; nonprofit rates are far cheaper.

There is an annual fee and postal requirements regarding minimum number of pieces and how they must be sorted. One mistake can prevent timely delivery. The local post office can get you started. Basically, a bulk mailing must have at least 200 identical items marked with a bulk mail permit number and indicia — placed where the stamp usually goes in the upper right hand corner. All 200 pieces must be sorted and bound by zip code. Bulk mail delivery varies, but it can take a couple of weeks even within local zones. Coast to coast can take up to eight weeks. Be sure to print *Time dated material — Please deliver by (date)* on the front of each piece.

Use your own mailing list, of course, to reach your known supporters. The artists' representative also might have a mailing list of interested fans in your area, and check with the performers' record company, groups for whom the concert is a fundraiser, and local similar-interest groups. The individuals on these lists are potential concert goers; they are interested either in concerts, the artists, or the cause. You may get mailing lists with *no strings attached*, but it is also common for groups to exchange lists (or portions) or to charge a one-time rental fee. If the budget allows, direct mail is often the most cost-effective method to reach a targeted market. Since bulk mail provides reduced postal costs, it is often cost effective to broaden your mailing to include individuals or groups you would like to develop as audience members. But plan for the extra time it takes to prepare bulk mail before it goes to the post office, or build in the cost of a direct mail service.

Tag-alongs and Shared Mailings. Mailing lists of similar-interest groups will contain overlapping names. Be sure to spot check the lists for duplication. As an alternate to increasing your direct mailing list, friendly organizations may have mailing lists to which they mail regularly. They may be willing to include your announcement, flyer, or ad in their publication. While you save postal costs and handling, you must print additional pieces.

If any organization has a publication that would be out in time for your event, it's an option to reach the people on their mailing list through an ad. Even if there is a charge (and a graphic design fee), it may be worthwhile in terms of the people-energy and money you save by not printing and mailing flyers. Keep in mind, however, that as a rule of thumb, ads are not as effective as a mail

ing. You will have to be flexible regarding their printing and delivery dates.

Personal Contact. Don't overlook the simplest method of publicity: word of mouth. Encourage everyone you know to tell all their friends about your event. Nothing can replace the energy created by personal enthusiasm for an event. Making an event the highlight of the season for a community may be exactly what you need to do.

Some producing organizations routinely use the technique of contacting people on membership lists by *phonebanking* or telemarketing. Getting a group of volunteers or staff together to make calls and speak to each person is a very strong way to promote an event, especially if the event is closely identified with an issue or organization and the caller supplies pertinent information at the same time. People who support your efforts often are touched by the personal attention a phone call represents.

Even if your organization is not particularly set up for telemarketing, you may want your staff to pinpoint their contacts and do a little phoning. Personal contact can have a dramatic impact on ticket sales, especially if you ask supporters to buy a ticket or two and adopt as their own project a goal of selling 10 or 20 tickets to others. You can offer one to two free tickets for each 10 to 20 sold if there are not computer ticket seller restrictions.

Leafletting at events where your potential audience will be is also a great way of targeting your audience, networking, and having personal contact.

Ticket and Album Giveaways
Giving away tickets often stimulates interest and ticket sales. If you anticipate a sell-out, you don't need to give any tickets away, but nothing is lost in giving some away if there might be a number of empty seats anyway. The size of your hall will help determine how much to use this approach.

You may want radio stations to give away tickets. A typical arrangement is to play a cut from an album, talk about the artist, and offer two free tickets to the first (or sixth or whatever number) caller who gets through to the station. You may be able to arrange to give away as many as 10 pairs of tickets during the two weeks before the performance, giving the disc jockey several opportunities to play your artists' album and promote your event.

The advantage of giving away tickets is that they carry no actual costs, unlike giving away record albums. However, if you are in a very small hall and are concerned about keeping your tickets available for sale, consider giving away albums as a promotion. Promotional copies may be available at no cost from the local distributor or from the artists. Negotiating the giveaway of albums is the same as for tickets, but because of the cost of albums you may need to purchase some to have a reasonable number to give away. Sometimes a public radio or television station is willing to work a record giveaway into its own membership drive, offering albums as premiums for new members or for members joining at a certain sponsorship level.

Keep in mind, however, that as a rule of thumb, ads are not as effective as a mailing.

Paid Advertising
Getting feature articles, calendar listings, or photos into the press is cheaper than taking out an ad, but you can't always get free press. Sometimes you can increase the effectiveness of publicity with advertisements. The repetition of the same graphic design for your event, as discussed in depth in Chapter 8, on posters and flyers may be used effectively in advertisements, too.

A paid ad might be the only way to get into a particular paper. Although the editorial and advertising departments of a paper or magazine are supposed to be completely independent, this isn't always true. Editors sometimes are more interested in running a story if you advertise.

Place your paid advertising after researching and targeting the markets you think will be effective or necessary. If you produce events that appeal to the progressive community, support the alternative press by taking out paid advertising. They often are more inclined to cover your events and run stories or calendar announcements, and their ad rates often are lower than mainstream media. Many of the smaller, specialized papers are struggling for financial stability and benefit greatly from advertising revenues. If those papers hit your most likely markets, it could be advantageous to get exposure there.

Advertising in major daily newspapers is both an expensive and an untargeted approach. But if you want to attract the general public, you may reach people who don't read the alternative press. Advertising in the daily paper conveys an image that the event is open to all, rather than only to special interest groups. In this sense, mainstream advertising legitimatizes the event. Often the best exposure for a paid ad in the major print media, although sometimes the most expensive, is in the weekend entertainment section — usually Friday or Sunday. As mentioned previously, the hall may allow you to take advantage of its advertising contract with the paper for discounted rates.

Research for Advertising. You probably already know which are the most widely read publications in your community and what markets they cover. Nevertheless, ask the ad representatives of various publications for demographic information (age, sex, income, interests, etc.) so you can set advertising priorities for your targeted audiences. Analyze the cost effectiveness of each publication. Get rate cards, which include information on ad costs, discounts available, deadlines, graphic specifications, and other information.

The two deadlines for paid advertising are the space reservation deadline and the copy deadline. Publications want to know in advance the size of your ad so they can plan their layout. Although you sometimes can make your space reservation over the phone, it's a good idea to put it in writing, too, so you can confirm the discounts for which you are eligible. Space reservation deadlines are often a week or two before copy deadlines, when the publication needs camera-ready copy. Some publications will design, typeset, and lay out an ad for a charge — usually more than what a freelance graphic artist would charge. Copy deadlines vary a few days in advance of publication for daily papers to more than two months in advance for monthly magazines. If you mail in your ad, follow up with a phone call to the ad representative to make sure it arrived.

The usual kinds of discounts available are:

Frequency Discount (Contract). If you contract to take out a certain number of ads within a certain timeframe, you can get a discount on each ad. This is particularly good if you plan to produce several events a year. Otherwise, you may be able to use the hall's contract or find another organization or business who will let you use their contract.

Agency Discount. Publications often give a 15 percent discount to an advertising agency, which charges the client the full price and keeps the 15 percent discount as a fee. If the rate card offers a 15 percent discount, by claiming to be an in-house agency you may be able to keep some discount yourself. Let the ad representative know so you will be billed accordingly.

Cash Discounts. The usual term for paying for advertising is 30 days, but many publica-

tions offer a two percent discount if you pay in advance. If you are a new advertiser with the publication, they may require payment in advance until you establish credit.

Advertising Budget and Timing. In placing your advertising you will have to make budget choices between size and frequency. Larger ads are not necessarily better. A small ad with an appealing design, run several times, is usually more effective than one large ad.

Generally, for the monthlies, if your concert is in the second half of the month, you can advertise just the month of the concert. If your concert is in the first half of the month, it's good to place an ad the month before the concert as well as the concert month. If your event is in the first few days of the month, it's only worthwhile to advertise the preceding month.

For weeklies, generally the two to three weeks before the concert are best, as most people don't want to commit to buying tickets until then anyway. On the other hand, early ads build advance excitement. You also can plan to run the ad the third and second week before the concert, and then re-run it the week before only if necessary. For the daily papers, a week ahead is fine. Ads in Sunday and weekend special editions also can be run the third and second week before the concert.

Because size specifications vary so much, each ad might have to be designed separately. Once the basic design is agreed upon, it is the dimensions around it which vary. You can reduce or enlarge up to 15 percent without needing to use a different line screen. When you plan your advertising budget, figure in the costs of graphics as well as placement costs. Also, as was discussed earlier, save some ad money for a last-minute push in case you need it.

Co-op Advertising. You may be able to work out co-op advertising — sharing the cost of paid advertising with someone else, such as the local record distributor, a record store, the record label (particularly if the artists recently have released a record or are on a record-release tour). For example, you could design an ad for your concert that also advertises the record and lists where it is available. Or the record store or distributor might do a record ad and include your concert date. You also can work out co-op deals on other forms of publicity besides paid ads. For example, if you list the record and where it is available on your flyer, the distributor, record store, or label might pay for part of the printing. However you work it out, co-op advertising benefits your promotion budget.

Sponsorship. Similar to co-op advertising, commercial businesses, nonprofits, radio stations, etc., may want to co-sponsor the concert to have their name on the publicity. They may offer in-kind or monetary contributions for the chance to advertise with you and the artists. Always get the artists' permission before agreeing to a sponsorship as many economic and political issues may be involved.

Radio Advertising. Paid advertising on commercial radio may not be worthwhile if the kind of music you're producing generally does not get commercial radio airplay. However, a particular station may attract your intended market, so in your discussions with the artists' representative you might decide to try radio advertising as a market development strategy. (In this case negotiate with the artists' representative about the promotion budget.) Sometimes by taking out paid advertising you can encourage or negotiate airplay, an on-air interview, or promotional ticket giveaways with the station. Radio advertising then can be worth it, since you will get added air time and exposure in return for your money.

If the stations that play your kind of music are noncommercial public and college stations, they won't run paid advertising. Aim instead for PSAs, interviews, and ticket giveaways with them. They may be very valuable sources of promotion and exposure. Cultivate individual show hosts and programmers, too.

Evaluating Promotion
If you're going to produce concerts, you must develop a means of evaluating your promotion methods and strategies to find out what is effective and what isn't. If you produce extremely varied events that appeal to different markets, it is still important to evaluate and compare the results. Watch the effect on ticket sales after different promotions. It's important to know if there's a jump immediately after a paid ad, your direct mail is sent, or a feature article appears. It is helpful for future concerts, as well as for the evaluation, to chart ticket sales in relationship to the timing of different kinds of promotion. Another evaluation method is to do a market survey. If your show is fairly informal, you can ask your audience directly from the stage how they found out about the concert. Ask for a show of hands of how many people saw a flyer, how many saw an ad in a particular paper, how many heard about it on the radio, how many heard about it from a friend, etc. This kind of survey is easy to do, and it provides a general sense of how an audience finds out about events.

> *You must develop a means of evaluating your promotion methods and strategies to find out what is effective and what isn't.*

You also can include a printed market survey in the program, and ask people to fill it out. This involves more energy — convincing people to take the time to fill out and return the forms, collecting them, and tabulating them. Audience members may respond less readily because writing requires more effort than simply raising one's hand; however, the results you get will be informative.

CHAPTER EIGHT

Developing Graphics and Using Them

Contributors Lincoln Cushing, Caryn Dickman, Sheila Kahn, Peggy Kiss, Pam Wilson

V arious forms of printed communication are an essential part of promoting your event. Whether you design the graphics yourself or hire someone, your printed promotional pieces reflect the quality of both the event and the producer to your potential audience. A well-designed, clearly printed flyer, poster, ad, or mailing piece should present the facts clearly. And it can create interest in your event, even among people who have never heard of your organization or the artists.

Printed Publicity

Clarity, appropriateness, and visual interest are the key goals of your printed publicity. Type faces can be sophisticated and formal, casual and cheerful, old-fashioned, or nostalgic. Developing an eye for their impact is a valuable skill you will need. You don't have to do the graphics yourself, but allow enough time to come up with something you approve of in design, typesetting, and printing.

In planning graphics, start by deciding who your audience is — whom you are trying to reach and what is the most important information you need to get across to that audience. The answers to these questions will help you decide what type of graphics you need (i.e., ads, flyers, mailing pieces, or other material).

The artists may supply photos, type recommendations, or other graphic components to maintain their own publicity style. However, on each graphic piece produced, the performers' names (and photos or drawings), date, time, place, address, ticket prices, and ticket sellers must be listed. Setting graphic priorities for this information will depend on the focus of the event and the people you are trying to reach.

As mentioned earlier with regard to billing the event, if you are doing a fundraiser and want people to come to the concert to support the cause as well as to hear the artists, then highlight the name of the cause. If the artists are the major draw, the performers' names should be featured. Display your company name in a smaller, but visible location. If you have been printing your company's name with a logo, think about using it in the ad if there is room. When there is an immediate association with a familiar typeface and logo, people will read the ad.

Printed pieces also should include secondary information such as ticket prices; names and phone numbers of ticket outlets; availability of child care or interpreting for the hearing-impaired, deaf, wheelchair accessibility, and a phone number for further information.

Visual Emphasis

Once you have determined your audience, decide on the importance of specific information based on what will attract that audience. Using visual emphasis, target your communication to your audience. You can create emphasis within a design in many ways. For example, by making the most important information bigger or bolder, setting it apart by space, or using a type style or ink color for important copy which is different from the type or ink used elsewhere in the piece, you will set up visual interest and emphasis.

All of these methods make use of contrast. Something is perceived as large or small, light or dark, important or unimportant, only in relation to what surrounds it. This holds true both within the graphic (an ad, for example) as well as for its context (the entire page of the newspaper where the ad appears). If you were to use the same big, bold type for all the information, the effect would be similar to using small light type for everything: without contrast, you leave it to the reader to decide what is important.

Like the headline on a news story, the few words of major information in your graphic (ideally combined with a picture) will attract the attention of readers so they will take the trouble to look more closely for the details. If you use many different styles of type or in-

clude too much copy, the effect is of many different elements clamoring for attention. The result is that the ad won't be read at all. Often, the most effective ads are those which use a lot of white space with an easy-to-read, relaxing typeface. A good practice for those unskilled in working with type is to choose only one type family, introducing a second typestyle only for special emphasis.

You rarely have much control over the context of your graphics. You don't know on which page of the newspaper your ad will appear or what else may be posted on the bulletin board where you put your flyer or poster. The best approach is to make use of as much information as you have, combined with common sense and an eye for contrast. For example, familiarize yourself with the places where flyers are posted in your community, and look at what's posted there. If everyone uses flyers on white paper, colored paper will stand out vividly by contrast. If the bulletin boards already are covered with brightly colored flyers, consider a white or pastel paper.

Without contrast, you leave it to the reader to decide what is important.

Repetition is an important factor in promoting your event. For this reason and for cost effectiveness, it is a good idea to create a single visual style for each event. A single image seen on the poster, the flyer, and the ad, such as a photo or logo paired with a particular typeface for the title or event will promote recognition of the event.

Using different images for the poster, flyer, and ad, however attractive each may be, may cause confusion. It may not always be technically possible or desirable to use an enlargement or reduction of the identical art for these three pieces, but in adapting the image to the various formats see that each retains the same visual theme to encourage recognition.

Printing

Usually the cheapest printing is black ink on inexpensive white paper. Introducing color almost always adds to the cost, but it's often well worth it in increased eye appeal. Most printers charge only minimally more for using one color ink other than black on regular stock. And it costs less to print black ink on a colored paper (thus getting something like a two-color effect) than to print two colors of ink.

If you're doing your own graphics, you should have an understanding of what each part of a job will cost before you make final decisions about graphic elements. Ask at least three typesetters or printers for cost and time estimates, especially on a big job or if you have not worked with them before. Keep in mind that any time you make a copy change after your type has been set, it will cost additional money. Typesetters usually have a minimum charge, and repeated changes can add up to more than the original cost of the type. It is best to have your copy finalized before you go to a typesetter. This will save time and money.

You may cut down on costs by doing part of the job yourself. For example, if you're creating a flyer and you have artwork, you can order your type as galley proofs, meaning the type shop will supply the necessary type and you will put the pieces together yourself to create a mechanical.

Show your artwork to your printer so she or he can tell you what you need, be it a halftone or stat. There are many quick print businesses that do various types of camera work for less money than type shops or large print shops, and it might be worth your time to check this out.

Discounts can be worked out from designers and printers for materials produced, especially if the event is a benefit. It is always important to ask. Printers often are more inclined to give a discount or donation on work which is simple and well-prepared than on rush work which is messy or over-designed, involving complicated and time-consuming printing techniques.

Desktop Publishing

Another option you might try is desktop publishing. If you have a computer, you can create a disk which has all your information on it and bring the disk to a quick print shop with desktop publishing services. Many of these places allow you to rent time on their equipment or provide the service for slightly more money. Step-by-step instructions are given so you can create your own artwork and incorporate graphics into your written piece on the computer. This is called *WYSIWYG* (what you see is what you get). It allows you the flexibility of seeing your piece and changing it in many ways right in front of you.

Many of these places have two types of laser printers. Both laser printers work by a heat process of putting dots together to create a letter. One type of laser printer prints 300 dots per square inch, another 600, and yet another, more sophisticated laser prints 2,400 dots per square inch. Of course, the latter is the highest quality printer out at the moment and costs more money to use. However, the money you've saved by doing the job yourself may allow you to get this type of output.

As mentioned in the discussion of adbook production, printers quote on a job only after you furnish the details: quantity, size, paper stock, inks, number of illustrations, photos, etc. You can phone this information to printers or write up the specifications and submit them in advance, then again when you deliver the job. For a first quote of costs from the printer you need to give very specific details. Ask for the quote in writing. Also ask if it would be possible to check a blueline. It may cost a little more, but it enables you to check the photo quality and make sure all your type is showing. It is also a last chance to catch errors. Although it is expensive to make changes at this stage, it is more expensive to reprint a job with the wrong date!

The larger the quantity of each printed piece the lower the cost per unit. Be as accurate as you can in estimating how many of each project you will need printed. For example, you might begin by ordering 500 posters. As it turns out, you actually need 1,000 posters and must go back to the printer and order an additional 500. Your 1,000 posters will end up costing you nearly twice as much as if you had ordered 1,000 in the first place.

On the other hand, if your original estimate is too high you also will spend extra money and will have wasted paper.

Size of the printed pieces is also an important cost factor. Sometimes a minor alteration (for example, to take advantage of a standard paper size or to run it on a smaller printing press) can mean substantial savings in printing costs.

> Printers often are more inclined to give a discount on work which is simple and well-prepared.

Review your ideas with the printer before investing a lot of time and money in creating art for your graphics.

Depending upon the event, it is often a good idea to use a union printer because it shows general support for the labor movement. In general, union printers charge more, but they also are known to give discounts to nonprofit and community-oriented organizations if you ask for it.

A major variable in the cost of printing is the cost of the paper. Tell the designer and the printer you want the least expensive paper that will work both for the visual concept and the budget.

Discuss *rush work* with your printer. The sample checklist in Chapter Nine outlines how to come up with a timeline that will leave enough time to complete the job. If parts of your job are not completed according to this timeline, you might be able to give your printer part of the job to work on, such as the program cover so work could *begin* on time while waiting for the inside pieces.

Graphic Artists

Before selecting a graphic artist, see samples of her or his work. Talk to others who have worked with this artist to make sure she or he does not have a pattern of missing deadlines or having budget overruns. Ask your printer about the artist you're thinking of hiring. Some artists create artwork that is clean and easy to print from, some don't. Graphic designers have varying abilities, skills, and interests. For example, some can illustrate, but others work strictly with type and layout, using photos or drawings.

If a graphic artist is using someone else's art, permission should be obtained from the artist. Then make sure credit is given. If you need someone to create an illustration, the graphic designer might handle that part of the job, adding in a management fee in the job price.

When you've found the right graphic artist for the concert, make a very specific agreement (a written contract is best, especially on big jobs) that includes deadlines, budget items, and a list of the final products you expect.

Design can be tricky — what you need is easy-to-read (from a distance) information, using attractive graphics. Be sure to see at least one rough design or sample layout so you can recommend changes or give approval before the artwork is finalized into camera-ready form. It's also helpful to solicit the opinions of other people. It's a typical procedure to change the typeface or position of the photo, or any element of the design, during the rough stage. But if you want to make changes later, you are likely to incur additional costs.

There is a vocabulary for graphics just as there is for other aspects of concert production. We have included many terms in the glossary. But don't hesitate to ask your designer or printer for clarification about any graphic design or production matter you do not understand.

To pick up information without spending a lot of money, browse through books at your local art supply store or at the library. *Pocket Pal* and *Getting It Printed* are good reference books (see Resources in Appendix).

CHAPTER NINE

Concert Program/ Adbook

Contributors Caryn Dickman, Cathy Fink, Melissa Howden, Sheila Kahn, Peggy Kiss, Nikki Roy

---

A program book or adbook can be a money maker and image enhancer for you. The written program you offer to the people attending your event is your opportunity to say something to them about your group, your cause, and your artists or concert.

In addition to short articles and informative text, the program book also can be an opportunity to produce a promotional piece that will sell your organization and ideas. It can lead to added credibility with future business and media contacts.

By including advertising in the program book, you also have the opportunity to talk about your organization, your cause, and your artists without having to bear the costs. By offering the opportunity for local businesses to connect with your concert-goers, you are providing a service that can generate a profit for you through sales of ad space. And if the publication is of high quality, it can be used to your advantage in making positive impres-

sions on businesses you want to approach for support in the future.

The cost of producing a high-quality program can be considerable. However, you may be in a position to have some labor or materials donated to your organization. Many talented and supportive individuals or businesses might, in exchange for public acknowledgement in the program, be willing to donate design, graphic artwork, printing, or paper costs. The more donated labor costs, the better quality product you can produce within your budget and/or the more money you can make with the project.

Preparing the adbook's design and layout will entail back-and-forth communication be-

> *The program book also can be an opportunity to produce a promotional piece that will sell your organization and ideas.*

tween you, the printer, and the graphic artist. Size, quantity, ink colors, paper stock, bleeds, photographs, and screens or illustrations are elements the layout artist needs to know about, and they affect the cost of printing. The layout can be done one page per board, two/board, or four/board. It *will* make a difference in the price of printing, so check out which layout plan is most advantageous for you.

If you decide on four pages per board, the layout artist must pay close attention to the final order of pages. But extra care required at the setup stage may save printing costs in the end.

Because creating an adbook is a complicated task having a number of specific deadlines, it is helpful to work backwards in planning your timeline.

For example, when is the event? When does the printer need camera-ready copy to have the book printed in time for the event? When does the layout artist or typesetter need copy to have camera-ready art to the printer on time?

Plot the time necessary for each step, and set an absolute deadline for accepting ads. Each deadline in the process must be met to prevent time shortages in the later steps.

Checklist for Producing a Program Book
The following steps will help you prepare your schedule:

1. Schedule all due dates and delivery dates.
2. Compile lists of potential ad buyers.
3. Get estimates on layout, typesetting, and printing costs.
4. Plan contents — how many pages for text, how many for ads? (Figure on a 50/50 ratio.)
5. Price ads and set placement deadlines.
6. Draw ad size guide and rate chart.
7. Write information letter with order coupon, and mail with size and rate chart to potential advertisers.
8. Make follow-up phone calls to potential buyers.
9. Take orders and payments *(in advance)*.
10. Take ads and copy to typesetter/layout artist. Proofread; make corrections.
11. Have graphic artist lay out and paste-up the mechanical. Make one final review.
12. Bring mechanicals to printer, review details of order and delivery date.
13. Deliver to hall. Be sure ushers give a copy to each attendee.

Detailed Instructions for Checklist
Lists of Potential Ad Buyers. These lists should be completed throughout your work on the program book — until the last space is sold. There are two kinds of ads and groups of buyers.

Individual Listings. A page or more can be used to list names of individuals. The section might be titled Friends, Sympathizers, Supporters, Co-workers, Sponsors, In Solidarity, or whatever sounds best to you and your event. Listings can be sold for whatever you think you can get — from $5 to $75. It is customary to have a sliding scale for different categories (student, family, senior citizen, etc.). Membership and contributors' lists can be used to solicit potential donors.

Ad Space. (Full-page, half-page, quarter-page, middle spread, business-card size ads, back cover, etc.) Many producers are selective when they approach individuals or businesses for ads, preferring to work with those whose goals are compatible with those of the producer. In this way, the program book as a whole can convey a certain tone, rather than being a random presentation of advertisers. However, it may be worthwhile to solicit support for the event in any way possible, including advertisements from businesses with no connection to your enterprise (like a beverage company or insurance agency).

Advertising Goals. Consider your goals in acquiring advertising. Lists of those to approach could include: local groups involved in similar issues or types of music; any group with money; progressive newspapers, journals, magazines; businesses that deal with or would like to deal with progressive organizations (typesetters, printers, copy shops, mailing houses, stationers, computer centers, etc.); businesses that might like to reach progressive audiences (coffee houses, professionals, doctors, lawyers, therapists, clothing shops, chiropractors, health food stores, yoga centers, etc.); sympathetic cultural groups (dance companies, theater companies, art galleries, bands, etc.), especially those which have performances coming up.

Layout, Typesetting, and Printing Estimates. Talk to the person who will be pasting up your mechanicals (artwork) for the printer, or a graphic artist who can help you make decisions on specifications. Sometimes a nationally distributed program is provided in connection with a long tour the artists are undertaking. If so, you need to produce only an insert to the program. While this saves you from having to obtain special cover stock and cover design, you do need to get specifications on the program being provided so your insert is in harmony with the size and look of the outer sections.

The printer will need the following information from you:

- Description of job (program or adbook or insert).
- Quantity (number of seats in the concert hall, unless you know it is not a sell-out concert) plus the amount needed for ad buyers, future promotional uses, etc.
- Flat size before folding.
- Size after folding (finished size).
- Number of pages (remember that the cover takes up four pages).
- Paper stock: your printer will show you samples and prices. Covers can be printed on the same stock as the rest of the contents or on special cover stock, which is more expensive. Ask for estimates on both.
- Ink: how many colors? Which colors will they be? (Black is counted as a color.) One option is to print only the covers with extra color.
- Binding: folding, stapling, stitching, etc.
- Number and size of half-tones, including photographs.
- Other special printing features: screens, bleeds, reverses.
- Printing schedule: the date you'll bring camera-ready mechanicals; delivery deadline and instructions.

Plan Contents. Figure the approximate number of pages you'll need for text (including cover pages). Calculate a high estimate of how much it will cost to produce that many pages (layout, typesetting, printing). You'll need to have at least the same number of pages of ads and charge twice as much per page as your estimate of costs per page. In this way, each full-page ad will pay for its own production as well as for one of your information pages. If you think you can fill more pages with ads, this obviously will add to your profits.

Price Ads and Set Placement Deadlines. Once you have figured out how much a full page of ads should cost to cover production expenses, you can raise that price if you think you can get more money for single, full-page ads, or you can leave that sum as the full-page price and make your profits by dividing other pages into parts.

> You'll need to have at least the same number of pages of ads and charge twice as much per page as your estimate of costs per page.

In other words, if you're charging $200 for a full page, you can charge $125 or $150 for a half page and $75 or $100 for a quarter page. Rate differences sometimes encourage people to take out larger ads. Remember, if individual listings take up one or two ad pages, they can produce a lot of revenue for the space involved.

Everyone purchasing ad space (not listings) should be asked to supply *camera-ready copy—* an ad the exact size or larger than the space purchased. You can reduce the artwork and maintain quality good enough for the printer to make plates from it. Ask your printer for specific requirements.

Also, get a cost estimate from your type-setter for setting a pre-determined number of words. If the purchaser cannot supply artwork, this typesetting charge can be added to the cost of ad space for messages up to that number of words.

Ad Size Chart. It will help your ad sales if you can provide a simple chart showing the program book page divided into the various-sized ads you're offering, with prices listed in their respective areas (Form 9:1).

Information Letter. A letter should be sent to potential ad buyers offering ad space in the program and explaining who the artists are, how many people will see the program (anticipated audience size), when and where the concert will be, brief description of the theme of the tour (if relevant), why it will be an exciting event, and how any remaining proceeds from ad sales will be used.

Or include a press release with similar information about the performance. The letter should be sent along with an order coupon and the ad size guide/rate chart.

You can use another version of the same letter to solicit individual listings. Using Form 9:2, keep track of the names of the people to whom you mail the letter as well as the results of the contact. Use one form per business. Even if you talk to several people there, put them all on the same sheet. If you have more than one person doing sales for

you this is very important. Don't end up soliciting two ads from different departments of the same business.

Contacting Potential Buyers. Sort lists into three categories:

1. Individuals who should receive a mass mailing soliciting individual listings. These letters can go into other mailings to cut postage costs.
2. Groups, organizations, and individuals who should receive the letter, coupon, and ad size/rate chart and should be called personally if there is time.
3. Best bet — groups, organizations, and individuals who are most likely to purchase ads. These require personal attention.

This last list should be called first, then sent materials and called again. Do as much soliciting as time allows. A space reservation deadline in advance of needing ads and money is helpful to gauge if there are enough ads to make the program book successful or if you need to sell more ads.

Take Orders and Payments in Advance. Collect ad payments with each order. All ads must be paid for by your deadline date.

Ads Preparation. Write the copy for the program book's information pages, and come up with a design for the cover pages well before your deadline date. Try to get these materials to the graphic artist at least a week before the ad deadline.

All ads and names for individual listings should go to the graphic artist and typesetter as soon as the placement deadline has passed. Late additions usually incur additional typesetting costs and may create layout problems.

Printing. When you bring mechanicals to the printer, review the specifications of the job and the estimates you were originally given; make sure that your delivery deadlines and instructions are still appropriate.

Formula

The following is a formula to compute the facts and yield some strong advice for creating a profitable adbook. Using this formula correctly could be worth several hundred dollars to your event.

Collect the following components:

T = Number of pages of text. Estimate the number of pages in the program book that will not carry advertising, including front cover page, program schedule, background on performers and organizations, etc. The better the text, the more likely it is that people will keep the adbook — benefiting the organization, the performers, and the advertisers.

A = Number of pages of advertising. Set the number of program book pages that will be sold to advertisers. Advertising pages should not overwhelm the text pages, e.g., six pages of text and 22 pages of advertising.

C = Cost per page. By talking to your layout artist and showing a rough design to a type shop or print shop, estimate the total cost to lay out, typeset, and print the adbook. Then divide this cost by number of pages.

L = Cost of labor. Estimate the value of the labor invested in this project for collecting ads, writing text, and laying out the book. Sometimes ad sales people take 15 percent off the top. Sometimes they do it as a labor of love for the cause. An obvious measure of cost of labor is salaries.

But when the laborers are fundraisers, another kind of labor cost presents itself: the *opportunity cost* or the money lost by having the fundraiser do something besides fundraise. For example, a canvasser with an $80 quota who is paid by the organization to do something other than canvass has an opportunity cost to the organization of $80 per day.

P = Price per page. This is the number that our computation yields, the amount you have to charge advertisers if you want to break even.

If you want to make a profit, you have to charge more. The formula is as follows:

$$\text{Price} = \frac{(A + T)C + L}{A}$$

Price = Advertising *plus* **Text** *multiplied by* **Cost** *plus* **Labor** *divided by* **Advertising**

For example, let's plug in some numbers.

$$A = 22 \text{ pages}$$
$$T = 12 \text{ pages}$$
$$C = \$30/\text{page}$$
$$L = \$600.00$$

Add:			
	Advertising		22
	+ Text	+	12
	number of pages	=	34

Multiply:			
	number of pages		34
	x Cost/page	x	30
	subtotal cost	=	$1,020

Add:			
	subtotal cost		1,020
	+ Labor	+	600
	total cost	=	$1,620

Divide by:			
	total cost		1,620
	Advertising	÷	22

Price/advertising page   = $73.64

To break even on the adbook, then we should sell ads for $73.64 per page (round this off to $75). If you sell 22 pages of advertising, all the costs associated with producing the adbook will be covered. And you will be able to hand out an attractive, commemorative program to all attendees. This program will serve to remind them of an important event, as well as of a cause or organization they supported.

Additionally, if well done, the adbook will help reinforce your professional image as a concert producer.

Making a Profit
To find out how much profit can be made on ad sales, use this version of the same formula:

$$\text{Profit} = \text{AP} - [(\text{A} + \text{T})\text{C} + \text{L}]$$

Profit = Advertising *times* Price *minus* number of pages of Advertising plus Text *multiplied by* Cost *plus* Labor

Let's use the same numbers as in the previous example to determine the profit we can expect.

A = 22 pages
T = 12 pages
C = $30/page
L = $600
P = $200/page

Multiply:	Advertising		22
	x Price/page	x	200
	price of advertising	=	$4,400

Add:	Advertising		22
	+ Text	+	12
	number of pages	=	34

Multiply:	number of pages		34
	x Cost/page	x	30
	subtotal cost	=	$1,020

Add:	subtotal cost		1,020
	+ Labor	+	600
	total cost	=	$1,620

Subtract:	price of advertising		4,400
	- total cost	-	1,620
	Profit	=	$2,780

Where price (**P**) = $100/page, profit = $580. Again, this is true only in a case where the numbers are exactly equal to the sample. If you have different numbers, you will have a different profit.

Don't underestimate the value of your ads. A full-page ad is very reasonable at $200 or $250. Many program ads cost a great deal more.

Remember, too, that you will not be sharing the profits of adbooks with the artists. This is your chance to make some money.

It's always an option to offer discounts or incentives: for example, 10 to 20 percent discount for nonprofit or community organizations, or a 10 percent discount for multiple advertisers who reserve space early. Be sure to account for discount options in your planning.

Adbooks offer several special opportunities. One is to provide a tangible memory of your event to all attendees. Another is to enhance your reputation as a concert producer. And finally, if priced attractively and well-marketed, the adbook could help make your event even more profitable.

CHAPTER TEN

Staffing

Contributors Mary Conn, Sheila Kahn

This chapter provides a description of the personnel you will need, how far in advance of the concert they should be hired, and the range of duties each job entails. The skill level required for these positions and the extent of duties will depend in part on the complexity of your event. Sometimes, some of these jobs can be done by a trained volunteer; others will need to be filled by a (probably paid) professional. We will use the concept of *hiring* in either case. For example, if you are doing a theater or dance presentation or a highly produced concert with a light show, you will need a professional stage manager to call sound, light, and curtain cues, cue actors' entrances, etc. But if you are producing a solo folk musician, an alert and intelligent volunteer can serve as stage manager, standing by to receive word from the house manager that the audience is inside the hall, she or he can then dim the house lights and signal the emcee to step in

front of the curtain. Some of the people you hire will not be able to see the concert; be sure they understand that.

Working with Volunteers
There are many advantages to recruiting volunteers to help with the tasks of putting on a concert. The most obvious advantage is to your budget. The volume of work usually is more than an individual producer can manage. At times, for even the smallest concert, it is more than the entire staff of a small organization can handle. But jobs must be done, and the alternative to hiring and paying personnel is to find people who want to donate their talents and time to the effort.

Another advantage of identifying people with energy and commitment is that when special projects or crises require augmenting your regular staff with good volunteer workers, you easily can draw on a pool of reliable people. Using volunteers also will tie your organization closer to the community, strengthening the foundation of your organization and encouraging more involvement in this event and future ones.

You can find volunteers by posting announcements in schools, coffeehouses, and women's bookstores, or advertising for help in folklore society newsletters (see Form 10:1). Referrals from these sources usually are competent, eager to work, and reliable. You can send this same announcement as an attachment to your *advance invitation* letter. Many people think it is exciting and fun to be on the inside of a concert or big event and will be delighted to have the opportunity to work. Be ready for their calls after you've placed these notices. You don't have to pitch a hard sell, but do state clearly why you are asking them to volunteer, what your group is, what the event is, and what tasks need to be done.

Note their preferences for jobs and for good times to meet, and make sure you know how to get in touch with them. In selecting volunteers be alert to *groupie types* volunteering their time. They will want to do jobs only where they have contact with the performers. In many cases they are bothersome to the artists and often are not helpful with tasks that require leaving the performers' presence. And they will not want to miss one moment of the show.

> *Using volunteers also will tie your organization closer to the community.*

Volunteers can provide excellent help in the weeks before the event with tasks like putting up posters, typing press releases and address labels, helping with mailings, baking goods for sale, working on outreach to targeted groups (such as hearing-impaired or ethnic organizations), telephoning for press information, silkscreening tee shirts, and picking up or redistributing tickets from ticket agencies.

On the day of the show you can use volunteers to usher, take tickets, set up chairs, make and place signs, unload equipment, work in the concessions area, assist disabled members of the audience, answer the backstage phone, drive the artists to interviews and to their lodgings, etc.

One of the keys to working with volunteers is to respect their generosity of effort. Show this respect by carefully planning the tasks you give them. It is easiest for volunteers to commit to do a specific task at a specific time, because they can plan their time accordingly. Of course, you should be flexible enough to accommodate their schedules.

Another way to show your gratitude is to compensate volunteers with a perk: free tickets, an invitation to the artists' reception, a free tee shirt, or whatever you feel is appropriate and affordable. You might choose to pair this reward with a fixed amount of volunteer time donated.

Call a meeting of your volunteers. Distribute a list showing each task, when it needs to be done, and a space for names and phone numbers next to each (Form 10:2). This meeting is important for assigning tasks and for building a sense of camaraderie. Keep the meeting fun but organized; do not waste volunteers' time, and be sure they understand what their tasks are. You may want to select one volunteer to coordinate all of the others, or assign a staff person this responsibility.

Build check points into the tasks so you will know what progress each volunteer is making. In this way you can commend helpers for a job well done, make adjustments for less able or less energetic workers, and verify that tasks are being accomplished.

Volunteers should be supplied with all the materials and support they need to complete their jobs successfully. Task closure is a more rewarding feeling than knowing that others must finish the final details. For instance, you might be doing a mailing where one group of volunteers has prepared all the envelopes and labels, but one of the mail inserts is missing. When this first set of volunteers leaves they see all the envelopes still open and know that someone else has to go through and handle them again, inserting the errant slip of paper. The careful sorting by zip code sequence may get out of order, and the workers will find it less fulfilling to end in the middle than to take the mailing to a mailbox or postal bag and send it on its way.

While some of the effort involved in putting on a concert can be managed by volunteer workers, for some tasks -- like running sound or lights -- it is very risky, and we advise strongly against it. But if the cause is appealing, professional technicians may wish to donate their services. In return, write up a receipt as if you had paid them their regular fee, but write on it *Services Donated*, so they can deduct it for tax purposes.

Make sure all volunteers get thank you notes or some other appropriate recognition for their efforts, including information about the accomplishments of the show (e.g., money raised). Include volunteers in any post-show evaluation of the event. Give them as specific feedback as you can on their work emphasizing the positive as well as concretely identifying problems. This is especially important if you expect to use the volunteers in future productions.

Staff Positions

Production Coordinator. This is the person who supervises the whole enterprise, doubling as producer. Everyone else has a piece of the puzzle, but the coordinator makes sure that all the pieces come together. This individual hires the artists, finds the hall, completes the estimated budget, hires all other personnel, supervises the graphics and printing production, designs the publicity strategy, administrates ticketing, pays attention to the artists' needs, and supervises the show. It's a comprehensive job which requires a detail-oriented, organized person with plenty of time.

After consulting with the stage manager and others as needed, the production coordinator should prepare a timeline (Form 2:1) as early as possible and make sure everyone follows it. In addition to her or his own responsibilities, the coordinator is the chief problem solver for everyone. She or he helps others most by providing them with the materials and support necessary to do their jobs.

On the day of the show the coordinator arrives early and plans to stay. The specific work on that day is to ensure that all workers are doing their jobs and are on schedule. The coordinator introduces the crew members to each other if they haven't already met and introduces the key personnel to the artists when they arrive. Before the show, the coordinator decides when to open the doors (which means checking if sound, lights, stage, and lobby are ready). This sometimes is determined by house policy. If last-minute sound and light problems still are being worked on, the production coordinator has the authority to keep the audience from entering until all is in place. Consulting with the stage manager and artists, the coordinator decides when to start the show -- to the minute. Before the show the production coordinator keeps in close contact with the box office, making sure no problems arise over the guest list. Invariably, people appear who think they are on the list. Their names have been left off, or they are listed under a different name, or the performers just forgot to put them on their list. And they may be people who just don't want to pay. Each one has to be checked and verified and approved before the box office can issue them a complimentary ticket.

During the show the production coordinator keeps an eye on everything going on around the production. She or he checks with the

> *Do not waste volunteers' time, and be sure they understand what their tasks are.*

box office when it closes to get a final ticket count; keeps in touch with the stage manager; makes sure the ushers are doing their jobs; inspects sound and lighting of the stage from various positions in the house; and usually just circles to make sure things are going smoothly until intermission. During intermission the production coordinator will check in with the artists or road manager and make sure the second set starts on time. After intermission she or he meets with the theater manager for settlement of the show. At this time the box office statement must be checked. The number of tickets sold, the number of tickets unsold, and the comps should add up to the capacity of the house. In every case you should be able to get this number, as all tickets must be accounted for. Once the correct gross has been established, the production coordinator then goes over expenses with the theater's manager. Costs for the theater are subtracted from the gross.

It is expected that any and all costs can be questioned at this time. The coordinator should know in advance what the charges are going to be, but if there are any surprises, she or he should ask for backup and explanations. In most cases a deposit is kept by the theater for up to a month for any last minute expenses that are billed. This deposit should not be more than $500. You may have to call more than once to get the deposit returned to you.

At the end of the production, the coordinator thanks the volunteers, pays anyone hired, then pays the artists or their road manager — going over all expenses and giving them back-up receipts and copies of the box office statement. She or he is also responsible for organizing the post-concert evaluations.

Sound Technician. The responsibilities for sound involve selecting the equipment and carting it to the hall, setting it up, troubleshooting, mixing the sound, and tearing it down to cart the equipment away. These tasks can be done by the same person or company or by two groupings of people. Sound people should be hired early. Contracting well in advance should enable them to secure the most appropriate, good-quality equipment for your concert. (The artists will probably have a technical rider specifying the equipment needed.) If a separate person is doing the mixing she or he should be hired at least one month before the concert, allowing enough time to become familiar with both the equipment and the music that will be performed. It is always helpful to the sound company to get a tape of the performers' latest recording so they can become familiar with the material and the mixes.

Sound reinforcement usually requires additional personnel: people to carry in equipment and carry it out when the show is over, set up mics, etc. Often the sound technician will want to bring in her or his own assistants. If so, make sure the fee quoted includes payment for all the personnel involved. The sound people also may need headsets, particularly if any of the equipment is being run from backstage. These sets are usually provided by the sound company at no additional cost. It's best if both the monitor and house mix people are familiar with the types of music being presented, since different genres have different mixing requirements. This is not a position for an inexperienced person who wants to learn how to do sound; bad mixing is very obvious and upsetting to artists and audience alike and can literally ruin the show.

The chapter on sound provides a more comprehensive discussion of the sound technician's responsibilities.

Lighting Designer. Some events do not require sophisticated lighting, and a technician can set the light levels (how strong the lighting should be) and aim the light instruments carefully so that the artists are adequately lit and no strong shadows are cast. The hall may provide a lighting technician. So there will be adequate time before the sound check to set and adjust the lights, plan time for it into your day of show schedule (Form 13:1). Technicians prefer to start on lights one hour before sound loads-in. You'll need to know how much pre-sound check time you'll need before contracting with the hall.

If the hall's lights are inadequate, you'll need to bring in lighting equipment. The rental price might include personnel to bring in the lighting and set it up for you; if not, you or the lighting designer should get all the cables in proper lengths for your stage set-up and clear directions for doing it. Make these arrangements as soon as you know your needs and what the hall provides. Double check that the hall will provide gels.

> *One of the primary functions of the stage manager is to ensure that everyone is working on schedule.*

Setting up is not hard — if you have one person focusing from each *tree* of lights, people of comparable heights standing in for the artists in the right places, and someone in the house giving directions to those focusing the lights. Turn the intensity of the lights down low when focusing so they won't get too hot to handle so quickly, also so the people onstage can look into the light comfortably and tell you when the brightest part is on their faces. These adjustments should be done before the sound check, not during, because the light instruments at low intensity may create a buzzing in the sound equipment.

At the end of sound check, turn up the lights to see if there is any buzz and if the focus and levels are correct for the artists. Be prepared to make any final adjustments then and to correct the buzz with the sound system.

If the production is going to have lighting changes for setting the mood and added vi-

sual interest, you will need a lighting designer. The lighting designer should be hired as far in advance as possible. She or he designs the lighting plan for the concert, rents whatever light fixtures and gels are needed, and gets them to the show. As with the sound crew, the lighting designer may require other hands (usually their own associates) to help with equipment and focusing, cut gels, etc. Again, the lighting designer's fee should include all personnel costs.

In many halls the dimmer board is located backstage. In that case the designer will probably want to sit in the audience and give the lighting changes to the technician who is running the board backstage. To do this, they have to have some kind of walkie-talkie or intercom system.

Chapter Twelve on Lighting gives a more complete description of the lighting designer's responsibilities. A sample light plot (Form 12:1) is included as an example of adequate lighting coverage for a large group of artists. Each stage and artist configuration will need a different plot, gels, cues.

Stage Manager. Unless it's a complicated production, the stage manager can be hired as late as two weeks before the concert, but you might as well do it at your earliest convenience especially for scheduling the day of show. On the day of the show this person should be at the hall all day. If the concert is being produced in a union hall, it is the responsibility of the stage manager to ensure that an adequate number of stage crew members and loaders are available to unload equipment, to set up equipment, to design the stage, to change sets, and to reload equipment on the day of show.

The stage manager's primary functions are ensuring everyone is working on schedule, getting the stage set up properly for the artists — the drum risers in place, the piano where it's supposed to be, arranging for any props the artists need onstage (such as a stool or table), and dealing with any problems that arise with sound or lights.

The stage manager also makes sure that the food and drinks the artists have requested before and during the conjunction are there when the artists arrive. Unless the artists travel with a road technician who does it, the stage manager is responsible for running the tech check.

The stage manager is also responsible for scheduling the day of the show in conjunction with the coordinator. She or he should look over the artists' rider and get it to the sound company and lighting technician. Then in discussions with them, she or he will find out how much time is needed to set up and get ready for the sound check and also what the crew needs are — how many people are needed and for how long. The stage manager then devises a schedule to suit everyone's needs, taking into consideration the artists, the necessary breaks, and the sound and light checks. With these in mind, load-in is scheduled.

When the stage manager runs the tech check she or he coordinates between the technicians and the performers. It is extremely important to get them on stage when needed and make sure their sound and lighting requests are met. Paying attention to the time is important as well. You have to keep in mind when the crew needs to break for dinner so that a meal penalty does not occur. If you are in a time crunch, let the performers know so they can work on their most difficult numbers in the allotted time, and get the problems worked out before breaktime.

The stage manager should tell everyone -- sound, lights, interpreter, artists, emcee -- what time to be at the theater. Then they always should check with the stage manager when they leave for any reason.

Once the doors are open and the audience is arriving, the stage manager is in touch with the key personnel, letting them know when to start the taped music (if any) and how close to starting on time the show will be. It is highly advisable that in a large hall the stage manager also have a walkie-talkie. She or he is backstage for the entire performance, but must be able to communicate with sound, lights, and possibly the lobby or box office during the show. The stage manager also gives artists their time warnings -- as often as artists request, but at least 15 minutes before show time. At five minutes before starting time everyone should be in their places and the emcee, interpreter, and artists ready to go onstage (unless the emcee has many long announcements, in which case the artists can come out a bit later). As soon as the emcee and interpreter are ready to come out, the stage manager lets sound and lights know -- *"Emcee and interpreter are entering stage left"* -- so the correct microphones are turned on and the lights and spotlight are on the emcee and interpreter when they enter. This procedure is followed every time someone enters the stage.

After intermission, the stage manager lets lights know when to blink the house and lobby lights or bring them to half, and then bring them all the way down to indicate that it's time to get started again. Lobby lights may not be controlled by the house switch, in which case the stage manager must signal the house manager when to blink the lights.

The stage manager is always backstage during the concert, no matter how small the event, to handle any backstage problems or emergencies that may arise. For example, an artist may be well into her set and realize she has left her guitar capo in the dressing room. Or the next group to perform might be rehearsing in a nearby lounge, and the sound could distract the performer onstage. It's the stage manager who smooths out the small hitches while the show is in progress, working quietly and efficiently so that the audience never perceives any disruption of the program.

Lobby Manager. This position should be filled by the time publicity is out if you plan to have an active lobby. The job is to supervise everything that happens in the lobby. The lobby manager should clear with the theater manager what is and what is not allowed in the lobby. Can signs be tacked to the walls or is tape allowed? Will tables be provided? And, very importantly, does the house get a percentage of all sales? If that is the case, the lobby manager should meet with the theater manager to inventory the materials being sold before the doors open. Everyone selling should be alerted that a percentage will be taken, as in many cases they may find that it is not worth it to sell merchandise.

The standard percentage taken by a house is 15 percent, but in some cases it is as high as one-third. It often can be negotiated down in advance or at the end of the evening, with a little bit of savvy and sometimes a free album or tee shirt.

If people are using tables to sell goods or mount displays, the lobby manager assigns them their tables and checks to see that they observe house rules. This person should be someone trustworthy who can handle problems that may arise over tickets, masking tape, tables, information questions, wheelchair needs, and all other lobby activity. However, if you're working in a small hall or there is not much lobby activity and someone else can handle problems, you don't need a separate lobby manager.

House Manager. The house manager needs to know where the light switches are and the manner in which you will let the audience know when intermission is over. She or he takes cues from the stage manager. This is not an optional position. In larger halls the house manager comes with the venue. If not, she or he should be hired at least two weeks before the performance, especially if she or he is not already familiar with the hall.

The house manager supervises and orients the ushers to the house, instructing them how to deal with double printed tickets (usually they have been misread), to seat the audience between numbers, to distribute programs, to seat VIP guests, and to handle special seating problems.

The house manager should be familiar enough with the facility to know whom to contact for any emergencies or problems that arise. She or he stays in touch with the stage manager regarding how the house is being seated. Is there a long line at the box office close to show time? Are many people arriving late because of traffic or parking problems? These are all matters that need to be considered by the stage manager in deciding when the show will begin. The stage manager usually decides to start later than the ticket reads about five minutes before curtain. She or he lets the house manager know the new curtain time, so the house lights can be flashed and the audience seated.

> *One or two people should stay at the doors at least until the intermission, because people do arrive late.*

Ticket Takers. Decide how many doors you're going to open and line up twice as many people to take tickets (tear them in half or stamp hands). One or two people should stay at the doors at least until the intermission, because people do arrive late. This avoids the possibility of upsetting concert-goers who had reserved tickets or of losing money because no one was available to direct people to the box office to collect their tickets. When the box office closes, any comp or will-call tickets that have not been picked up should be given to one of the ticket takers for those latecomers.

Ticket takers usually do not have time to hand out programs as well.

Also, ticket takers are responsible for counting the ticket stubs. This is called a *drop count*. It should let you know how many people actually attended the event. (It should not be relied upon for an income figure because of no-shows and the occasional ticket that may not have been collected and torn.)

Ushers. If seating is reserved, hire ushers who know the hall and can help people get to their seats. In an unreserved hall, ushers can be useful in identifying where available seats are and in encouraging people to sit together, not leaving one empty seat between each party. Ushers also hand out programs. For some concerts these people will double as your security workers, assuring the comfort and safety of the audience and solving problems as they arise. One or two ushers could be posted at the press seats to make sure those seats are saved for the press or critics.

Security Coordinator and Staff. This person should be hired about one month before the concert so she or he can hire the security workers. The security coordinator consults with the production coordinator to determine how many workers will be needed in the hall, in the lobby, and perhaps backstage; hires them; acquaints them with the hall on the day of the show; supervises them; and deals with problems they can't solve. The security coordinator can meet with workers an hour before the door opens to give them their assignments and acquaint them with the hall.

The term security does not imply guards with guns on their hips. Security usually handles relatively minor problems: drunk people who get rowdy and must be asked to leave, people trying to get on stage before and during the show, people smoking in the hall or taking photos in a distracting way. Often, security workers don't have to do anything so they can enjoy the show while keeping a watchful eye for any problems.

They essentially serve as symbols of authority, so they should be identifiable with an armband, tee shirt, or large button. They should be able to direct people to bathrooms, child care, and the medic as well as assist

with wheelchairs and be helpful to the audience in any way needed.

One security position that is of the utmost importance is backstage dressing room security. A guard should be at the door from the moment the artists arrive at the facility. There is so much traffic backstage that sometimes things *disappear*. This is a position where the guard may be able to hear the show but *probably* will be unable to see any of it. If necessary, it is better to pay someone and know they will be there throughout the day than to use a volunteer who wants to see the show.

A volunteer runner should sit with the medic so the medic can treat someone while the security person calls an ambulance if necessary. Be sure to have security guarding entrances to the stage, instrument storage area, and other areas of concern.

Sign Language Interpreter. If you hire an interpreter you are in effect adding another artist, and you should do so as soon as possible (see Chapter Fifteen on Accessibility). The featured artists and the interpreter must understand each others' performance needs and agree (or compromise) about them before contracts are signed.

> Ideally, the usher in that part of the hall will be able to sign.

Get the typed lyrics and tapes of the performance material to the interpreter quickly; this requires cooperation from the artists, who may not be used to (or may resist) planning a firm set list far in advance. These materials are needed early so the interpreter will have plenty of time to learn the artists' material, translate it into American Sign Language (ASL), find a poetic expression for the translation, and preview the material with deaf individuals prior to the concert to get their feed-back about the interpretation. The chapter on accessibility includes a more detailed discussion about whether to interpret the event.

Technical concerns will include:

1. The interpreter's position on the stage needs to be set with the artists' approval.
2. There must be sufficient lighting to give the audience a full view of the interpreter's facial expression and body movements, which all are part of the interpretation.
3. Sound is critical: ideally, the interpreter needs two monitor speakers (one for voice and one for the music). Minimally, one monitor with the sound of the artists' voices is required to hear accurately and synchronize the interpretation with the performance.

For general admission seating, post a notice about the hearing-impaired section at the box office and in the lobby. Hearing friends often want to sit there, too. Ideally, the usher in that part of the hall will be able to sign.

Piano Tuner. When artists request a piano, they mean an acoustic one, not an electric keyboard. The piano must be tuned professionally on the day of the show. Often the facility you are renting has a piano you can rent. Usually, there is a piano tuner available who is familiar with the instrument.

If the facility does not have a piano, the company you rent one from will almost always provide a tuner.

Tuning should be scheduled before any of the load-in occurs. There are some tuners who will not work if there is even whispering going on, while others use electronic strobe tuners and can tune with any amount of background noise.

If the artists want a touch up done, the best time to schedule it is during the dinner break, before the house opens. Have an agreement with the tuner about returning if there are any post-tuning problems.

Tuning a piano usually takes two hours. Once the piano has been tuned it should be moved as little and as carefully as possible. Arrange for it to be in position before the tuner starts work. Pianos should be tuned where they will be played, not tuned and moved. Under no circumstances should it be lifted, and room temperature should be kept stable.

Medic. Hire a nurse, a paramedic, or a first aid specialist to assist with any medical problems or emergencies that arise. The medic should be in an aisle seat at the rear of the hall wearing an armband for easy identification. Mention her or his presence when making announcements or in the program. Ushers and security personnel should know the medic's seat location. Medical personnel, like other technical professionals, may be willing to donate their time and expertise.

Box Office Manager. The box office should be managed by someone you can trust with money. The job involves selling tickets, giving out comps to people on the guest list, and helping with the accounting of both tickets and money. It's a high pressure job for a short time and needs an organized, responsible person who has clear directions.

In addition to the box office manager, at least one other person should work in the box office the day of the show. If the comp list and will-call lists are long, you should have a separate window (line) for people just picking up tickets, where no money will be handled. When there is no one in that line, ticket buyers can be served there, too, and things will go more quickly.

Mistress or Master of Ceremonies (Emcee). The emcee is the first person your audience sees, and the impression she or he makes will be important. This person makes all announcements before the show and at intermission and introduces the artists. The emcee can enhance the performance and even be a draw if it is a well-known or respected person — for instance, someone from the media or associated with a particular cause. She or he should be someone who speaks clearly, knows how to use a microphone (which you can demonstrate before the house opens), and is comfortable and personable when standing in front of your audience.

The production coordinator should approve any announcements and schedule the time limit for the emcee. A brief meeting with the artists to go over how they want to be introduced is a good idea. In fact, some artists stipulate approval of introductory comments in their contract. An emcee is not mandatory. Some artists do not want to be introduced at all. Others can be introduced from an offstage microphone by the stage manager. How the show begins should be decided between the artists and the production coordinator after sound check.

> The coordinator should be an experienced child care provider.

Publicist. You can either hire a publicist or do the job yourself. The publicist should be hired as early as possible, well before any publicity begins. She or he works with the production coordinator in planning the media and publicity strategy. The publicist supervises all the work described in the section on working with the media: compiling press lists, pitching specific angles for stories to editors and freelancers, writing and disseminating press releases, supplying photos, following up with phone calls, often coordinating poster and flyer usage, and much more.

Ideally, a publicist is someone with media contacts and savvy. Or at least she or he is willing to learn and compile lists quickly!

She or he also should be knowledgeable and enthusiastic about the artists you are pro-

ducing. If the artists are out-of-the-ordinary for the media, the publicist may function as an interpreter of the art form to the media, rather than simply planting the *who-what-when-where* kinds of stories. These can be the best angles to pursue. Supply the publicist with the artists' biographical information, photos, and recordings in time for her or him to develop enough familiarity to be effective with media contacts.

Poster Distributors. Once your posters and flyers are printed, you need people to put them up all over town and as far out of town as you decide is realistic. Make a list of all the places where you might attract people to come to this concert: bookstores, coffeehouses, grocery stores, gay bars, laundromats, women's and ethnic studies centers, nonprofit organizations, disabled student centers, clubs for the hearing-impaired, community bulletin boards, etc. Then get someone to put up posters in those places; the first time, about a month before the concert and at least once again (depending on how long the posters stay up), one or two weeks before the concert. Professional postering services are available in many cities. They are expensive compared with the coverage you can get with good volunteers. However, their relationships with some stores and use of their developed lists may be cost-effective when you are trying to reach new people.

Child Care Coordinator. The child care coordinator should be secured at least one month in advance so that she or he can look at the available space, hire the other workers, arrange for the supplies, and plan a program. The coordinator should be an experienced child care provider. The coordinator will need to arrive early enough on the day of show to ensure that everything is well organized before children begin to arrive. Chapter Sixteen on Child Care outlines the basis for deciding whether to provide child care and further describes the tasks involved.

Custodian. Many halls have a professional custodial staff, and you may be charged for the service. However, it's a courtesy to take some responsibility for cleanup, especially if there is an active lobby and programs. If you have a group selling cider and cookies, either ask them to bring a broom to sweep up the crumbs and a rag for accidental spills or provide these to the group. The ushers who handed out programs could go through the house after the show to help pick up programs left behind. Bag up any garbage and find out where to leave it for pickup.

Hospitality Coordinator. The hospitality coordinator is responsible for ensuring that the artists are comfortable. She or he should be hired two to three weeks before the show. The artist may prefer staying at someone's home, enjoying her or his hospitality, or lodging at a hotel. Always supply a private room with a bed, clean linens, and quiet space.

The hospitality coordinator also takes care of transportation to and from the airport or train and from home to the concert site. Often an *artists' friend* is assigned to each group or performer to provide transportation, etc. Hospitality workers may be responsible (and reimbursed) for buying the food items that the artists requested and setting up the dressing room at the hall. The hospitality coordinator may arrange a reception or post-show party if the artists have agreed to it.

Caterer. If one is needed, the caterer should be hired three to four weeks in advance and given very clear guidelines. In some halls you have to use the building's caterer. Check with the theater manager on this. The number of meals and amount of food needed will depend upon the time of day and length of the event and the number of people to be fed. For most evening concerts, dinner is provided for the artists and production crew. Sometimes the union crew is included.

The meal should be well-organized, on time, located and served in a manner as non-

disruptive as possible to the preparations for the show.

Usually a buffet served in a convenient space near backstage works best. The food should be attractive. It is important to check with the artists' representative to find out if they have special dietary requirements and if they prefer to eat with the crew or privately in their dressing room.

The caterer should be responsible for clean up after the meal. It is nice to offer leftovers to the artists for after the show as many artists eat very little before a show. Frequently, leftovers are given to the production crew, a battered women's shelter, or a program for the homeless.

Union Personnel. Some facilities require a union stagecrew. This is a very important aspect of your budget because there are often hidden costs that may surprise you after the event.

In some halls, you have to talk to the theater's head technician about your crew needs. In others, you call the local International Alliance of Theatrical Stage Employees (IATSE) union office directly and talk to the head steward. Rates of pay and minimums are different in every city. What you should expect is a minimum call per show. This is usually a master electrician, carpenter, sound technician, and property manager.

On some very simple shows, for example, a solo acoustic piano concert, you sometimes can negotiate the crew call down. In other cases, if you underestimate your crew needs to save money and there is too much work for your crew in the allotted time, they will be angry about your poor planning and more than likely will go into an overtime situation that will end up costing more money.

There is also a minimum amount of hours for each crew member called. It is usually four hours, but in some cases it is eight. Some crew members are called only for a *show call*, for example, spot operators. In that case, they are paid a set amount for the show.

In some unions you pay the crew hourly for the load-in set up time, a set amount for show call, and then hourly for the load-out. As the producer you need to find out not only the hourly rate, but the show call rate, when overtime occurs, the overtime rate, and the percentage added to all of these for health, vacation, payroll, etc. You need to find out when breaks are necessary.

Meal penalties occur after a certain amount of time. For example, if the crew takes an hour break, you don't have to provide their meal. However, if you allow only a half-hour break, they need a meal which you provide at the hall. In some cases there is flexibility with the union, but this is not something you should expect. Most important, your show will go more smoothly if you have a good relationship from the beginning with your crew.

CHAPTER ELEVEN

Sound

Contributors Leslie Ann Jones, Paul Reisler, Mike Southard

As a producer, you're trying to present a memorable experience for both the audience and the performers. Both need to be able to hear clearly so they can be comfortable and concentrate on the music.

In fact, sound may be the most important aspect of successful concert production, and it is certainly the one people will notice and complain most about when something goes wrong. People will overlook lines at the bathroom, non-dramatic lighting, funky halls, and many other production hardships, but what they really came for is the music, and it's the producer's job to assure sound reproduction of top quality.

The Sound of the Concert Hall
When planning a concert, pay particular attention to the choice of halls. A good technician with the right equipment can make most places sound acceptable, but it's important to know problems that sound will need to accommodate.

Gyms and churches with high ceilings and hard walls generally sound boomy or muddy. If the seating curves around the side of the stage, it is difficult to deliver the sound to all the seats. Balconies and overhangs create acoustical problems, and the sound will not be as clear under them as elsewhere. Hard surfaces cause the sound to bounce, especially with loud music.

Also consider the size of the hall. Hypothetically, on an outside flat surface — as the distance from the sound source (speakers) doubles, the sound power needed to cover that area quadruples. Any formula taken literally can result in unrealistic requirements and unnecessary costs. Again, it's best to rely on the opinion of a well-informed and competent technician.

Ideally, you should go hear a concert in the hall, listening from different places, and give notes to the technician about problems. Hall managers most likely have had a lot of experience with their hall's specific problems and can tell you about them. Get a second or third opinion if the hall manager is defensive about problems or glorifies the hall's acoustical advantages — possibly from a musician who frequents the venues you have in mind.

Finding a Technician
Mixing sound, like playing music, is a skill which can be elevated to an art. Since you won't be doing the sound yourself, make sure you hire an experienced, qualified sound technician. The sound technician is often one of the most important links between the audience and the performers. The failure of a thirteen-cent part can bring the show to a dead halt. The tech must be able to keep calm and correct the problem quickly so the show can continue.

The performers' confidence in the sound engineer is a key ingredient for on-stage happiness and ability to relax and perform well. Given this critical role in the success of an event, once you find good engineers, treat them with utmost respect and consideration.

Most music performances can be placed in two categories: those where the audience attending will expect the music to be very loud, and those where the audience will be upset if it is very loud.

Both of these categories require special, but in many ways, different skills from the technician. It is very important to find a technician with experience and a good reputation for working with the type of music you are presenting.

Where do you find a good sound person? Start by asking musicians who play the type of music you're presenting or ask other producers. It would be inappropriate, for example, to hire a sound technician with only heavy metal experience to do sound for a bluegrass concert. When possible, it's great to hire technicians who support and enjoy the music you are presenting.

Above all, look for someone with a professional, responsive attitude.

Advancing the Concert
Most artists' contracts include a *technical rider*. This rider sets forth specific technical requirements, which may include staging, lights, sound, scheduling of rehearsals and performances, and other specifics. These riders can be extremely complex and demanding, not to mention confusing, to anyone not familiar with technical terminology. Sometimes these riders must be followed to the letter, but just as often the rider was written for the largest venue the act might encounter and may be scaled down for smaller shows. Also, these riders are many times outdated or simply incorrect.

The failure of a thirteen-cent part can bring the show to a dead halt.

Advancing the show means to make personal contact with the artists' representative in charge of that particular aspect of the show and to review carefully the technical rider, as well as other details including lights, dressing room, hospitality, etc.

It is very important that the show is *advanced* by the person responsible for any aspect of the show where specific requirements are outlined in the rider, in this case, the sound technician.

An option to the technical rider, or as a double check system, is for the artists to fill in requirements on a Sound System Worksheet (Form 11:1) and stage diagram, and send two copies to the producer. The producer should have the sound contractor list available equipment and return the original copy to the artists for approval. This should be done at least a month before the concert. Please be specific as to equipment — list model, description, and the number required. Even if the artists provide a technical rider, it may be easier to use the information in it if it is transcribed onto a sound system worksheet.

Finding Equipment

As for stage equipment, such as guitar amps, keyboards, etc., be sure to respect the artists' particular brand and model requirements in renting equipment. They've had a lot of experience and know what works for them. If the artists require specific brands and models which you cannot find, locate equivalent equipment and get approval for the substitution before renting it. Don't allow a rental company to dissuade you from your artists' legitimate needs.

As for the sound system, the artists' technical rider should give you a clear idea what is required, and may even go as far as to request specific components. Below are some sources for procuring a sound system for your concert, along with some pros and cons for each:

Concert Sound Companies

Most cities have one, if not several, professional sound companies. You can locate them in the yellow pages, through ads in trade publications, or, best of all, by asking performers and promoters who use sound often.

Pros

Professional sound reinforcement is an extremely competitive business, so any successful company must do good work to stay in business. Sound companies normally offer the best quality and the most reliable sound equipment. Many offer a large selection of equipment and can more easily tailor the system to the needs of the performance, as well as meet the specific requirements set forth in the technical rider. Many companies routinely carry backups for key components, so a failure is remedied with a replacement instead of a repair, which could mean a minor delay instead of a disaster. Sound companies deal with many different acts on a day-to-day basis, so they may be more proficient at adapting quickly to different performers and unexpected situations.

Cons

Using a professional company is usually the most expensive choice for sound, especially if your concert is located far away from the company you want to use. Many companies require at least partial payment in advance. Large companies usually have several working systems and reconfigure often. If you get a new technician and/or a recently reconfigured system, you are paying for on-the-job-training. One should be careful to avoid the presumption that using a professional company necessarily ensures good sound — your odds are probably better, but it is still important to use discretion when selecting a company.

Bands with Sound Equipment

Many bands have invested in high quality sound systems and often are willing to rent the system out when they aren't playing, or to sell a package as an opening act that supplies sound for the headline act.

Pros

This is often a much more economical option, particularly if you get an opening act and sound for less than you would have paid for sound alone. Your choices are greater, for there are many more band systems around than sound companies. If you are extra careful in selecting, you can sometimes get good sound and a real bargain.

Cons

The core equipment for a band sound system (speakers, amps, etc.) is often quite good. However, the peripherals (mics, equalization, signal processing, etc.) are usually tailored to the band and must be augmented and reconfigured for the headline act, which will make technical problems more likely. Band sound engineers may be inexperienced at working with acts other than their own. The experience factor is very important, for an engineer can make a barely adequate system work and keep everybody happy, or make a terrific system sound terrible and leave everyone disappointed.

In-house Systems

Many venues have permanently installed sound systems. These can range from state-of-the-art to adequate to junk.

Pros

A well-installed in-house system is carefully engineered and designed specifically with the needs and peculiarities of the room in mind, and sometimes by virtue of its physical placement can provide more consistent and even coverage not possible with a rented system. Permanent systems also can be "fine tuned" over long periods of time. These systems take very little physical abuse, so they can be more reliable. The sound system may be included in the price of the venue. In-house engineers also may be available and are sometimes quite good.

> *There is a fairly clear distinction between the quality of consumer and band level equipment as opposed to pro line equipment.*

Cons

Maintaining, improving, and updating permanent sound systems is very expensive and may have a low budgetary priority. A large percent of them are obsolete or may not be intended for the type of show you are doing. More specifically, many are systems originally intended for voice only or theater reinforcement and are totally inappropriate and inadequate for music performances. In-house engineers may be overly optimistic about the capabilities of their system, and personnel varies in quality as much as the systems themselves. There is sometimes a fixed add-on charge for the use of these systems, which can be inordinately high if your technical requirements are modest.

Music Equipment Stores

Many cities have music businesses that rent stage equipment, components, and complete sound systems.

Pros

For very small concerts and for augmenting existing systems, these sources are the most convenient and usually the most inexpensive. As retail sales outlets, music stores may be receptive to trading the use of equipment for promotional opportunities, for example, including the store's name in advertising and pre-concert promotions.

Cons

A sound *system* implies an integration of many complex electronic components that must be carefully connected and matched to perform properly as a whole. Systems rented from music stores are usually made up of demonstration items of equipment models and brands the store wants to sell. Even if the store offers a complete system rental, there is a fairly clear distinction between the quality of consumer and band level equipment as opposed to pro line equipment, and music stores rarely carry or rent pro line equipment.

The importance of providing good sound underscores the impact your choice of sound can have on the outcome of the performance. Good sound is good business. Showing care in the technical aspects of your concert is certainly a part of establishing a good reputation among concert goers and performers.

Unfortunately, there are no absolutes in selecting the best source of sound equipment and engineers for your concert. As with almost any service, you get what you pay for, and usually the most reliable and highest quality is the most expensive. No one, of course, recommends that you write a blank check for sound or anything else. We do recommend you take the time and effort to locate the best sound possible within your budget. If you look carefully and you know exactly what you are looking for, you can find good sound without always paying top dollar.

Cost

Since sound is such an important part of the concert, it is false economy to scrimp in this area. However, it doesn't make any sense to blow your budget on a system that will fill a 2,500 seat hall with three balconies when you're producing a concert for 200 people. It probably would be reasonable to pay $500 for sound equipment and a technician in a 500-seat hall. As the size and complexity of the concert increases, the cost will increase. You may have to spend $600 to $1,200 for a major concert hall. Obviously, these costs vary based on different geographical areas, supply and demand, access from loading area to stage, and general pricing. The above figures are only rough guides in advance of budget preparation.

Sound Check

Leave enough time for setup in your schedule: generally one hour more than what everyone thinks necessary is about right to compensate for all the things that can go wrong. The technician should be prepared to troubleshoot the system and replace any bad wires, fuses, etc. If there is broken equipment, it should be fixed before the artists appear for sound check. Artists should be notified of delays so they don't have to wait at the hall longer than necessary.

Everything should be set up and tested before the appointed time for sound check. Make sure that all mics work, and there are no hums or buzzes in the system. Check this with the stage lights on as they often cause buzzing problems if sound and lights are on the same circuit. See that the monitors are working and the system has been equalized to eliminate feedback.

When the system is ready, which should be at the time scheduled for sound check, bring in the performers. This is the time to set levels; make sure that mics, chairs, etc., are in the right place; and fine-tune the system. The sound check is a critical part of preparation for the concert. The audience should be kept out of the hall until sound check is completed.

A good sound engineer can make sound check a pleasure, an inexperienced one can make it a nightmare. The engineer should direct sound check from the mixing board with a microphone, asking the artists to play instruments and sing until each level and blend is determined in both monitor and hall speakers. There is no need to rehearse whole songs at sound checks unless it is requested by the artist in advance or the engineer needs it. Quiet in the hall is necessary to help it go as quickly and with as few distractions as possible. The producer, technician, and artists' representative all will want to be assured during sound check that the sound in the hall is the best it can be. Walk around to several different spots to hear the balance, blend, and frequency range. Keep in mind that when people are in the hall the sound will be absorbed and changed by their presence.

Some artists will reserve the right to have a person of their choice (for example, road manager or technician) supervise the mixing during the sound check and performance. This is not meant as an insult to your chosen technician; instead, it is a great help when the technician isn't familiar with the performers' music. When the road manager calls to advance the concert, it is wise to find out if the artists will be bringing their own mixer. If so, it's sometimes helpful to have their mixer and your chosen technician speak several days or weeks before the show to make sure the equipment provided is to the artists' specifications.

Sound check should be finished no later than two hours before show time, allowing artists and stage crew time to eat, meet friends, and prepare. For example, if the concert is to begin at 8 p.m., the sound should be all set up and working by 5 p.m. so the check can proceed between 5 and 6 p.m. This also is often the time to check light levels or run through light cues. Complicated cues can take up to an hour to run, so be clear in advance what is wanted by both artists and producer and schedule the appropriate amount of time.

During the Concert

You may want to play recorded music before the concert and during the break. This should be cleared with the concert artists in writing as some people feel that this takes away from the impact of the concert. Of course, only music which is appropriate to the mood of the concert should be used.

> *Never play music by any artist performing at the concert.*

Never play music by any artist performing at the concert, unless approved by the featured artist.

If you intend to tape the concert for any purpose, including your own use, this must be approved in writing by the artists or their management in advance (see Forms 7:6 and 7:7). Taping for broadcast often requires a separate mix that includes audience mics for ambience. This should be worked out well in advance with both the artists and technician.

During the performance, walk around the hall to make sure that the sound is clear. If there is any problem, alert the technician immediately.

A Journey through the Audio Chain and Sound Glossary

Producers, while not needing to be technicians themselves, find that a working knowledge of sound, equipment, and technical vocabulary is quite essential.

The sound passes through a great deal of equipment, and literally miles of cable, on its way from the performers to the audience. Since a sound system is only as good as its weakest link, be certain that everything is well matched.

A block diagram of the audio chain might look like this:

Diagram 1

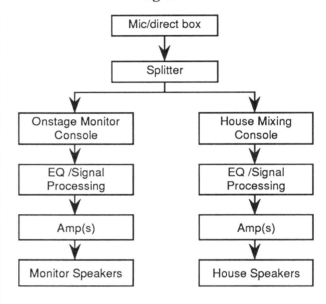

or

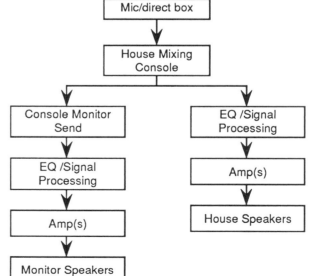

Note that the signal divides at the splitter box to feed both the house and the (onstage) monitor systems. The second diagram illustrates another configuration where the monitor levels are controlled by a discrete (separate, unaffected by adjustments to the house mix) monitor mix sent from the house console.

1. *Microphones* (mics) convert sound waves into electrical energy. Different mics have different characteristics which make them suitable for certain applications. Words such as condenser, dynamic, ribbon etc., refer to the nature of the element that transforms sound. Omni, cardioid, and figure-eight refer to the directional characteristics of the mic.

   Generally, dynamic, cardioid mics are used for live applications; dynamic mics are able to take more level before *distortion* (see 14 below), and cardioid mics are less susceptible to *feedback* (see 15 below).

   Mics also are rated as to impedance. Try to avoid high-impedance mics, which are designed for nonprofessional use. The signal from a high-impedance mic degenerates quickly over lengths of cable, and it often picks up unwanted radio frequencies.

   Remember: good mics are critical! Use the fewest number of mics necessary to minimize feedback.

2. The *mixer* takes signals from two or more sources and blends them together at levels the technician can set. The number of channels on the mixer determines the number of signals which can be mixed together. Mixers often have a number of other useful features which help control the sound. Input equalization works like the tone controls on a home stereo to shape the sound of each microphone. Only equalize as needed. Proper mic selection can eliminate many problems.

3. The *equalizer* (EQ) divides the audio spectrum into different frequency bands and provides control over those frequencies. Unlike the equalization provided with the mixer, which is used to adjust the sound of each microphone/input, this EQ is much more elaborate and can control the sound of the total system. It allows the engineer to reduce frequencies which are too loud and are causing feedback and allows for boosting ones that may be lacking. Since feedback occurs at certain frequencies which are often room dependent, it is important to control those frequencies.

   It is advisable to have EQ for both house speakers and monitors, as they each have their own problems. Some of the problems requiring equalization are caused by the particular resonance of the room, others are due to the characteristics of the equipment or the physioacoustic properties of the ear. However, overequalization can cause more problems than it solves. Where possible, solve acoustical problems with acoustical solutions, not electronic ones.

4. *Amplifiers* boost the signal fed to the speakers. Your main consideration is that sufficient power is available through the amp to adequately supply your speaker. Figuring the power requirement is a difficult equation best left to your sound technician.

5. *Speakers* convert the electrical energy back into sound. Most speaker systems use different components for the various parts of the audio spectrum. The low end is often handled by woofers, the midrange by horns, and the high end by tweeters. Column speakers (such as the Shure Vocalmaster), which use several speakers of the same size aligned in a vertical column, generally are not acceptable for music reinforcement. Arrays of many

small speakers (such as those made by Bose) work well in certain instances (small clubs, etc.).

Some systems combine the functions of mixer, equalizer, and amplifier into one integrated unit for portability and ease of operation. The Electrovoice Entertainer and Shure Promaster are units that work quite well for small concerts. The old warhorse, the Shure Vocalmaster, is not suitable for professional concerts.

6. The *monitors* are speakers pointed toward the performers so that they can hear themselves. Some solo performers may choose not to use monitors. Good stage monitors are absolutely essential when performances include an interpreter for the hearing-impaired/deaf. Interpreters need to hear the words clearly to do their job. When an ASL interpreter is being provided, make sure the monitor console is capable of providing a separate vocal-only mix for the interpreter if requested by her or him.

7. A *snake* is an extra-long cable that is really many cables all bundled together. It can be used to connect the mics to the mixer. A mic input box splitter usually is at one end of the snake which is placed on the stage to plug in the mics. The splitter splits the signal from each mic. The other end of the snake is then connected to the mixer. This eliminates a lot of separate cables going from the stage to the house mixing position.

8. An *electronic crossover* is used to divide the sound into separate low-, mid-, and high-frequency bands and route them to separate speakers designed to handle those frequencies. In speaker systems composed of different components, this allows for a more efficient use of amplified power and results in a cleaner sound.

Some multiple-component speaker systems use multiple amps and others have a passive crossover built into the speaker to route the frequency bands to the appropriate components.

9. *Gaffers tape* (also known as duct tape) is used to bind and place the cords and cables so people don't trip over them. Have plenty, and use it liberally.

10. A *direct box* is used to match the signal level of musical instrument pickups to the level needed by the mic inputs of the mixer. Direct boxes are generally used for electric bass, synthesizers, and sometimes acoustic guitars. They can eliminate the need for a microphone which could potentially add feedback problems.

11. *Stands* for mics extend to whatever height the musicians desire. Some performers are specific about needing boom stands or straight stands; this information is probably in the technical rider or stage diagram. *Boom Arms* allow horizontal or angled extension of the mic stand. *Goosenecks* are flexible extensions for the mic stands.

12. *Windscreens* are added to vocal mics indoors to prevent popping sounds and to all mics outdoors to prevent wind noise. Some mics have built-in windscreens.

13 *Monitor Mix.* Some mixers have a separate set of controls which adjust the sounds coming out of the monitor but do not change the sounds the audience hears. This means the performers can hear a different mix which may help them play better as they will be able to hear more clearly what they are doing.

14. *Distortion.* Distortion refers to the alteration of the frequency range created by increasing some frequencies or eliminat-

ing others. One very common kind of distortion occurs when too much signal is sent to a system. It overloads the circuitry and produces a crackly and unclear sound.

15. *Feedback*. An unpleasant sound which can be ear-piercing or an irritating hum created when a room is so reflective that the sound hits the walls and bounces back into the microphones to be re-amplified. It occurs at high or low frequencies.

The Stage Diagram Layouts (Form 13:3) are generic representations that will change with each venue and artist. These diagrams show roughly where you'll place speakers, monitors, microphones, and instruments, as well as other props, on stage.

Since sound is such a crucial element, be sure you've put together a complete and competent crew, advisors, and system. Your audience and the artists who perform will find the extra planning well worth it.

CHAPTER TWELVE

Lighting

Contributors Virginia Giordano, Ellen Goldstein

Lighting is a vital element in any production and should be carefully planned for in advance and monitored closely when the technical elements are being put together during the sound check. Lighting is a subtle support system for the performers — lighting reinforces the healthy look and upbeat attitude that most concert artists project.

Lighting also creates mood and atmosphere, but this is secondary to the primary purpose of lighting which is to *light the performers*. It is more important to light the performers well, sculpt and enhance their features and costumes, than to blanket the stage in colors and effects to artificially create a *mood*. The performers create and dominate the mood, the lighting supports that mood.

When there is ample equipment and a skilled designer, it is pure joy to create lighting effects. Practically speaking though, many situations are inadequate, so it is better to do performers. Remember, the audience is there to watch the performance, not the lighting.

There are a few terms vital to understanding this chapter and how lighting is assembled.

The *lighting design* is the finished product. Just as the set design is the finished scenery you see on the stage, the lighting design is all the lighting, moods, and variations you finally see during a performance.

A *plot* is a map for all the lighting instruments — it shows where the instruments will be hung in the theater, the focus, any additional trees or pipes which are brought in, and the color for each instrument, known as gel. The plot often indicates use of follow spots. Form 12:1 is a sample plot for a band or group production.

A *cue sheet* lists when the lighting changes take place in numerical order, and a *cue* is the individual pattern and the brightness of lights used to create each look.

Lighting Design
Lighting design can be as simple as having

one lighting cue and using it throughout the show, or it can be more complex with changes for different moods. The more complex the design, the more expensive it is to implement, particularly if you are in a space which is not well-equipped.

Even if you are familiar with lighting, you will want to hire a designer or work with the technical director sometimes provided in the hall rental. Working with you and the production coordinator or stage manager (that person most familiar with what the artists want), the lighting designer will sort out the logistics regarding lights: designing the plot, ordering, picking up, installing, striking, and returning rental instruments, supervising the lighting crew, and running the lights during the show. Before they begin to work, lighting designers need a budget, which includes their fee. They will get estimates on rental costs and provide crew fees if it is their crew, not yours. Often designers have a crew with whom they regularly work, or they can put one together. If not, you need to provide people to help with the put-in (setup) and strike.

Be sure to pick the right amateurs, so you don't spend in time or aggravation what you save in dollars.

People may volunteer for crew in exchange for admission and to learn a skill. It's harder to use volunteer help in technical areas, but using volunteers can save money on the budget, allowing for more lighting instruments! Be sure to pick the right amateurs, so you don't spend in time or aggravation what you save in dollars.

The first step in planning lighting is to find out the performers' specific needs and preferences.

Some have a standard technical rider defining lighting requirements — for example, no dramatic lighting, no blackouts, specific colors that should or shouldn't be used. If the performers' contract does not specify lighting, contact their road manager, artists' representative, or agent for this information. Then check the hall and get a list of the equipment and capacity of each instrument. If you're not using the hall's technical director, your designer will do an on-site evaluation of the equipment. Obviously, bigger halls require more equipment. A fully-equipped hall will have front lights, overhead lights, backlights, spotlights, and a dimmer board. Often spotlights cost extra to use and require hall personnel to operate. Some halls charge for each instrument; in others, the lights are included in the rental.

Check the equipment, don't take for granted that because something is hanging it is working. Whatever the hall doesn't have, you can rent — instruments, dimmer boards, and cable. You generally have to buy gel, and color numbers are often specified in the artists' rider.

It is desirable to work with a lighting designer who is familiar with the artists and material to be performed. When that isn't possible, be sure to supply the designer with records and videos by the performer. Pop concert lighting designers are used to working spontaneously, but it helps them to become acquainted with the performers' style and tone.

Performers rarely submit a set list in advance, and you shouldn't insist they do so except when ASL interpretation is requested. The performers must, however, provide a stage diagram indicating the setup of musicians and equipment. The lighting designer will base the design and plot on this and her or his sense of the performers' work.

For theatrical and dance productions, the lighting designer and the director or choreographer will meet well in advance of the performance to work out design concepts, moods, etc. It is the designer's job to attend rehearsals, study the material, and understand the cues.

Technical Rehearsal

In theater and dance production it is referred to as the technical rehearsal; in concert production it is called the sound check. An experienced production manager knows that the schedule for the sound check on the day of the show has to accommodate many technical elements and demands. The production manager should establish the schedule taking into account: hall availability that day, union call, load-in time, sound setup time, lighting hang and focus, number of performers or groups to check, dinner, and house open.

Lights are focused after equipment (sound, piano, etc.) and performer locations are established. Except for a touch up, lighting equipment should not have to be moved or seriously refocused after it is set, because doing so is very time-consuming. Use crew members to stand in for performers during the focus. Before performers arrive, tentative cues can be set and adjusted. Sound equipment and performer positions should not have to move a lot to accommodate lighting, so although lights can be hung before sound is in place, they should not be focused until after the stage has been set up. Don't wait until the piano has been miked to discover that the pianist is out of the lights.

Be sure that during the sound check you see each performer in the lights and cues that they will be performing. A stand-in will not do here — each person's skin tone, height, and hair color look different from another person's in lighting. It is very important to see each performer in her or his lights. Darker and lighter skin tones respond to light in varying ways. Be sure to inform your lighting designer about the artists' skin and hair coloring so they can plan what gels to use. If possible, ask performers to approximate the color costume they will be wearing for performance. A lighting cue setup on a performer in a dark color will look different that night if she or he walks out on stage in a light costume.

Standard concert lighting is a term which refers to the kind of lighting generally used by an orchestra. Most concert halls are equipped for standard concert lighting, if nothing else. This light is usually ungelled or very lightly colored and washes the entire area in a uniform medium/bright light. Usually the cue does not change, so lights come on at the top of the show and stay in that cue until intermission. When there is not enough money, time, or expertise to do a full-scale lighting job, standard concert lighting is acceptable — and, in fact, is preferable to fooling around with cues and colors that don't work. Fresnels and PARs are the instruments which provide this kind of general lighting. They are inexpensive to rent, easy to focus, and provide even light. The only drawback to this kind of equipment is that the light can spill over. But this can be controlled, and it is a good solution in many situations.

Lighting Do's and Don'ts

Keep the following ideas in mind as you plan and execute the lighting.

Avoid shadows on the performer. Always rent enough instruments to cover the performers for good visibility — in limited budget or equipment situations, drop any consideration about color or mood and go for well-lit performers. Don't rent one spotlight and expect that to do the job if you don't have any other lights. One spot light straight on will flatten a performer's face unless you have other front and top lights to fill in. One spotlight is best thought of as a highlight, to punch up the performer in existing lights. Spotlights can be used effectively in pairs, without other lighting, usually for a dramatic moment. Two spotlights converging at a 45 to 90 degree angle on the performers provide a three dimensional feeling which a single spotlight (without other lights) cannot.

Avoid spillover of light into the audience or onto the wings of the stage. If the first few rows of the audience are lit, it may be distracting to the performers, and the audience seated there may feel self-conscious. Some artists like to have light on the audience. This is best accomplished by dimming the house lights to an acceptable level.

Selecting the correct gel colors is an art. A general guideline is that darker or heavier colors are used for effects — top, back, and side lighting to outline and highlight performers and sets — and on white backdrops (cyclorama) for color effects. The lighter shades and tones in the color groups are used on performers' faces. Pinks and ambers *warm* a performer's face and blues *cool* it; lavenders read as either cool or warm depending on the rest of the colors, though lavender is generally thought of as a cool color.

If you are using light trees in the audience, do everything you can not to block sightlines. If possible, don't sell the seats blocked by poles. When you have reserved seating, this will have to be planned well in advance so those tickets can be pulled. Use sandbags or guy lines to protect trees from falling over. Cables need to be taped down securely with duct tape, and this area should be kept free of traffic.

If your concert is interpreted, the interpreter should be in a steady light at all times, in front of a background which will not distract from hand movements. The interpreter must be visible whenever there is any singing, talking, or announcing on or off stage. Light should be lightly gelled or not gelled at all. The interpreter should appear well-lit, but not distracting to the performers. (The interpreter should not be as brightly lit as the performers unless specified by the performers.) The interpreter's stage position should be spiked (marked with tape) so that she or he can return to the same position after intermission. Discuss with the interpreter and the performer whether blackouts and fadeout will be syncopated with the rest of the lights or

whether the lights on the interpreter will remain constant.

If you are lighting a band and using a spotlight on different musicians as they perform solos, the spotlight operator should be familiar enough with the music so that the spot can be directed to each musician as the solo begins. An experienced spot operator instinctively will know how to do this. If this can't be done smoothly, don't use a spotlight to highlight solos.

Know where the houselights are and who will operate them. Often performers will request that house lights be up for a particular number. Some performers let the house manager know they're going to do this; sometimes, however, they don't decide until the last minute. In many halls the dimmer board is located backstage. In that case, the lighting designer may want to sit in the house and give the lighting changes to the technician backstage who is running the board. To do this, they need a communication system, an intercom. Often sound technicians are using an intercom, also. Intercoms are usually rented from sound companies. If the lighting designer calls cues from the house using an intercom, make sure she or he has adequate light to read a cue sheet and is located in a seat where she or he will not disturb the audience by giving cues.

Finally, make sure the lighting designer, production coordinator, and house manager have coordinated the lighting logistics for the beginning of the show and the end of each act. Make sure each person knows who is giving cues and from where they are taking cues.

The interpreter should appear well-lit, but not distracting to the performers.

CHAPTER THIRTEEN

Day of Show

Contributors Mary Conn, Penny Rosenwasser

By the day of the show you already know the artists' technical requirements (stated in the contract), the estimated hall and crew expenses, and the artists' itinerary, including arrival time at the hall. A couple of days before the show, it's a good idea to check in with the sound and light technicians to make sure they have everything covered. If they are substituting any equipment, the artists' booking agent should be alerted so she or he can let the performers know.

On the day of the show, two concurrent schedules are in operation: one for the production crew and the other for the artists. The more complex your production, the earlier you need to start at the hall.

Plan your day-of-the-show schedule backwards from showtime (see Form 13:1). The schedule revolves around the tech check and preparing for it, taking into account your crew's needs. Make sure you plan your sound and light load-in early enough so that every-thing is ready by sound check, and the artists don't have to wait unnecessarily. Form 13:2 is a more specific schedule for each job, providing space to write the person's name and hours of work.

The artists' rider most likely will include all of the specifications required for the show. (This is often not the case with *new* performers or established performers on the road with new bands. Riders are constantly amended while touring because new problems come up, dietary requirements are changed, etc. To troubleshoot this, the stage manager or production coordinator should speak with the artists' road manager or agent a few days before the engagement, to see if any changes have been made or are anticipated so they can alert the caterer, sound company, hotel, or those affected by the changes.) The rider first appears with the contract. At that time copies of it should be sent to the facility, sound company, light company, and caterer so they all can be prepared.

What the artists want may be very specific, and you should make every attempt to get everything required. A certain brand of crackers or bread may sound ridiculous when you know of something better, but get what is requested. Some artists may be willing to try the local product if it's there, but familiarity is something that touring artists really need while on the road.

On the day of the show, the production coordinator and the stage manager should keep a copy of the contract with them at all times. Enclosed with the contract/rider is usually a stage diagram (see Form 13:3). The stage manager uses this for placement of the microphones, monitors, drum risers, bass cabinets, piano, etc., so preliminary light focusing can begin. When the performers arrive they will do the final placement. Some minor lighting adjustments are normal. Stage diagrams do not have a universal key as you can see by the examples, but most are self-explanatory. If you have any questions check with the sound company or the artists' road manager or agent.

> *Build extra time into your day's schedule to keep nerves calm and things on time.*

The stage manager and production coordinator will arrive before load-in time to prepare for the sound and light equipment and crew. Make sure the building manager knows when you are arriving so you are not locked out. It is always a nice gesture to have coffee, donuts, bagels, and juice for the load-in crew. (Form 13:4 is a checklist of items to remember to take to the hall.)

The stage is the setting for the artists' performance. And the performance is the presentation of not only the artists' work but of your work as a producer. Everything that takes place on the stage during the entire day and night is interrelated and has an effect on many other variables, the two most important being the artists and the audience. Therefore, it is the producer's and stage manager's jobs to ensure a smooth running, on-time day; the artists have plenty to do without the additional stress which piles up when there are problems with sound equipment, piano tuner delays, or not enough glasses on the stage.

Build extra time into your day's schedule to keep nerves calm and things on time. If possible, have the piano tuner come soon after the piano arrives or before load-in occurs. It is not necessary for the production coordinator or stage manager to be present while the piano is being tuned, but the tuner should be available for a touch-up after the sound check when the pianist has checked it, to implement any tuning adjustments desired.

While all this is going on, it's important to have one or two people serve as artists' and/or producer's liaisons. They can serve as the artists' drivers, hospitality helpers, runners, and general resource people (such as for last-minute runs to the store for batteries or guitar strings, etc.). Under smooth and simple conditions, they may have little to do. However, you need to have them available, just in case. They should be patient, good-humored, flexible, responsible, and good caretakers — and they should have no other duties at the performance.

You can communicate with them about delays in sound check so the artists arrive in time but do not have to wait unnecessarily at the hall.

Your lighting crew usually starts the hanging and preliminary focusing an hour prior to the sound company arrival. The first couple of hours the stage manager oversees everything that is going on. During this time, sound is being unpacked and set up. She or he should verify that nothing has been forgotten and that the crew members are working well together.

Dressing rooms should also be checked. Are they clean? Well-heated or ventilated? Place stage furniture, rugs, props, plants, or flowers on the stage prior to the sound check.

The production coordinator makes sure that the lobby, child care rooms, and box office are clean and set up correctly; that the food, drinks, ironing board, etc., requested by the artists are there before the group's arrival; that the bathrooms are clean and functioning; hall carpets have been vacuumed; parking lot gates are unlocked, etc. She or he also can put up signs — for child care, wheelchair entrances, concessions, bathrooms, and so on.

It's vital to have separate rooms for the artists (as many rooms as possible), the sign language interpreter, and the production crew. Having private quiet space before a show is crucial to many performers. They also should be able to lock their dressing room doors or have someone available to provide security at all times.

With the sound check time approaching, the stage manager contacts the head sound person to see if everything is proceeding on schedule. If not, the artists should be called and warned about the delay, and given a later call (time to be at the theater). By the way, it is always better to tell people to arrive at the facility a little earlier than necessary to prevent possible problems from delaying their arrival (traffic, getting lost, bad weather, etc.).

Once the performers have arrived, the stage manager introduces them to the crew, directs them to the dressing rooms, and checks to see if they have any immediate needs. When the head sound person is ready, the stage manager is alerted, and performers are called to the stage. This is usually done individually, as each microphone is tested first and monitor levels are set for individuals.

Time needed for sound check can vary from 30 minutes to more than one hour, depending on the complexity of the music, the skill of the technicians and the artists, the level of initiative the artists take during sound checks, and the number of artists in the band or performing group. Beginning with the monitor speakers, the engineer will work to get the best instrument and vocal sound levels for the artists.

If the performers are travelling with their own sound and light technicians, this can greatly facilitate the sound check. There will be no question about placement of instruments, and these technicians have a clear understanding of the artists' needs. If that is the case, the stage manager's job is simply to communicate with them about the hall and crew requirements, the day's schedule with emphasis on time concerns, and advise them what can be done at the facility.

While sound is getting ready for the performers, so is the lighting crew. If no light plot is given to them they generally do some washes of the stage in various colors. In most cases the artists have color choices, and the production coordinator should check with the hall to see if they have the desired gels. In many cases they have to be supplied and are an additional cost in the budget.

The lighting director will need a volunteer to stand in on the stage for focusing. It is always helpful to have a runner available during the day anyway, and this is a job she or he can do. Spike marks are then made on the stage with colored cloth tape so that when the performers get there they can be shown where they should stand. Some final adjustments in the focus will need to be made, and the front of the house can be done during the sound check. Any overhead lighting will need to be done after sound check but before the doors open.

The artists almost always have some kind of idea about what kind of lighting is appropriate for various songs. The road manager should provide a set list and go over it with the head electrician or lighting designer. The electrician should be told what is to be done with the spotlight. Does it stay on the headliner the entire time or move to other musicians for their featured songs? If no cues have been established by the performers and there is no road manager, the stage manager should ask the performers what they would like, communicate it to the lighting designer, and go over the songs on the set list with her or him. Levels of the lights can be checked rather quickly during or immediately after the sound check. The stage manager should show the artists the general washes for approval and further suggestions.

If things are not going smoothly at sound check, and you are working in a union house, there are a few things that can be done. The artists should be told when the crew break has to occur and how many minutes are left to check out the sound. Suggest to them that they work on their more difficult numbers and get them right. Then ask the musicians: Can they live with it? Is it crucial to take a few more minutes? The crew can break at their appropriate time and return an hour before the show (which they would do anyway) and continue to work on the problems, while the house manager holds the doors.

Another alternative is to keep the momentum going and go into overtime and pay the penalty. In some cases if it is only a few minutes the crew will let it slide, but that is never to be expected. The decision to go into overtime should be made by the production coordinator, and sometimes it is decided by whether the budget can take it.

When sound check is finished (or break time occurs), the artists' meals usually are ready. It is their quiet time to relax and prepare themselves for the show. Crew members who are at the hall all day need to eat. You can provide food for the crew or allow enough break time so the crew can get their own meals. In either case, let them know what to expect. At the very least it's a good idea to have food at the hall for people to munch on. Check with the union in advance about meal regulations.

Sometimes the production coordinator and stage manager can eat during this time period, but not always. Contact has to be made

Crew members who are at the hall all day need to eat.

with the house manager to be sure the programs are available and to tell her or him about the length of the show. Is there one set or two? How long should intermission be? Should latecomers be allowed into the house and be told to stand at the back during songs or allowed in only between songs when they can be seated quietly? Sometimes the artists have very specific requests about these procedures. The house manager will want to know when you want the lights flashed to get the audience seated and will suggest a later start time if there is a long line at the box office, or when a good percentage of the expected audience is late in arriving.

If showtime is to be delayed by five or ten minutes or more, the performers and crew need to be informed about it immediately. This is something the stage manager does. It is important to open the doors as close to schedule as possible. If the hall has many doors and you are going to open only some of them, put signs on the ones you will be opening so people will line up in the right place. With general seating people arrive early to get good seats. Not only is it inconsiderate to keep them waiting, but in bad weather it can be very uncomfortable.

Additionally, people may have children with them who are going to need child care. If the child care crew is ready, you might let the children in early to get them out of the weather. If for some reason beyond your control (such as the artists arriving late or sound check being delayed), the doors cannot open on time, you should go into the waiting crowd and let them know what is happening and why, and at least let them mingle in the lobby.

During the day, the production coordinator periodically checks with the box office to see how ticket sales are progressing. Are there lots of calls? Will there be a good walk-up? People in the box office can help sell a show if they are informed about it throughout the weeks the show is on sale. The box office should be given an alphabetized, typed guest list as early as possible by the production coordinator. The artists' list probably will not be typed but an effort should be made to make it alphabetical and neat.

The doors open when the house manager is given the okay by the stage manager.

At this point the stage should be set with water and all props. The stage manager will have placed the set lists near or on the monitors for all of the musicians. Last minute adjustments can be done by the musicians (not the headliner), the stage manager, and the sound people. Too much action can be distracting to the audience, so keep it to a minimum.

When the doors open, the sound board operator begins the preshow music. The stage manager checks with the house manager once the doors are open and actual show time is decided. When decided the stage manager lets the sound and light people know and notifies the artists and the emcee. They should all be in place five minutes before the curtain.

At the start of the show the stage manager cues the lights — first, house to half, to get the audience settled, and then, house out. The light board operator is cued to bring up the lights on the stage, the emcee then goes on stage or announces from offstage, and the show begins. The stage manager stays in the wings and watches the show. If there are any noticeable problems on the stage, communication should be made through the backstage headset or via runner to either the sound or light technicians. The production coordinator should be checking sound and lights from the house and also checking with the box office.

The concert may be a large gathering of somewhat like-minded people in your community. Many producers and artists feel this is a good opportunity to bring the audience's attention to particular issues or other cultural events by making announcements at the beginning of the concert. A long series of announcements at the start of the show, however, will make the audience restless. In-

stead, choose one or two announcements of critical importance and use the program book or the tables in the lobby for other groups to get their message across.

To have a smooth and quick introduction, the emcee should make the announcements rather than spokespeople from the particular groups. The selected groups can write up a one-to-two minute statement for the emcee. The hall will be dark, so phone numbers may be lost in an announcement. Artists often want to approve the content and placement of these messages.

The production coordinator should know where the lobby coordinator is at all times. The lobby coordinator should know what the last song is in the first half so she or he and the crew can be in position before the intermission begins.

Intermission is a break for the audience, performers, and sound and light people, if things are going well. If that is not the case, it provides additional time to correct problems. Two-thirds of the way through the intermission, the stage manager should find the house manager and see how things are going. Is the line at the bathroom so long that the audience should be given a few extra minutes? Are concession sales going so well that people are waiting to buy? These and other factors may add an additional five minutes to the break. And, once again, the stage manager lets everyone involved know they have the additional time.

The second half of the show begins much the same as the first half. It is up to the production coordinator, with the artists' approval, as to whether the emcee goes back on with more announcements or just welcomes the performers back. And, of course, the artists may just want to walk out and start without the additional announcement.

Technicians all are cued the same as before. Before the artists return to the stage, the stage manager should let them know how much time is left before the show is scheduled to end — and before union crews go into an overtime situation. This will affect the set list for the second half and the number of encores performed. When the artists first come offstage at the end of the show, they should be told again how much time is left, then they can determine what song or songs they will do as encores.

After the intermission, the production co-ordinator settles expenses with the facility manager. The box office statement is review-ed (utilizing Form 6:4 or one that the box office supplies), and the hall costs are sub-tracted out of the receipts. Use the Contract/Budget Settlement Form (Form 2:4) to record all income and expenses. A check for the balance is usually given to the produc-er at this time. In some cases it may take a couple of days to get the money, and in most cases *final* costs are not given to the producer until as late as six weeks after the show.

After settlement with the facility, the pro-duction coordinator goes to the artists' road manager or the artists to settle up. If you're working on a flat fee with the artists, it is a simple payment after the concert. If the road manager is not a technician, she or he gener-ally prefers to do this before the show is over. In cases where the artists are receiving a per-centage of the net, the road manager will ex-pect to get copies of all receipts of expendi-tures, the box office statement, and hall costs, before getting the check. (Often performers will want to be given cash the night of the show. You should check with the road mana-ger beforehand and have the cash ready, if that is their preference. Prepare a check for payment, they then will endorse the check back to you for your records.) If some re-ceipts are missing or just cannot be copied at the time, they should be sent to the booking agent or representative as soon as possible.

When the artists are handling the settlement it will happen at the end of the night. It is good to have all of the figures ready and have double-checked the math, so things can be finished as quickly and

efficiently as possible.

When the artists are finished and have returned to their dressing rooms they may want to receive friends. These people should have been on a backstage list that was held at the box office where they would have received a backstage pass (something the production coordinator pro-vides). Alternative-ly, a backstage list can be given to the dressing room secur-ity guards, and they can screen who is admitted. Sometimes the artists will sign albums after the concert, so a table in the lobby should be readied and supplied with pens and comfortable chairs. Often the artists will want to spend a few quiet moments either alone or with close friends before going to the lobby. The production coordinator should let the record seller and the crowd know that the artists will be appearing.

Choose one or two announce-ments of critical importance, and use the program book or the tables in the lobby for other groups to get their message across.

Once the show is over the stage crew begins striking all the equipment. They begin as soon as the house lights are up. The stage manager oversees the work. The sound com-pany knows what they are doing and how they want things packed and loaded into their truck. And the head technician with the facil-ity knows what needs to be done to restore the theatre to the state it was in before the load-in. The load-out usually takes much less time than the load-in.

When load-out and settlement are comple-ted, the production manager and stage mana-ger thank everyone who has helped them throughout the day. With good planning, the day will have been an artistic and financial success for all.

CHAPTER FOURTEEN

Follow-up

Contributor Torie Osborn

A number of tasks are involved in *closing up shop* after your event is over. This is the time for assessing the strengths and weaknesses of the event and finalizing contacts with those who participated, from staff to artists to contributors.

The first task is the very pleasant one of writing thank you letters to those who were especially helpful. Thank media contacts who publicized or reviewed the event, board members who provided hospitality for artists, and staff members (including volunteers) who worked diligently to make it a success. Notes can be brief, but they should be personal; generic thank you notes just don't give that warm feeling you would appreciate yourself.

You may want to write a personal letter to the artists also, in addition to sending a complete set of press clippings. In this way the relationship concludes cordially and with a reminder to the artists of the success of the event. A follow-up note at this time is also a good idea if you hope to work with the particular artists in future productions. Showing a little extra consideration may well set one producer apart from many others in the artists' view.

Similarly, a thank-you note and a press clipping or two may be useful in building or continuing a relationship with those who have donated money or in-kind services (such as printing costs). Contributors appreciate some evidence that they've supported a worthwhile production — one that was artistically and financially successful and provided some visibility for the donating organization.

The next task is to go over all your notes to determine what went well and what parts of the production were less successful. Organize

> *When the project is over, the whirlwind dies down, and it's back to work as usual.*

the notes for easy retrieval — maybe according to budget item or job. Review these notes during the first week after the show, when their meaning is freshest.

As an evaluation, list the key areas and budget items (e.g., sound, hall rental, paid advertising) on a sheet of paper, and leave space for solutions or recommendations. In this space give a narrative description of both what went wrong and right. Evaluating the event systematically should save you from making the same mistakes again, and remind you of the successes to repeat. For example, if you note that the printer didn't have the programs ready on time, remember to leave more time or to get a different printer (and leave more time!). If the sound equipment was great, remember to use the supplier again and ask for the technician by name.

Obtain input from an Evaluation Form (Form 14:1) to review your production. It is helpful if everyone significantly involved in the event will complete a form, including the artists or artists' representative, if possible. Sometimes producers will solicit feedback from members of the audience through a simple form included in the program handed out to everyone or at a table in the lobby, often in conjunction with gathering names for the producer's mailing list. Make this feedback or an analysis of it part of your notes.

If your production was a collective effort, you may want to hold a *post-show* meeting to share your perceptions of the event. This is especially helpful after a large undertaking that required months of work by several key people. In this way you can obtain a more complete picture of the different areas of responsibility (publicity, artist management, technical support, etc.) and how they can be improved in future productions. It also wraps up the group effort for all participants.

A comprehensive review can be invaluable for producing your next event, particularly for an organization in which someone else will be in charge of a similar event next time. An important area to take stock of is first budget

estimates, second estimates, and final (actual) budget. Go over your budgets carefully to understand what happened so you can plan better next time.

Were your plans well-laid, but were there not enough people to carry them out? Could a small adjustment next time put you in the black? (If only you had gone with the Irish group instead of the folks from the British Isles — you forgot that St. Patrick's Day was coming up — or if only you had realized it was not just Sunday night, but Palm Sunday night.) Was the timing right in dealing with advance notice to the press? Was there enough time to do effective outreach and organizing? Did posters go up too early? Where were the discrepancies between your expectations and reality and why were they there? Were expectations unrealistic? Were there a lot of latecomers, so that it might be wise to adjust curtain time? Recording this kind of information simplifies the task for next time.

> *A comprehensive evaluation can be invaluable for producing your next event.*

Post-show also is the time to evaluate the media publicity your event received so that you can determine where to direct your efforts in the future. One way to do this, is to compile a file of press clippings — all print coverage in newspapers, magazines, and other publications. In addition, list each media person contacted (whether print or broadcast) on an index card, and make careful notes about what worked and didn't. It will be useful in the future to know which radio or TV stations and show hosts provided time for an interview, those which ran a PSA, and those who did nothing.

Perhaps your contacts can be groomed for the next artist, or a little more time can be devoted to pursuing a certain station whose listeners you'd like to reach. A form for the index cards (or other recording method) can include the name of the media, contact person, date of coverage, nature of coverage (interview, videotaped spot, etc.), and any comments. And don't forget to thank the media; the appreciation will be well received.

When the project is over, the whirlwind dies down, and it's back to work as usual.

There may be a letdown after basking in the glow of a job well done. When the stage lights become a memory, you start to have time to yourself again, though you may not know exactly what to do on your first free evening.

We know how many people deal with it — by beginning to plan the next event. It promises to be even better, easier, and more fun than the last one!

CHAPTER FIFTEEN

Accessibility

Contributors Leslie Cagan, Susan Freundlich, Marilyn Golden, Sheila Kahn

It is exciting to see large numbers of event producers working toward making events accessible to disabled people. The writers of this book want to encourage you to do this kind of outreach. We believe the following information will help you.

There are large segments of society that may be inadvertently excluded from cultural events because of special disabilities — some hidden, some highly visible. The efforts and desires of people with disabilities to participate, combined with the producer's care to have events publicized and made accessible to them, will propel forward their struggle for basic rights: acceptance and access.

Interpreting a concert is a full night's work, plus many, many hours of preparation and rehearsal to convey the mood and concepts of the music.

People with disabilities may be interested in concerts but their potential attendance depends on the producer providing some very specific services. While it won't be possible for you to accommodate every person's special need, it's important to be aware that there are people with disabilities, including being hearing-impaired, or in a wheelchair, or having back or post-operative conditions, who will want to attend the concert and be treated well.

Wheelchair Accessibility
A standard adult wheelchair is 25-1/2 to 27 inches wide, so doorways should be 30 to 32 inches wide. You have to check to see if the bathrooms, and all other areas of the hall you want your whole audience to have access to, are sufficiently wide and appropriately graded.

Discuss the wheelchair concerns with the representatives of hall management. They may have addressed this issue before and have good ideas on where wheelchairs can go. It's very important that the management is involved in this planning before tickets go on sale. People coming in wheelchairs should be confident that such details have been worked out before they arrive at the hall.

For our purposes, a wheelchair-accessible hall would be one which has:

1. No stairs, inside or out (including to restrooms), unless an alternate path of travel via ramp or elevator is available. Ramps should be sturdy and shallow, not exceeding one inch in height for every 12 inches of length (if space is very tight, certainly no more than one inch in height for every 10 inches of length). Ramps should be 48 inches wide (if space is constrained, no less than 36 inches wide).

    Either short curbs (a couple of inches high) or handrails should be provided on each side of the ramp to ensure no one falls over the side. Handrails are helpful to semi-ambulatory people as well.

2. Seating available to people using wheelchairs which is as integrated as possible; that is, a choice of places for wheelchair users to sit, similar to the range of choices available to non-disabled people. This may mean removing some seats. Many halls are not physically equipped to allow for maximum integration. Other options are: reserve aisle seats for wheelchair users and have them transfer into those seats (their chairs should be kept close by); flat seating at the top or back of the hall; aisle seating that does not block exits. In all situations, non-wheelchair friends should be able to sit next to the wheelchair users, often in moveable or folding chairs. Pathways to all seating areas should be approximately four feet wide (if space is constrained, at least 36 inches wide).

3. Wheelchair-accessible restrooms with doorways at least 32 inches wide (including the doors to restroom stalls), corridors approximately four feet wide (especially if a turn is required), and sturdy grab bars mounted near the toilet. A clear area, five feet in diameter, is ideal and helps maneuverability in restrooms.

4. All other public areas such as food/drink concession areas, literature/record tables, public telephone, drinking fountain, etc., in wheelchair-accessible areas should be configured as described above.

To make final decisions on the placement of wheelchairs, it is essential to go to the hall. When you designate an area specifically for wheelchairs, make sure that visibility and sound are as good there as elsewhere in the hall. The placement of wheelchairs should not block the flow of other people moving to and from their seats. When figuring out how many wheelchairs you can fit in the hall, plan for a wheelchair to take up about twice as much space as a fixed seat and figure the ticket count accordingly.

If you have to use a hall that is not very accessible to wheelchairs, a volunteer or an usher should be assigned to coordinate the wheelchair seating, making sure that people in wheelchairs get to their location and have the information they need. Other volunteers could be used to work at the show (before intermission and after) to post signs at the hall entrance, direct people to wheelchair-accessible seating, and help people in chairs go up or down ramps.

Sign Language Interpreting
According to the Gallaudet College Office of Demographic Studies, there are an estimated 18 million deaf and hearing-impaired people in the United States. American Sign Language (ASL), the language used by most deaf people in the United States with each other,

is a linguistically distinct and unique language. A sign language interpreter for a concert will translate the songs as well as everything else that is spoken from the stage, making the event as a whole accessible to deaf people. Deaf and hearing-impaired people have limited access to many events and information because they are often not signed.

If you and the artists decide to have a concert interpreted for the hearing-impaired/deaf, please make sure to have a competent interpreter who can translate songs into sign language. Call the local interpreter referral service, and ask for recommendations of interpreters with performing arts interpreting experience. These services often are connected with deaf community centers or to colleges (including community colleges) with deaf/hearing-impaired students. If you know people who work with the deaf, ask them to ask their friends to recommend interpreters. Or call the Registry of Interpreters for the Deaf in Rockville, MD at (301) 279-0555, for referral to a regional or statewide clearing house.

Interpreting a concert is a full night's work, plus *many, many hours* of preparation and rehearsal to convey the mood and concepts of the music. Include payment of the interpreter in your initial budget. Discuss fees and expectations as part of the budget and planning work.

Hearing-impaired/deaf people need seats close enough to the stage to see the interpreter. You might consider a special section for *Hearing-Impaired People and Their Friends*, or seats for the hearing-impaired/deaf could be scattered among the sections of the audience closer to the stage. However, some hearing-impaired people may prefer not to sit in specially designated seats because they would rather not draw attention to themselves. The interpreter will need to have good lighting, placement on the stage that is not obstructed by speaker systems, pillars, etc., and at least one monitor speaker. The interpreter must be able to hear everything

that is said on the stage.

To do the job well, the interpreter will need to receive a close approximation of the artists' set lists at least three to four weeks before the concert, lyrics, and a tape of all the music. It takes time to develop full, meaningful translations. If the artists indicate that this is not possible, ask them to provide all the material from which they will choose.

Many artists, although they might support the idea of providing interpretation, will refuse to supply firm set lists because they want the option of choosing material spontaneously, according to their own feelings or the audience's response. Therefore, your job is to be a good communicator between the artists and ASL interpreter — so there is understanding and agreement in advance. Some artists will cooperate fully because they understand the nature and needs of the interpretation.

The next step is to let people know about the accessibility.

Some artists have developed working relationships with specific interpreters. Find out if they would prefer to have one of them. Work for an arrangement that meets both needs as much as possible. Occasionally, some artists are not willing to send lyrics in advance. The producer, in those cases, needs to notify the interpreter as she or he may not want to do it cold.

If you are opening your doors to the deaf and hearing-impaired, everything must be interpreted, not just selected parts of the concert. Arrange for your interpreter to interpret announcements, introductions, and anything else that is not specifically the work of the artists, or have another interpreter lined up to do that.

In June 1988, interpreters were invited for the first time to participate in the AWMAC Conference (Association of Women's Music and Culture), held at the National Women's

Music Festival. Interpreters met to discuss issues of interpreting and translation in the performing arts.

In their caucus report, Sherry Hicks said: "We identified issues relating to the nature of our work. We work with music, a culturally bound art form, belonging to hearing culture. Interpreters attempt to mediate the auditory spoken language to the visual-gestural language, the natural language of deaf people. In this search for linguistic equivalence, we realize our goal may evolve to a linguistic and cultural translation with respect to art.

"Our work is seen as an emerging art form, another dimension added to the stage, one that the women's community has come to expect. There are mixed reactions from deaf audiences. Since we are unsure of what the deaf community wants, we are committed to having a creative dialogue with that community.

"Other areas we plan to discuss further include: how each of us prepares for performance, feedback strategies, how we translate English or ASL, is our work valid. We also focused on the dimension we add to a multicultural vision of the women's music industry.

"We all question the validity of the *art form* with respect to deaf people. Some interpreters have made the choice to discontinue performing arts interpreting, based on political, linguistic, and cultural information. Others continue, informed of the controversy, seeking answers.

"Much has come out of our caucuses. We have come together and recognized our differences as women and as interpreters. Our views of the work vary. This is healthy. Our styles of translating are unique — we work to respect each other's work."

Publicity and Ticket Distribution
Assuring that the hall is wheelchair-accessible and providing a sign language interpreter are the first steps toward making your show accessible. The next step is to let people know about the accessibility. On all posters, leaf-

lets, press releases, and calendar announcements include in either words or symbols a notice of the accessibility of your concert.

You can use the logos (see Form 15:1 for samples) which are gaining acceptance as meaning: *This event will be interpreted in sign language* and *wheelchair accessible.*

If not, state precisely what is/is not accessible — for example, *hall is accessible, bathroom is not; or, the concert hall is accessible once inside, and assistance will be available at entrance.*

If the front doors are not accessible, perhaps a side door is; in that case, publicity should indicate which entrance is for wheelchairs, signs at the hall should point to that door, and ticket takers and ushers should be stationed there.

Statements about accessibility do take up space on your leaflets and posters. Try to find the clearest, most concise way to state the information, without burying it or making it so small it is illegible.

Getting the word out also means making special contact with groups and organizations that work with persons with disabilities. Find out what publications exist and when their deadlines are. Drop off posters at hearing-impaired/deaf and disabled community centers and service organizations. Talk to staff and users of the centers about the concert and how to get tickets. Involve people with disabilities in your publicity and information-sharing if possible.

Some producers discount tickets for those who live on fixed incomes (for a full explanation see Chapter Six). If you choose to discount, hold out enough tickets in the wheelchair and hearing-impaired section.
You can set a date to release to the general public any which have not sold, but hold out a few to sell at the door.

Ticket outlets must be instructed that you are selling reduced-price tickets and know who can buy them. Obviously, it's best if all types of tickets are available at all outlets, but if that's not possible it should be clear on the publicity and at all outlets where disabled tickets are available. The important things for ticket outlet personnel to know are: where the tickets are available and that if people ask for discounted tickets, sellers shouldn't argue. Not all disabilities are visible. There is very little fraud in buying disabled tickets. Of course, if a disabled person is going to the concert with able-bodied friends, the friends should pay full price. Disability cuts across all economic levels, and some who could purchase tickets at a discount may choose not to. For example, computer programmers, office workers, or college professors who happen to require a wheelchair may be able to pay full price for a

concert ticket. As we mentioned with regard to seating, people with disabilities do not always welcome attention being drawn to their "specialness" by receiving discounts or other kinds of preferential treatment. Providing the service is enough, don't force it on anyone. Sometimes it's possible to find a relevant person or organization to handle disabled ticket distribution. For instance, a community center or university ticket office that serves deaf/hearing-impaired people and has a TTY phone (a telephone specifically designed for deaf/hearing-impaired) might be willing to sell tickets. By all means indicate the TTY phone number and location on your publicity.

CHAPTER SIXTEEN

Child Care

Contributors Bananas, Inc., Jennifer Leith, Marti Mogensen

Child care is a service that can make your event more attractive to parents who otherwise might feel they could not attend. It can be important in building both audience and community relations. The availability of child care may also make it possible to offer a sampling of events to older children who are unable to sit through the entire production. Child care makes cultural events more accessible to parents and may increase children's perception of culture in our society.

However, child care requires planning, a budget, a good coordinator, and compliance with the legalities.

Before making the commitment to offer child care, you need to examine the type of care best suited to your event, the expense of hiring staff, the availability and possible cost of space and equipment, and the organization required. You should check city or county guidelines for staffing, insurance, and space; however, for single events, most jurisdictions waive requirements, and a program set up by an experienced child care worker is sufficient. It is sometimes possible to provide child care for minimal extra effort and expense.

A realistic budget will provide for staff, supplies, renting space, insurance, and incidentals, such as photocopying forms. First, cost estimates will certainly be modified depending on the number of children (which affects the number of workers needed and quantities of snack and activity supplies). Some expenses could be recovered by charging the parents a fee per child. However, if you are offering child care as a social and political statement, it defeats some of your purpose to make parents bear the cost. As with other elements of the budget, be clear about your goals.

If you are unfamiliar with child care, the details can seem overwhelming, but an experienced child care worker will find them routine. Contract an experienced person at least a month (or longer if you want her or his help with budget, space location, and planning) before the event. This child care coordinator's duties can include the entire implementation of the program encompassing securing the site, arranging for staff, borrowing necessary equipment, and making legal and security decisions, all within your budget and with your knowledge and approval. The coordinator is responsible for developing forms including staff contracts, waivers for parents, registration and emergency care forms, and sign-in/sign-out sheets. And on the day of the show she or he will make arrangements with security and hall personnel, set up the child care site, supervise the care throughout the show, oversee the cleanup of the site, and return the borrowed or rented equipment. The coordinator plans and oversees the actual greeting and signing in of the children, the program and the closing, including the return of children and their belongings to the proper adult.

> *Child care makes cultural events more accessible to parents and may increase children's perception of culture in our society.*

Often there is a tendency to expect child care workers to donate their time. Although working with children can be delightful, child care is hard work, and you should expect to pay for this service unless workers offer to donate it.

Reservations for child care should be required in advance so you can plan the number of workers needed. Promotion and advertising should state that child care is available including the number to call for reservations, the ages of children accepted (if appropriate), fees (if any) and the basis for acceptance (such as *limited space available*), plus a deadline by which to register for child care. When parents call to reserve child care, ask for their name and phone number, the child's name and age, and any special concerns or needs they may have. At that time instruct the parents about what items they will be expected to provide.

Plan on one adult for every three children under two years old and one adult for every five children over two years of age. It's also a good idea to have a reserve of workers as substitutes and relief if you need to call on them. The coordinator will organize and go over the basic program plan and safe conduct rules with all staff. Guidelines for all of this can be found in *The Bananas' Manual on Event Child Care* (see Resources in the appendix). The following checklist can serve as a quick guide.

Choosing the Space
1. Is the space safe? Look for fire hazards, open stairs, clean carpets, etc.
2. Check for access to bathrooms and drinking water.
3. Is it easy to supervise children in this space? Ideally, there should be separate sections for different ages and activities. For example, babies may need a quiet space while older children need an open space for active play.
4. Can the children make noise and not disturb the performance?

Equipment/Supplies
1. Bring toys, books, crayons, markers, scissors, play dough, paper, and anything else that young people might enjoy and your budget allows.
2. Parents may be asked to bring blankets and diapers for babies. A few extras should be on hand also.
3. Always plan a snack. Children get hungry at different times, so it's a good idea to have apples, cheese and crackers, and other nibbling foods on hand. A sitdown snack also can provide a quiet time for the group. Don't forget — the workers will get hungry, too!
4. It's a good idea to have water and juice in

bottles and cups on hand.

5. Get a small first aid kit — bandages, gauze, antiseptic, and such. Parents also should sign a medical release form so the child can get medical treatment in an emergency.

6. Bring name tags, sign-in sheets, pens, pencils, and masking tape to mark items as children check in.

Advance Arrangements

1. Have all child care workers arrive well in advance. A preliminary meeting on the day of the show will usually be necessary with the coordinator and workers.

2. Decide what the rules are. Child care works best when there are definite boundaries to the child care area. When and under what circumstances may children go in and out? Safety rules are important, too, such as *walking* on the stairs. Rules may be necessary to protect the room you are using, such as writing only at the tables.

3. Have a plan set up for when the children arrive. How will each child be greeted?

Arrival and Greeting

1. The parent should fill in the sign-in sheet including the child's name, parent's name, parent's seat number if known, and any special notes above such things as allergies, toilet training, etc.

2. Mark any toys, food, clothing, or supplies the child brings along, particularly baby food and medications.

3. Tell the children any rules they are expected to follow, right away.

4. A staff member should greet each child. If a child is crying or fussing on arrival, the child care workers should take care of the situation. Let the parent know that the situation will be under control. Show confidence by taking the child and offering comfort.

Program

1. Plan different activities for different age groups as well as both active and quiet activities. Be clear about who is planning and carrying out each activity. For concerts associated with a cause or issue, or involving a specific culture (example, a choir singing African freedom songs), you may want to plan activities relevant to the concert.

2. For short-time care, one special activity often can be planned which will occupy most of the children most of the time. Examples are play dough, mural making, or a puppet show.

3. Be sure sleeping arrangements and outdoor activities are clear and well-planned with safety and health considerations.

Closing

1. Find out in advance when the event is scheduled to end, so everyone can be ready. Start clean up soon enough so that the children have a chance to participate.

2. Have a plan for signing each child out to the proper adult. Make sure children leave with all of their belongings.

3. For future planning, you may wish to ask children and parents how they liked the child care arrangements. Staff also may have a short meeting to evaluate the service.

CHAPTER SEVENTEEN

Children's Concerts

Contributors Cathy Fink, Nancy Raven

Producing a children's concert differs in some respects from producing other events, but it involves examining the same kinds of questions considered earlier in the book. Goals, technical details, budget, and promotion all must be considered carefully, and most of the sample forms can be used for children's productions as well.

Goals

First, what are the goals of your children's concert? Do you know a specific performer who does excellent children's concerts, or is it an idea you'd like to pursue without knowing which artists to approach? Do you want a full *family* event with a repertoire that caters more to children, or would you like to have mostly children there? Children typically can't get to concerts on their own, so you can plan on having a fair number of parents attend.

The financial goals of a children's concert should be looked at the same way as any other event. Your goal may be to make money, break even, or even lose money in exchange for community outreach.

Finding an Artist

Ask parents and children whom they would like to see. They may suggest a local favorite who would draw well for your event or artists whose records they have or whom they've seen before. Don't assume that a children's performer will charge less than a performer for an adult concert; children's artists are professionals, too.

Finding a Hall

The concert setting should be comfortable for children and for the way the artists like to work with that audience. Many children's artists count on audience participation so the setting needs to encourage that interaction. Do the artists prefer to have people sit very close to the stage? Would she or he like a gym, with everyone sitting on the floor and the artists standing? Make sure the seating is comfortable for children and that the stage is no more than three feet taller than their heads when sitting. If it's too high, the children will be straining to look up.

Safety features in the hall and the accessibility of bathrooms are very important. Make sure unneeded stairways are blocked off; there are no sound/light cords to trip over; balconies have good railings; and exits are easily accessible for emergencies. Children should not have to go up and down many stairs to get to their seats or to the bathrooms. Try to set it up so people coming with children who can't sit through the whole performance will have easy access to come and go without disrupting the performance.

Sound

For a small event, 50 to 100 people, you may be able to do without sound equipment. In fact, sound equipment could be a real bother and detract from the fun. However, for larger events, appropriate sound equipment is very helpful or necessary. The attention span of children is affected by how well they can see and hear the artist. See Chapter Eleven for specific information on sound.

Budget and Cash Flow

An average children's concert is 50 to 70 minutes long, rather than the 90 to 120 minutes typical for adults. In thinking about how much to charge for the concert, take into account the shorter length of the concert and the fact that you hope to attract families and people bringing children. Setting the ticket price should be done in conjunction with the artists, and reviewing your financial goals.

Here are a few options for determining ticket prices:

1. One price for adults, one price for children (usually lower).
2. One price per child, adults free with a child.

3. One price for adults (e.g., $4), one price per child (e.g., $2.50), with a maximum set price for a family (e.g., $12). This way larger families can still afford to bring their children to an hour-long event.

It's nice to supply refreshments *after* the show — during or before can create quite a disturbance for the performers. Besides interruptions for trips to the bathroom, it's no fun trying to distract kids from their popcorn to sing along.

Of course, as refreshments also produce income, you will have to make a judgment call based on your goals.

Networking

Be in touch with organizations that work with children, such as day care centers, children's museums, YMCA's, YWCA's, JCC's, schools, libraries, scout troops, etc. Some of these groups will publicize your concert at their events, share mailing lists, or otherwise offer support or advertising opportunities. Some may want to buy a block of tickets in exchange for a table with information about their organization.

PTA's and other groups of concerned parents also may be helpful. Stay in touch with children's bookstores that may support your event. They frequently have a good sense of the children's music market in your area.

Media

Here's an opportunity to get some publicity for a very special event. Right now, well-produced children's concerts are few and far between. If your artists have records or are locally or nationally known for their work with children, you have an excellent angle to pitch for feature articles or pre-event interviews. The broadcast media welcomes spot appearances or interviews. There is also a lot of public relations assistance — e.g., Parent's Press (has different names in different areas) and other weeklies that will run calendar information for your event.

CHAPTER EIGHTEEN

Outdoor Concerts

Contributors Leslie Cagan, Linda Ware

An outdoor concert or event has its own charms: enjoyment of the surroundings, opportunities to mingle and move about, a more informal and festive atmosphere. Many festivals choose outdoor sites to have several stage locations running simultaneously. In many ways producing an outdoor event is like producing an indoor one, but there are major logistical considerations that are different and require careful planning.

Finding a Site

When looking for a site consider power sources, stage locations and level ground, audience seating and parking, sound displacement, bathroom facilities, food and drink vendors, weather conditions, equipment and truck access, unloading and parking, barriers for security and ticket control, accessibility for disabled, and public transportation, etc. You must have the big picture in mind and visualize what you want to create and whether the site will allow it to materialize.

Some park service organizations will co-sponsor an event, providing you with some or all of your needs regarding location, sound, stage, lights, dressing rooms. Others may provide power and security only. Commercial venues may be available with more developed sites, but they are probably more expensive. You must have your goals clearly in mind before proceeding: is it a one-day show or two; one stage or more; rural or urban; why is it outdoors; does the stage need to be large enough to accommodate dancers; what if it rains; will you charge admission, thus needing to limit access with fences and security people? Once you have your site and your event clearly in mind, begin formulating all the details and variables of an indoor concert, plus more.

Weather Conditions

This is the one variable you absolutely cannot control. It might be possible to arrange a rain date, but consult your artists. How will that alter your budget? Be prepared, with sudden changes in the weather, to make last-minute changes in your show. A serious rain or wind might force you to cut off the show after it has started (your audience might not stay, or you could risk serious electrical problems with the sound system). If there is a chance of rain, add into your budget plastic sheets or tarps to cover equipment. Determine in advance who has the authority to stop a show and have them stay in close communication with the sound and light people. It is possible to get rain insurance to cover losses, although it is very expensive and complicated (rain insurance policies are usually written for a specific minimum amount of rainfall within a specific time frame). Check this out with a reliable insurance agent.

The other major weather consideration is the sun. Is the stage oriented so that it exposes the artists or the audience to hot sun for a long time? Is there any way to change this? Do you need to build a canopy over the stage and sound booth; will the site permit this? For any warm-weather outdoor event you should provide water and shaded areas for the comfort and safety of the audience. Hot, sunny days pose an extra risk, especially to senior citizens.

Site Structures
If you use an existing outdoor theater you will not have to build a stage, ramp, and stairs although you might still want to add a canopy, artist hospitality area, or other features. At some sites you will have to build a stage large enough to include speaker stacks, separate mixing and light platforms, and possibly press and or speaker platforms. At small events a flat bed truck can be used. Contact the companies nearby that build stages, describing precisely what you want and asking for a bid. There is the further option of literally building the stage yourself; if you undertake this project, use only competent, experienced (possibly licensed and insured) carpenters and

construction crews, and figure the building time and expense into your production schedule and budget. A railing around the stage sides is usually necessary. It might be possible to construct a ramp that can be used for wheelchair access as well as equipment loading and unloading.

Artists need dressing rooms or tents; the stage crew needs storage and work space; and there should be a general backstage area for hospitality. If you are expecting media, you might want to designate a press area backstage or to the side of the stage. Temporary additions can be constructed from wooden posts and plastic tarps anchored with rope, or you can rent tents of various sizes from companies that regularly supply outdoor events. While tent rental can be a significant expense, it is less labor intensive. Examine your budget and crew availability if you plan to build structures onsite; also discuss your ideas with the site manager, who may have access to materials or can advise you about restrictions regarding construction.

In many ways producing an outdoor event is like producing an indoor one.

Equipment
For larger events in particular, large equipment and vehicles will be needed. Trucks will bring in construction materials, sound and light equipment, chairs, tables, generators, AC cables, scaffolding, signs for check-in, tents, portable toilets, etc. A forklift may be needed for some of this equipment and construction for larger events. Many vendors are not open on the weekends so confirm in advance your pick-up and deliveries.

Sanitation and Medical Services
Since most outdoor sites offer few sheltered bathroom facilities, you'll have to investigate the cost of renting portable toilets. Com-

panies which rent this equipment or park managers can advise you on how many to rent for your estimated crowd size. If your budget permits, rent enough units for the largest crowd estimate rather than for the minimum. They can be distributed throughout the site in small clusters in inconspicuous settings (behind trees or sloping hills) so they need not be eyesores, and audiences appreciate short waiting lines and clean stalls. Have the emcee announce and also print in the program their locations.

Providing medical services is even more important at outdoor events, given the additional stresses of weather (especially heat) and the mobility of the audience. For events attracting a large crowd -- say, several thousand people -- consider soliciting a hospital or medical center to donate its emergency care unit, in return for acknowledgement in printed advertising or the program and possibly by the emcee at the concert. These units, usually housed in a trailer or ambulance, should be situated in an accessible place. If the event is small, one or two nurses or paramedics should be sufficient. Again, set them up accessibly and include information on their services among the stage announcements.

Sound travels very differently outdoors than indoors.

Security

If you're not working in an outdoor theater, or other site with controlled access, it will probably be difficult to charge admission unless you can figure out a way to enclose and secure the entire area. The site may offer security personnel, but in most cases hiring and coordinating security will be the producer's responsibility. You'll also need security for artists' instruments, equipment, and personal belongings. The backstage area should be secured; ropes, fences, security

people are options. In addition to around the stage and backstage, security personnel should be in visible points in the audience, by merchandising areas, the box office, and entrance doors. If the event runs more than one day, secure storage is needed for sound equipment and concession materials.

Power

Running sound and lights requires a power supply. Some sites have outdoor power but you may have to bring in one or more generators. However, don't assume a sound person or electrician can hook-up the generator — it is a specific skill. They also will need feeder cable connectors! Check with your sound and light people about what they'll need. Sound and lights should run on separate power supplies to avoid getting a buzz in the sound from the lights. Have an experienced, licensed electrician check out the site with you and help you choose your power supply.

Sound

Sound travels very differently outdoors than indoors. In addition, other noises near your concert location (airplanes, traffic, playgrounds, sirens, church bells) could affect sound. Ask your sound technician to visit the location to advise you on sound possibilities, difficulties, equipment, and cost. When using more than one stage or performance area, don't have sound overlapping or interfering. Also, be aware of the neighborhood and surrounding environment. Consider changing the site if the sound problems are too severe. A canopied area must be provided for the sound mixer and soundboard; a raised platform with a tarp covering, located in the audience seating area, should be sufficient.

Lights

Of course, night concerts will require light, but daytime performances also could need lighting. Ask your lighting technician to go to the site during the time of day your show will take place. The technician should be able to predict if lighting will be necessary because of shadows (from the angle of the sun at a certain time of day, buildings and trees causing shadows, daylight savings time changes).

Night lighting will involve scaffolding to hang stage lights overhead and on the sides or behind. Spotlights may project from a platform in the audience. You also may need work lights for constructing and striking the stage equipment or the stage. Of course, work lighting is much different from stage lighting.

Refreshments

What refreshments to offer for sale at an outdoor event depends on the estimated crowd size, site, health department restrictions, and your budget. Selling food and drinks can be a good source of income. Outdoor concerts often are much longer than a typical hall event -- many are all-day celebrations -- and the audience is more active, and particularly more thirsty, on a warm, sunny day in a park-like setting. A table of baked goods and cider donated by supporters works fine for an indoor show, but it won't be adequate for an audience that includes frisbee throwers and dance enthusiasts among the quietly seated listeners. If you want to attract a *family* crowd, it might be best to avoid selling beer. Publicity that specifies *no alcohol sold or permitted on premises* conveys an image of a tame event for people of all ages, not especially welcoming rowdy participation. Or set aside a family area where alcohol will not be permitted. All national parks prohibit the sale of alcoholic beverages, and other sites also have restrictions.

A convenient way of selling refreshments (and it's sometimes required) is to contract with a professional concessionaire. Many serve the standard fare of hot dogs, burgers, and soft drinks; others specialize in vegetarian or ethnic foods. Check with the local health department for advice and restrictions concerning foods, especially perishables. The producer (or the site) receives a percentage from the concessionaire's sales (ranging from 10 to 30 percent — check local arrangements); this might be income for you. The contract should specify terms for settlement and for liability of each party. You could invite many vendors to sell food, drinks, crafts, records, tee shirts, etc., or to distribute literature, depending on space availability, site restrictions, and suitability.

Accessibility and Seating

Is it general seating on the lawn, or reserved seating, chairs, benches? Can people in wheelchairs move easily to the restrooms, merchandise, and food areas? Will elderly people be comfortable? If the general seating is on the ground, plan to provide some chairs for people and mention lawn seating in your publicity so that people can bring blankets or folding chairs. Will people be able to get to the site easily enough (especially important if it is far from public transportation or not well known)? If you expect much of your audience to travel by car, check the adequacy of parking facilities. Maps to the event should be prominent in your printed publicity, signs should be posted, and guides should be available to assist with parking as people arrive.

An outdoor concert can be exciting, fun, and sun-filled. People love to listen to a good concert outdoors. As producer, weigh the potential problems against the positive points of outdoor concert production, and do as much as you can to ensure the success of the show.

Liability Insurance

As with indoor concerts, you will need liability insurance. Since there are more variables and risks to an outdoor venue and event, your coverage will probably cost more.

CHAPTER NINETEEN

Visas

Contributors Cathy Fink, Mark Van der Hout and staff

An immigration visa is legal permission for an alien to enter the United States. It is obtained from the United States Consulate abroad if the individual is outside this country. For performing artists, the visa is obtained following approval of a visa petition by the INS (Immigration and Naturalization Service). There are two types of visas, and a performing artist is required to have one of them if she or he is not a citizen or legal resident of the United States.

If you are considering producing a concert with a non-U.S. citizen or resident ask the artists' representative how the visa will be handled. Do they expect you to apply for it, or will they take responsibility for obtaining it? If your concert date is in the middle of a tour, it's likely that you will not be the person applying for the visa, but do make sure that it's been handled. Generally, the U.S. agent/ artists' representative will apply for the visa, especially if it is for a tour, but if you are inviting a performer for a single event, it may

be your responsibility. Make sure that this issue is very clear and included in your contract for the performance. If there is no visa and INS becomes aware of your event, both the artists and producer may have legal difficulties. This is especially true now, in light of the employer sanctions provisions in the proposed Immigration Reform Control Act of 1986.

Applications for visas are handled initially through the INS. If there is no branch office where you live, phone the head office in Washington, D.C., and ask for information about the office nearest you. In many areas of the country, the visa petition is mailed directly to one of four regional adjudication centers. You should find out in advance where the petition is to be sent or precious time will be lost.

The two categories under which performing artists may apply for work in the United States are contained in one form, the I-129B, or Petition to Classify Nonimmigrant as Temporary Worker or Trainee. The categories are:

H-1. "Alien(s) of distinguished merit and ability to perform services of an exceptional nature requiring such merit and ability."

H-2. "Alien(s) to perform temporary services of labor for which a bona fide need exists."

Performing artists may not submit their own petitions. The petition must be submitted by the employer, agent, or artists' representative in the U.S. Under the *current* regulations, this is the person who must guarantee payment. Only one petition is needed for several gigs or a tour, and it may be submitted in any locality where there is an engagement or the district in which the petitioner (employer, agent, etc.) resides. Under *proposed* INS regulations, the petition would need to be filed where the first engagement is to take place or in the city of the petitioner's place of business. It is unclear if and when these regulations will be enacted. Find out if new regulations have been enacted before filing, as the proposed regulations make several other changes.

> *If the press kit is written entirely in a non-English language, pick out the best pieces and translate them.*

H-1 Visa
The H-1 category traditionally has been reserved for more well-known artists. Distinguished merit and ability can be proven without stardom, but it is a little harder. It is essential to provide strong documentation of the artists' talent, popularity, uniqueness, etc. (see Form 19:1).

When providing documentation for a traditional Quebecois group to perform in the Washington, D.C., area, letters of support were obtained from The National Council for Traditional Arts, Society for Ethnomusicology, American Folklife Center (Library of Congress), Canadian Embassy, Folklore Society of Greater Washington, congressional representatives, and other publicly elected officials. Each letter documented the writer's credibility as an expert in the field; the group's originality, talent, validity; and served as a reference for any further questions.

The INS looks at many applications on behalf of singers, folksingers, guitarists, etc. You need to make your artists stand out in the application process.

It is also essential that the visa application be filed with the INS at least ten weeks in advance of the entry date. This allows the INS time to process and allows you time to appeal in case of an initial rejection.

Other Important Documentation
A Full Press Kit. If you can't show a demand for the artists in the U.S., show how well-known, loved, and respected they are in their homeland or other countries and what the potential is here. Include any articles written on the artists in the U.S. — reviews, press clippings, etc. Document their record sales in the country of origin.

Information regarding sales of records or cassettes through U.S. distributors or record companies is also helpful. For example, Redwood Records was able to help document Ferron's popularity in the U.S. with sales figures of her recordings.

If the press kit is written entirely in a language other than English, pick out the best pieces and have them translated. Summary or precise translations may be done. A biography and perhaps one press clipping also would help.

Include a complete itinerary and contract for the performances. As an agent or artists' representative, you may include all the information in one contract (i.e., dates of shows, total guarantees, etc.). The itinerary should list tentative dates, concert halls, hall capacity, and ticket price range.

It's worth contacting the embassy or consulate of the performers' country of origin in some cases. They may be thrilled to know you are helping one of their nationals and may be willing to write a letter as well as show some interest in the tour. They sometimes arrange receptions if the artist is performing near the embassy.

H-2 Visa
H-2 status has been suggested by several INS officials for artists who are not yet of *distinguished merit and ability*. The application process is more complex than for the H-1 visa, but the actual judging is less harsh. The artists' agent or employer must submit a Temporary Labor Certification Application to the state's Department of Labor or Employment Development Department. The application needs to show that recruitment efforts were made in the locality of the job offer, including with the musicians' union in that area. Employers also must show that they have advertised for the position by submitting a copy of ads and results. The ads can be specific but not too tailored to the individual (see Form 19:2).

Once again, attach an itinerary showing dates and places of performance as well as contracts regarding the performance. The state employment agency will forward the application to the U.S. Department of Labor after advertising is completed. You should contact the Alien Certification Unit of the state agency *before* filing to make sure you are meeting all requirements.

The U.S. Department of Labor (DOL) then will issue, hopefully, a temporary labor certification which advises the INS that there is a labor shortage for this job and that foreigners may be hired. The final step is to file the non-immigrant H-2 visa petition (Form I-129B) with the appropriate INS office along with the labor certification received from the DOL and all supporting documentation. A minimum of three months should be allowed for this three-step process, if possible, but

expedited processing can be requested if justification can be shown.

If you are applying for an artist's visa for the first time, either as an H-1 or H-2 (especially) it is highly advisable to consult a lawyer who specializes in immigration law. A specialist may be able to save you considerable time, energy, and frustration.

The current cost of having an immigration lawyer handle this for you will differ with each law firm, but you can expect it to cost between $75 to $250 an hour. It will take several hours of their time. Be sure to discuss the fee and time estimate before plunging in. It may be possible to make an arrangement where you do most of the legwork and consult with the lawyer at several stages to make sure you aren't missing anything. Do not wait until you already are having a problem before consulting a lawyer.

> *The two most important things when applying for a visa for an artist are: lots of lead time and excellent and complete documentation.*

If you are planning a festival where several visas will be needed, consider filing one petition for all the performers who need visas. This may work out if there is only one event in one location. If you are bringing in a several-person musical group, only one petition is needed.

Also, if several tours for a given performer are being arranged over a several-month period, file one petition to cover all tours, and ask for a period of time to cover the later dates plus travel time. This will save you a good deal of time and expense (especially if you are using a lawyer). The performers need to remember to request a *multiple entry visa* at the consulate abroad if they will be travelling in and out of the country.

Whenever you are talking with INS officers about a specific application, be sure to write down the names of the officers in case you need to refer to them or the information they gave you. Also write down your application number so it can be easily found on future inquiries.

If, by unavoidable circumstances, you are applying late for the visa, you may submit the application with a request that it be expedited, giving reasons why the delay was unavoidable. It really is a last resort since you'll have no time for appeals or resubmissions should anything go wrong.

If your visa application is denied, there are appeal procedures. These must be acted upon quickly in order to expedite the appeal.

It has been suggested that INS procedures would better serve the community if the INS would:

1. Acknowledge receipt of the visa application within three working days.
2. Report visa status (granted, rejected, challenged) within 20 working days of receipt of the application.
3. On a response to an INS challenge, report reviewed status within one week.

These are only suggestions which are not part of INS current practice.

To summarize, the two most important things when applying for a visa for an artist are: *lots of lead time* and *excellent and complete documentation*.

CHAPTER TWENTY

Fundraising and Organizing around the Concert

Contributors Leslie Cagan, Cathy Fink, Sheila Kahn

Producing a concert presents a great opportunity for fundraising and organizing. You may use it to distribute literature about your organization, increase your mailing list, recruit volunteers for other projects, promote upcoming events, and develop greater visibility for your organization in your community, as well as provide a vehicle for focusing on the issue(s) of concern to your group. You also may want to use the opportunity to do fundraising. Keeping your original goals in mind, you may wish to select some of the activities described in this chapter to help you reach your objectives regarding both organizing and fundraising.

It is important to remember that while there is no inherent contradiction between organizing and fundraising, you do need to consider the balance between these two somewhat different activities as you plan your concert and the other activities tied to the event.

Organizing

Concerts have been used as organizing events to greater or lesser degrees of success. How much organizing you can do through your concert will depend on how much effort you put into advance planning, as well as how much the artists are willing to get involved. In many concert halls it will be possible to set up literature tables for your group or for other groups you invite. Your ability to do this will be shaped by the actual space available in the hall, but it also should be guided by some political considerations. Is it more important for you to reach people with one particular message or information about one particular piece of work, or do you want to make your audience aware of a range of groups?

In addition to general literature tables and leaflet distribution, it is often possible to generate support for specific petitions or postcard/letter-writing campaigns. It is critical to decide on the best form for distributing such materials. Sometimes you can put postcards you want everyone to sign on each seat in the hall before the concert starts. Or materials might be collated into the program you hand out. You can consider having volunteers circulate in the crowd as people arrive, during intermission, and at the end, asking people to sign a petition or take leaflets. If you plan to do this make sure you have enough volunteers to handle the size of the audience, and be sure to train people in ways to be assertive without being pushy. Of course, any organizing goal needs to be discussed or cleared with the artists and hall management at the time you book and/or confirm. It is also important to discuss your organizing approach and any special concerns with the artists before the show begins.

Your confidence should be high, but your expectations reasonable.

Discuss possible options for the artists to help in your organizing effort. Are they prepared to give any sort of rap from the stage about your effort? Will the artists encourage people to sign the cards or petitions or encourage people to stop by the tables during intermission and on their way out of the show?

What the artists do from the stage can make all the difference in terms of how receptive people in the audience are.

It is important the artists have as clear a sense of your group and the work you do as possible. The best raps artists can give are those that are integrated into their own material and come across as part of the program, not as something tagged on as an afterthought. However, most artists don't want to be deluged with reams of reading material on the organization. Provide them with simple, complete, clear information.

Fundraising

The types of fundraising activities you choose to do will depend in part on the dollar amount of your fundraising goal and your resources. Your confidence should be high, but your expectations reasonable. Remember, especially if you have never produced a show before, that things will come up for which you haven't planned, and even what appears to be the *easiest* thing to organize always will take time, energy, and important people-power. Be realistic about your resources. It is wiser to plan activities you are sure you can accomplish so you can count on the income than to plan events which might be risky and could even end up costing you more money than you make.

Selling tickets is the basic way to raise money at an event. Make sure that you know how many tickets you must sell to break even. If you cannot sell that number of tickets then you will end up losing money on your primary fundraising source. Make sure that you have a clear and workable plan for selling out your hall.

Another way to generate more funds from ticket sales is to reduce as many of your costs as possible. Sometimes with benefit shows, a concert hall might be willing to negotiate on certain prices. Printing, or its labor, may be donated. Ask the people doing the sound and lights to consider reducing their fees, although you do not want to force people into donating services which they can't afford to donate. Remember, technical people will work hard at a show, and you should not assume they can afford to reduce their rates. But it doesn't hurt to ask.

Fundraising can include sponsorship ticket sales; corporate or individual sponsors; raffles, door prizes, and auctions; producing a program book where you sell advertising space; receptions and dinners; and concessions and bake sales.

Many nonprofit groups have adopted a policy of having the expenses of an event covered before the event begins. In that way, the organization already has paid for the event before selling a single ticket. This is not the *normal* way to produce a concert since ticket sales are usually the largest source of income, but your group may have a special opportunity to fundraise around a concert and accomplish all your goals.

Sponsorship Tickets
A sponsorship ticket provides a special opportunity for supporters to contribute an amount that exceeds the regular ticket price. Grassroots organizations may have a major donors' list as well as individuals who support their work; both groups of people should be contacted and offered sponsorship tickets. The sponsorship ticket should be an *attractive offer,* priced both to sell and to make you a profit. Sometimes the sponsorship ticket includes a pair of tickets to the event and listing as a sponsor in the program, or it can include both the event and an invitation to a reception. It also could be a package that includes tickets and an autographed poster or record album.

Leave plenty of time to sell tickets to the sponsors. About three months before the concert date, ask everyone in your organization to go through their card files and pull out the names and phone numbers of possible sponsors. Everyone should then add names from their personal address books. Compile all the lists, check for duplicates, and make sure the notes are legible. Prepare a simple accounting sheet of who called whom, the date, the time, the response, and follow-up, if required. Find five people who can volunteer phone time, hook up your phones, and six to eight weeks before the concert, begin your calls. Make it fun; keep enthusiasm high — plan refreshments for an hour into the evening — to keep them on the phones. A willing effort will bring better results than relying on overworked staff to squeeze in these calls between their other work.

Depending on the experience of your callers you may want to prepare a *rap sheet* for them with a brief explanation they can read or paraphrase over the phone: the organization's goal, how you are going about achieving it, and how the individual could be an important part of your effort by becoming a sponsor of your concert.

People already supportive of your regular program are likely to make a small, tax-deductible contribution to your organization. If your organization does not have tax-deductible status you might be able to find another group to serve as your fiscal sponsor. If so, make sure people know the correct way to write out their checks. You can offer them a great package — two tickets, an invitation to a private reception with the artists, and a record of their choice (which they can have autographed at the reception). Say your tickets are $7 at the door, but the sponsorship ticket costs $50. The sponsors get $14 worth of tickets, some small dollar amount of food (say $3 per person if wine and hors d'oeuvres are served), and an $8 record or cassette of their choice; the remaining $25 is a contribution that can go directly to your organization.

> *A willing volunteer effort will bring better results than relying on overworked staff to squeeze in calls between their other work.*

If your package includes anything which involves the artists (reception, signing records, etc.), make sure to have a clear agreement with the artists before you start the publicity.

Raffles, Door Prizes, Auctions
Raffles and door prizes are favorites in many fundraising efforts. If you have good relationships with local merchants, this may be easy to do and beneficial to you and your neighbors. Often, the easiest to do in this category is the 50/50 raffle. There is no prize that needs to be promoted: the prize is the

money that everybody puts in. As in state lotteries, many people will put in a dollar or two for a chance at winning their own money back and everyone else's, too. In a 50/50 raffle the winner gets half, and your organization gets half. All you need to supply are printed forms for people to fill out with their names and addresses — one for each dollar they put in and a box for all the forms.

If this idea is appealing, you can print up booklets of these tickets and sell 10 forms for a bargain of $8. And you can sell them in the lobby right up until the time you have the drawing. This kind of raffle includes the additional benefit of providing names and addresses for future mailings. If participants come to this concert, they'll probably be interested in finding out about your next one and in being on your regular mailing list. They may even become regular supporters of your group.

An alternative to the raffle idea is to offer door prizes. Although giving away prizes often is not a money-maker for your group, it can be a great way to generate mailing list additions. It's especially good to get some door prizes donated from local businesses. If your giveaway includes items that are exciting and big enough (like giving away a waterbed), offering door prizes may even sell tickets for you. However, it may be easier and almost as effective to give away an album or cassette of the artist.

If you can easily get more elaborate merchandise or services donated, you may want to organize a silent auction to take place before the concert and through intermission. On a table, under the description of the merchandise or services is a box. People can write down their bid, identifying the item with a number, along with their name, address, and phone number. At the end of the evening, the high bidder can pay for and take the merchandise or be given the information on receiving the items they won. Be clear about who's responsible for delivery up front — don't get stuck delivering a big object unless

you want to and have the ability to do so.

Should you decide that you want to do any of these (raffles, door prizes, or auctions), be sure to discuss it in advance with the artists or the artists' representative. If you want to draw a raffle ticket during the show, that will have an effect on the character of the event. You should discuss whether or not the artists will be asked to be directly involved in this effort. For instance, do you want the artists to actually draw the winning ticket? Anything that might require the participation of the artists or have an impact on the show should be talked through with the artists or their representative before you start promoting it. The more you have worked out before the show the more smoothly everything will flow during the performance.

The Program/Adbook
A program book/adbook can be a great money maker for your organization. Its success depends on good planning — number of pages available, quantity to be distributed, plenty of time to solicit ads and charging an appropriate amount for the ad size.

An adbook/program book can be a financial success if:

1. It is planned early enough (90 to 120 days prior to the event).
2. People are willing to work hard to produce it.
3. Good graphics are used to represent the sponsoring organization.
4. Budgets are worked out carefully to account for all labor and printing costs and to establish proper ad rates.

An adbook/program book is less likely to be a money maker if:

1. It's a last-minute decision.
2. The budget is not planned in advance.
3. Paid labor or volunteers are not available to sell ads.
4. The graphic work is not high quality.

The production of a program/adbook can be a separate project from everything else — as long as the timelines work well with those of the concert. This is discussed in depth in Chapter Nine.

Please keep in mind that there are many options when producing a program/adbook. You may want to look at samples of what others have done in your community. They range from the glossy playbills of major theaters and professional associations to the two-page, copied 8 x 5 flyer with *thank yous* on the back sheet. Some include self-addressed, stamped envelopes for contributions to be mailed, others have tear-out coupons. But all of the successful ones share elements of the careful planning and considerations listed above.

Make sure you discuss your plans for a program/adbook with the management of the hall. Some halls have strict rules on what they will allow to be distributed; some produce their own programs and do not allow any others. Make sure there will be no problem with distribution of your program/ adbook and that you have a clear agreement with the hall on distribution. Will the hall's employees distribute it? Or will your volunteers? Depending on your relationship with the management of the facility you are using, you may want to get a written agreement on this item.

For a more detailed discussion, please read Chapter Nine.

Receptions/Dinners

Receptions are another avenue for fundraising. It may be an occasion that entices people to buy sponsorship tickets if your artists will attend or if you invite a special guest to be host/hostess. It may be an opportunity to give a direct fundraising pitch to all assembled guests. The pitch should be clear, precise, and as short as possible. Remember, while the guests probably support your cause, they are out tonight to have a good time and enjoy the concert.

Make it easy for them to contribute. You may want to have self-addressed envelopes for them to drop off (with checks inside) as they leave the reception area or let them know you also will be collecting checks near the concessions at intermission — and make arrangements to do so!

Instead of a reception, potluck dinners can be planned to precede the event. Planning the dinner is an entirely separate project. If you can recruit a volunteer community group to cover this end, you will be relieved of the details of planning this function, get new people aware of and involved in your work, and sell more tickets. If PTA or church members are bringing family favorite dishes to the dinner, for example, it is likely that spouses (and children, if there is child care) will come, too.

In fact, it may be worth co-sponsoring the whole event with another group to get the extra people to help with these auxiliary events and to get the support and attention of these potential allies and extended audience members.

A word of caution about taking on the planning for a reception or potluck dinner. Such an event can become a major effort. Be sure to evaluate carefully your resources, and take into account how much other work you already have to cover with the show itself, as well as the fundraising potential for such an additional event.

If you do decide to go ahead with a reception or dinner there are a few practical considerations.

1. Is there an adequate room in the concert hall for such an event? If not, is there a location convenient to the hall?
2. For a pre-concert event you need to think about timing. How much time will be needed for the sound check? What kind of time do the artists need before the show to dress and prepare?

3. If the reception is after the show, do the artists need a break between the show and the reception?

If your reception or potluck is built around the artists, be sure to work out all the details before you start advertising. Make sure you have a written agreement addressing any money issues. For instance, are the artists donating their time for this event or are they expecting some percentage of the income from the reception? It is important to work out as many of these details in advance so that everyone involved knows what to expect and what others are expecting of them.

Concessions
Concession sales are potentially good money makers, too. Baked goods and drinks always sell well at intermission. Often people who won't offer other kinds of support will be happy to donate baked goods and their time selling the goods at your table.

If your goods are all donated (some companies may contribute their beverage/ product), you can estimate an income of $1 per person. If you are buying things to sell, budget no more than half that for purchases. In addition to the cookies, brownies, and drinks, anything that is nonperishable should be displayed for sale in your lobby space, including literature, memberships, merchants' coupon books, buttons and bumper stickers, tee shirts, and extra posters.

Anything you are planning to do in the lobby or other public space of the hall should be cleared in advance with hall management. Most halls require that you give them a percentage of the money you take in from concession sales, and many places simply will not allow you to sell food or drinks (because they sell it themselves).

Do not be afraid to negotiate on the percentage that the hall wants to take from your sales — you may not win but it is worth trying. Also be clear with the hall on such items as who will provide tables (do they or will you

need to bring your own?); hanging things on the wall; can you sell your own records, tee shirts, or do they have a merchandiser, etc.? As much as possible, work out the details before the day of your show so you are not caught up in negotiating with the hall at the last minute. Depending on your relationship with the hall, you might request whatever agreements you work out be put in writing.

Artists or their distributors may retain exclusive rights to sell the artists' books and records, but check. You may be able to take a percentage if you supply volunteers to sell these items.

In some cases for fundraising concerts, the sponsor is able to purchase the artists' records directly from the company or distributor at a reduced price and sell them for profit. If the artists and record company are agreeable, you may make anywhere from $2 to $5 per album. If you sell a lot of records this will add up. If you buy outright you may be able to sell them for a greater profit, but this can be risky. You could get stuck with a lot of albums, and this upfront cost may strain your normal cash flow. Check it out before you begin to make deals so you know what kind of a deal you want and what you can accept.

To *ballpark* this idea, in 1988 you could buy albums from the company in quantities of 25 (open boxes unreturnable) for $4.50 each plus shipping. If you were to sell them at $10 each, your profit is $5.50, minus shipping, each.

Co-Sponsorship
If you are interested in coalition-building and in attracting new volunteers, you may consider co-sponsoring the whole event or certain aspects of the *fundraising activities* with another organization whose assistance would benefit you and the production.

The potluck dinner and program book might be more successful with new input from people you don't normally reach. The event as a whole may attract a new audience of potential members if you share mailing lists with another organization.

You also may cut your costs if you have an insert in the same mailing, and you share the cost of doing a mailing.

Co-sponsorship also may expand the media interest. There are ways to work with other groups without formally co-sponsoring this event. You might be able to trade or rent their mailing lists, groups might be willing to publicize your event in their newsletters, you might invite groups to have tables in the lobby in return for helping to get word out about the show.

There are pros and cons to working with another group on a concert. Consider your options and be clear about the advantages of either approach, as well as the potential difficulties. If things go well, working together on such a project could lay the foundation for future joint efforts. At the same time, if for some reason things do not go well, you may be jeopardizing a potentially important relationship. If you decide to work with another organization, be sure that there is a clear division of work and that you both have copies of a written understanding of that division. It is critical that things do not fall through the cracks, that there is clarity on your joint decision-making process, and that there is a system for accountability.

You can do it!

Corporate Sponsorship

Corporations are at times interested in associating their name and logo with an event because it provides them with valuable publicity and promotion.

If it is a company that is compatible with your goals and philosophy you may gain some extra income by having them as sponsors. Usually their name and/or logo will appear on all ads, posters, mailings; they can provide a banner to hang in the lobby; and they have an ad and respectful placement in the

When appropriate, they can sell their product at the concessions, too. You receive an amount of money that is relative to the size of the production. For example, the primary sponsorship of a concert budgeted at $15,000 could be $500 to $1,000.

Artist Fees

Artists have many different approaches to benefit concerts. Sometimes they drop their fees. Often, however, artists who are likely to perform for your organization do benefit events on a regular basis and cannot afford to lower their rates. Feel free to ask, but get clear on this early in the booking stage.

Also be clear that the publicity is worded in a way which receives the artist's approval. Benefits and fundraisers are special events and the publicity needs to be carefully chosen so no one is misled.

Do It Well

Concerts and special events can generate a loss of income, break even, or make hundreds to thousands of dollars.

As demonstrated by the Farm Aid type of event, the potential to raise millions of dollars for a cause does exist. Special events can be media events or tempests in a teapot. It takes money to make money and resources to create resources. You will want to ensure your investment will be recouped plus make a profit. To do this takes careful and fastidious planning and good management of the efforts of your volunteers and your staff for both the concert and other fundraising efforts around it.

You can do it!

Appendix A: FORMS

Appendix A: FORMS

Table of Contents

TIMELINES

Times scheduled will vary according to your specific needs, but they are useful as guidelines. For example, you may not be able to contract with the artist until your budget has been accurately estimated and presented. Many of the fundraising suggestions need artist approval before you adopt them as strategies.

Checklist of Tasks

AS SOON AS YOU KNOW YOU WANT TO HAVE A CONCERT

Date
Projected Completed

_____ _____ 1. Set organizational and financial goals.
_____ _____ 2. Research halls (costs, capacities, insurance needs, etc.). Check lighting, sound company, and equipment. Put hall dates on hold.
_____ _____ 3. Do a tentative budget.
_____ _____ 4. Initiate contact with artists for date, fee.
_____ _____ 5. Decide what fundraising/promotional activities you want to pursue.
_____ _____ 6. Contract for suitable hall and artists simultaneously; make deposits, if necessary.
_____ _____ 7. Develop media leads with quarterlies or bimonthlies, get your event in their calendar listings, and pitch for a feature article — deadlines are usually very early.
_____ _____ 8. Send announcement to other concert producers, community organizations, interested influential people, asking them not to schedule conflicting events and soliciting help if appropriate. Ask them about including an insert in one of their future newsletter mailings.

TWELFTH WEEK BEFORE THE CONCERT

Date
Projected Completed

_____ _____ 1. Confirm prices and services of lighting equipment and personnel if not provided by hall; contract for services.
_____ _____ 2. Confirm prices and services of sound technicians and suitable equipment; contract for services.
_____ _____ 3. Prepare budget with accurately estimated expenses and projected income.
_____ _____ 4. Prepare cash flow estimates.

Date
Projected Completed

_____ _____   5. Decide if you want to do a program book. If yes, set goals; get cost estimates (graphics, typesetting, layout, printing, deadlines).

_____ _____   6. Begin work with graphic artist on poster, flyer, and ads. Get all the copy together. Include artists, date, time, hall, ticket outlets, information number, date tickets go on sale, accessibility information, other relevant information as design and space allow.

_____ _____   7. Decide what other promotional activities you want to pursue.

_____ _____   8. Research and develop lists (name, address, phone) for media (print and broadcast), potential sponsors, volunteers, block ticket sales, potential ad sale contacts (if program book).

_____ _____   9. Begin fundraising activities — plan ad selling campaign if you are doing a program book; plan how to sell sponsorship tickets (decide what you will offer, put together a package to mail or make calls); look into design of tee shirts production, and plan sales; plan reception; decide what kind of auction or raffle you want to do; plan for lobby sales.

_____ _____   10. Firm up ticket outlet places, send confirmation letter.

TENTH WEEK BEFORE CONCERT

Date
Projected Completed

_____ _____   1. Develop name and address labels for media contacts (monthlies, weeklies, dailies, radio, and TV).

_____ _____   2. Draft press releases.

_____ _____   3. Print posters and flyers.

_____ _____   4. Assemble material for media mailings (biographical material and photos supplied by artists' representative).

_____ _____   5. Mail to monthlies (per their deadlines).

_____ _____   6. Place ads in monthlies (per their deadlines).

_____ _____   7. Draft targeted press release or design flyer for inclusion in other groups' mailings.

_____ _____   8. Mail press releases or flyers to these groups (per their deadlines).
Note: If you have more than 200 labels and they won't include your material in their mailing, it may be worthwhile to get a bulk mail permit and mail the packets yourself.

_____ _____   9. Put together sample packet for adbook sales.

_____ _____   10. Hire ad salesperson and begin sales if you're doing an ad/program book.

_____ _____   11. Continue compiling list of potential sales contacts.

Date
Projected Completed

_____ _____   12. Decide if concert will be signed. Contact American Sign Language
                              interpreters — contract for services and promotional work.
_____ _____   13. Decide whether to use a popular emcee — begin negotiations now and
                              put name on posters.
_____ _____   14. Firm up budget estimates — make adjustments; check cash flow
                              projections.
_____ _____   15. Have tickets printed and numbered (if you have a Bates machine, you
                              can do the numbering yourself and save some money).
_____ _____   16. Decide whether child care will be provided. Begin preparation —
                              develop forms for callers reserving space.

EIGHTH WEEK BEFORE CONCERT DATE

Date
Projected Completed

_____ _____   1. Make follow-up calls to monthlies, remail as necessary.
_____ _____   2. Mail or deliver tickets to all outlets; use easy accounting forms. Tickets
                              should go on sale when first publicity goes up.
_____ _____   3. Put up one-third or so of your posters in prominent places.
_____ _____   4. Develop list of volunteers; have some put up posters.
_____ _____   5. Recruit your production staff.
_____ _____   6. Prepare promotional package for weeklies and dailies.
_____ _____   7. Mail public relations packet to weeklies and dailies.
_____ _____   8. Draft ad/program book copy.
_____ _____   9. Call radio and TV stations regarding interviews and mail promotion.
_____ _____   10. Begin block sales — contact special groups.
_____ _____   11. Continue fundraising activities.

SIXTH WEEK BEFORE CONCERT

Date
Projected Completed

_____ _____   1. Finalize program book copy (articles, biographies, photos, artwork);
                              order type or use computer-generated copy — ask your printer (and get

Date
Projected Completed

_____ _____   confirmation of price and time for printing booklet when you have a
                     firm idea of number of pages, halftones, artwork).
_____ _____   2. Decide what activities volunteers can help with — schedule what they
                     will be doing and when.
_____ _____   3. Gather volunteers, have a get-together (if possible, you can all meet at
                     the hall). Plan a postering night, a silkscreen party for tee shirts, a "get
                     the mail out" party, etc.
_____ _____   4. For children's concert: Contact schools for volunteers and help from
                     PTA members.
_____ _____   5. Make follow-up calls to radio and TV stations — artists' representative
                     can help schedule interviews. Ask about ticket giveaway promotions.
_____ _____   6. Continue fundraising — ad sales, sponsorship ticket sales, etc.
_____ _____   7. Continue block sales — to corporations, unions, allied groups, hearing-
                     impaired; ongoing development of your list of these groups.
_____ _____   8. Mail lyrics to ASL interpreter with tape or record album.
_____ _____   9. Place space reservations in weeklies or dailies (per their deadlines and
                     your budget).
_____ _____ 10. Get ticket count from all outlets weekly; prepare ready report for the
                     artists.

FOURTH WEEK BEFORE CONCERT DATE

Date
Projected Completed

_____ _____   1. Using simple accounting sheets, check and record ticket sales from all
                     outlets.
_____ _____   2. Continue block sales and fundraising — continue developing list.
_____ _____   3. Line up emcee or a local radio/TV personality for introductions/pitches
                     from your organization; send letter of confirmation.
_____ _____   4. Re-poster, put posters up everywhere.
_____ _____   5. Draft public service announcements (PSAs).
_____ _____   6. If artists have approved them, send PSAs to radio stations.
_____ _____   7. Prepare tee shirt artwork and silk screen (don't forget ventilation, space
                     for drying, volunteers for folding), or send design to tee shirt printer.
_____ _____   8. Finalize program book ad sales, and obtain all artwork; finish lining up
                     sponsors.
_____ _____   9. Lay out the program book.
_____ _____ 10. Contact other groups about having literature or tables in your lobby
                     (develop this with ad sales).

Date
Projected   Completed

_____ _____   11. Make follow-up calls to weeklies and dailies.
_____ _____   12. Get ticket count.

THIRD WEEK BEFORE CONCERT DATE

Date
Projected   Completed

_____ _____   1. Call all ticket outlets; redistribute tickets as necessary.
_____ _____   2. Continue group sales.
_____ _____   3. Decide if you are having a reception. Send invitations with directions.
_____ _____   4. Plan food concessions menu with volunteers (according to their talents —
                       even food you buy and sell will make a small profit, but nothing
                       compares to donated, homebaked goodies).
                    5. Find door prize/auction donations. Pick up items as available.
_____ _____   6   Make follow-up calls to PSA directors at radio stations.
_____ _____   7. Complete program book layout by midweek.
_____ _____   8. Take program book layout to printer by midweek (or as your printer
                       needs).
_____ _____   9. Meet with sound and lights personnel at hall to confirm equipment
                       needs and time for set-up.
_____ _____   10. Receive records to sell from artists' representative; check inventory.

SECOND WEEK BEFORE CONCERT DATE

Date
Projected   Completed

_____ _____   1. Call all ticket outlets for count; redistribute as necessary.
_____ _____   2. Make second follow-up calls to dailies and weeklies — do they need
                       photographs; do they want to arrange for complimentary tickets for a
                       review or an advance interview?
                    3. Continue group sales.
_____ _____   4. Confirm artists' travel arrangements.
_____ _____   5. Meet with volunteers to plan specific logistics for the day of the show —
                       who will pick up the artists at the airport, who will help unload sound

Date
Projected   Completed

                             equipment (if needed), who will help get equipment and paraphernalia to the hall, clean up, etc. Set assignments, meeting places, and times.

_____ _____   6. Get biographic notes to the emcee.

_____ _____   7. Try to get radio phone interview in next two weeks, or pre-produced artists' interview tape.

_____ _____   8. Begin radio promotion — album/ticket giveaway.

ONE WEEK BEFORE THE SHOW DATE

Date
Projected   Completed

_____ _____   1. Get program book back from printers.

_____ _____   2. Call all ticket outlets daily; redistribute unsold tickets as needed.

_____ _____   3. Put up last of posters.

_____ _____   4. Check hall for sign placement — what signs will you need? Will you need stands or will tape work?

_____ _____   5. Try to get media coverage with artists in town a day or two before the day of the show.

_____ _____   6. Day of show comes! See Forms 3:1, 13:1, 13:2, 13:3, 13:4, 14:1, and 16:1.

ONE WEEK AFTER CONCERT

Date
Projected   Completed

_____ _____   1. Pay any remaining bills.

_____ _____   2. Write out actual budget and assemble with copies of receipts, invoices, and accounting sheets.

_____ _____   3. Mail thank-you letters to media, volunteers, artists, sponsors, and others.

_____ _____   4. Evaluate this concert production experience.

CONCERT BUDGET

The following worksheets are designed to help you plan and record all income and expenses related to producing a concert or event. The first two pages, labeled Concert Budget, serve as a checklist for the kinds of expenses you may incur when producing an event.

The next worksheet lists items related to fundraising. Keep income and expenses in this category separate from concert expenses. What you earn in this area often does not have to be shared with the performers, although record money, related to their albums, may be an exception.

The final worksheet may be used to recap your overall income and expenses.

The worksheet of columns may be taped to the right-hand side of the Concert Budget and Fundraising Activities to extend these forms to cover entries over a period of several weeks or months.

These worksheets serve as guidelines. Feel free to adapt them to your specific need, use them as a checklist or reminder.

CONCERT BUDGET

Expenses	Estimate	Actual	Actual	Total
HALL				
Deposit				
User Fees				
Other				
ARTISTS				
Fee				
Lodging				
Traveling				
Other				
GRAPHIC DESIGN				
Ads				
Ad/program book				
Flyers				
Posters				
Press releases				
Tickets				
Other				
PRINTING				
Flyers				
Posters				
Press releases				
Tickets				
Other				
POSTAGE				
INSURANCE				
SOUND				
Equipment				
Personnel				
Piano Tuner				
Other				

	Estimate	Actual	Actual	Total
LIGHTING				
Equipment				
Personnel				
Other				
PERSONNEL				
Box office manager				
House manager				
Lobby manager				
Security guards				
Stage manager				
Ticket takers				
Ushers				
Other				
CHILD CARE				
A S L INTERPRETER				
TICKET AGENCY				
CREDIT CARD FEES				
ADVERTISING				
Radio				
Print				
TOTAL EXPENSES				
INCOME				
Tickets Sold @				
Tickets Sold @				
Tickets Sold @				
Tickets Sold @				
TOTAL INCOME				

Fundraising Activities

	Est. Expenses	Act. Expenses	Est. Income	Act. Income
LOBBY SALES				
Beverages				
Food				
Manager				
Records and Tapes				
Table and Chairs rental				
% to hall and artists				
% to record company				
GRAPHICS/PRINTING				
Buttons				
Invitations				
Literature				
Printing				
Program/ad book				
Tee shirts				
RECEPTION				
Beverages				
Food				
Space rental				
Decorations				
Equipment rental				
POSTAGE				
RAFFLE/AUCTION				
Manager				
Prize				
Raffle/auction tickets				
GRANTS				
DONATIONS				
TOTALS				

Income/Expense Recap

		Est. Expenses	Act. Expenses	Est. Income	Act. Income
TOTAL INCOME					
Tickets					
TOTAL EXPENSES					
Concert					
CONCERT SUBTOTAL					
TOTAL INCOME					
Fundraising					
TOTAL EXPENSES					
Fundraising					
FUNDRAISING SUBTOTAL					
NET TO PRODUCER					
NET TO ARTIST					

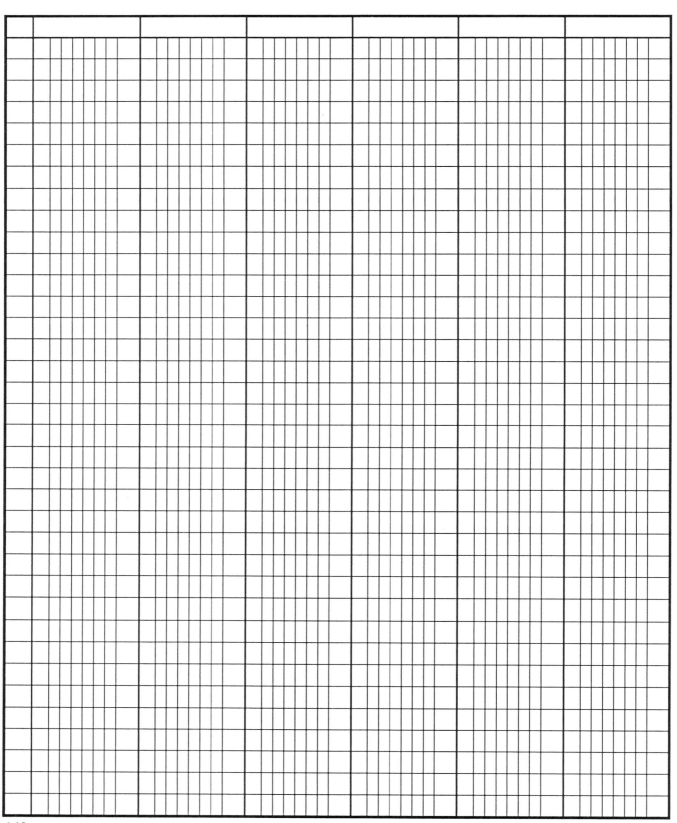

CASH FLOW PROJECTIONS

The following categories of expenses are listed in the order they usually are paid. As estimates are given or payments are made, enter the amounts on the appropriate pages of Form 2:2, or Form 2:4. Put total actual expenses on this form to use for planning future events.

	Estimated	Actual
90 to 120 days before event:		
Artists' transportation and/ or fee deposit	_____	_____
Hall deposit	_____	_____
60 to 90 days before event		
Calendar notices	_____	_____
Graphic design	_____	_____
Layout of ads	_____	_____
Printing and postage for press releases	_____	_____
Tickets printed	_____	_____
30 to 60 days before event		
Advertising	_____	_____
Mailing list rental charge	_____	_____
Printing, labor and postage for mailing	_____	_____
Printing posters and flyers	_____	_____
30 days before event		
Run advertising for 2 weeks	_____	_____
Phone	_____	_____
Putting posters up	_____	_____
Last week or day of show		
Artists' fee balance	_____	_____
Balance paid to hall, sound, and equipment, personnel, lights, child care personnel and supplies, insurance	_____	_____
Food for artists and crew	_____	_____
Lobby manager	_____	_____
Local transportation	_____	_____
Lodging	_____	_____
More posters and flyers up	_____	_____
Musical equipment rental	_____	_____
Program printing	_____	_____
Stage decorations	_____	_____
Stage manager	_____	_____
Union and non-union crew	_____	_____

CONTRACT/BUDGET SETTLEMENT STATEMENT

SHOW INFORMATION

Date _____ Performance Date _____

Concert _____

Showtime begins _____ Ends _____

Artist _____

Address _____

City _____ Phone _____

Venue _____ Capacity _____

Address _____

Contact _____ Phone _____

Scale: _____ @ _____ $ _____   Actual: _____ @ _____ $ _____

_____ @ _____ $ _____   _____ @ _____ $ _____

_____ @ _____ $ _____   _____ @ _____ $ _____

_____ @ _____ $ _____   _____ @ _____ $ _____

Subtotal: $ _____   Subtotal: $ _____

Crew _____ @ _____ $ _____   _____ @ _____ $ _____

Disc. _____ @ _____ $ _____   _____ @ _____ $ _____

Comps. _____ @ _____ $ _____   _____ @ _____ $ _____

Taxes _____ @ _____ $ _____   _____ @ _____ $ _____

Net gross potential $ _____   Actual gross $ _____

	ESTIMATE	ACTUAL	OVER/ UNDER	RECEIPTS
FACILITY EXPENSES				
Box office/day of show	_____	_____	_____	_____
Box office fee ___ %	_____	_____	_____	_____
Custodial	_____	_____	_____	_____
Facility advertising	_____	_____	_____	_____
Hall rental/flat or minimum	_____	_____	_____	_____
Hall _____ on G.P. maximum	_____	_____	_____	_____
House lights	_____	_____	_____	_____
House sound	_____	_____	_____	_____
House staff	_____	_____	_____	_____
# ___ @ ___ x ___ hrs.	_____	_____	_____	_____
# ___ @ ___ x ___ hrs.	_____	_____	_____	_____
Loaders	_____	_____	_____	_____
Piano tuner	_____	_____	_____	_____
Stage hands/crew	_____	_____	_____	_____
Security	_____	_____	_____	_____
# ___ @ ___ x ___ hrs.	_____	_____	_____	_____
Spots # ___ @ ___	_____	_____	_____	_____
Ticket commissions	_____	_____	_____	_____
Ticket printing	_____	_____	_____	_____
Other facility expenses	_____	_____	_____	_____
Subtotal	_____	_____	_____	_____

	ESTIMATE	ACTUAL	OVER/ UNDER	RECEIPTS
PRODUCER EXPENSES				
ASCAP/BMI				
Additional box office				
Additional loaders/runners				
Advertising				
Backstage security				
Equipment rental				
Graphics				
Hospitality				
Insurance				
Light expense				
Mailing				
Poster/distribution				
Print/alternative				
Print/major				
Printing				
Programs				
Radio				
Sound expense				
Stage manager				
Transportation				
Subtotal				
Total expenses				
Artists' guarantee				
Producer's Fee (%)				
Total show cost				
Gross potential				
Total show cost				
Split amount				
Terms/split				
Artists' (%)				
Producer (%)				
Potential artists				
Potential producer				

CONTRACT/BUDGET SETTLEMENT WORKSHEET

SHOW INFORMATION

DATE *(budget prepared or revised)*

	Preliminary	**Revised**	**Final**
Artists' representative	_____	_____	_____
Co-producer	_____	_____	_____
File	_____	_____	_____

CONCERT OR EVENT
Name _____

_____

Actual billing for advertising _____

_____

Contact person for artists _____

_____

Address _____

_____

Phone _____ /day of show _____

PERFORMANCE DATE (actual date) _____

TIME
Doors open _____
Start time _____
Latest start _____
Length of performance _____
Intermission _____
Must end by _____
Artists' travel considerations _____

PRODUCER AND/OR CO-PRODUCER
Name _____
Address *(include street for express mail)* _____

_____

_____

Phone _____ /day of show _____

VENUE (facilities on hold)
Name _____
Address _____
Capacity _____
Contact *(name and phone)* _____

Dates Available   Deadline for Deposit

_____
_____
_____

Name _____
Address _____
Capacity _____
Contact *(name and phone)* _____

Dates Available   Deadline for Deposit

_____
_____
_____

Name _____
Address _____
Capacity _____
Contact *(name and phone)* _____

Dates Available   Deadline for Deposit

_____
_____
_____

VENUE (facility confirmed)
Date _____ In writing _____
Address _____
Contact advance *(name and phone)* _____
Contact day of show *(name and phone)* _____
Other facility personnel *(name and phone)* _____

_____
Box office manager *(name and phone)* _____
Union steward *(name and phone)* _____
Back stage entrance *(phone)* _____
Parking _____
Loading dock _____

SCALE
Work up gross potential at different ticket prices/scales/numbers.

Scale	_____ @_____ $_____	Actual	_____ @_____ $_____
	_____ @_____ $_____		_____ @_____ $_____
	_____ @_____ $_____		_____ @_____ $_____
	_____ @_____ $_____		_____ @_____ $_____

	Subtotal $_____		Subtotal $_____

Crew Discounts	_____ @_____ $_____		_____ @_____ $_____
	_____ @_____ $_____		_____ @_____ $_____
Comps	_____ @_____ $_____		_____ @_____ $_____

Taxes	_____ @_____ $_____		_____ @_____ $_____

	Net gross potential $_____		Actual gross $_____

SOUND AND LIGHT SEATS (number to be held and location)
Hall preference _____
Sound company _____
Lighting company _____

Check final decision and notify all parties including box office.

DISCOUNT AND COMP TICKETS
Requested by _____

_____
_____
_____

Approval *(hall/act)* _____
Details on dollar amount of discount/maximum number available:
　　　Where available for sale _____
　　　Special instructions _____

Complimentary tickets *(number and location)* _____

_____
_____

Facility requirements _____
Artists' requirements _____
Authorization to give list *(name)*_____

_____

Producer number (___); press (___); others _____
Holds to buy *(number/location)* _____

_____

Holds for artists (___); record company (___); producer (___)
Procedure for complimentary lists/to buys at hall box office _____

_____

_____

Release date/time
    Complimentaries _____
    Will calls _____

TAXES AND OTHER CHARGES (withheld by facility)
Facility coordinator asked *(details)* _____

_____

Tax information on tickets _____

_____

FACILITY EXPENSES
Minimum or flat amount versus percentage *(maximum)* _____
Calculate gross potential _____ x _____ % = _____ maximum
Contract
    Received _____
    Sent _____
    Deposit required *(amount/date)* _____
    Hall cancellation policy _____
    Insurance requirements _____
    Copy of contract sent to agent *(date)* _____
    Certificate sent to hall *(date/cost)* _____
    Time facility available load-in _____
    Hours including basic rent _____
    Overtime charge starts _____
    Calculate overtime estimate _____

STAGE CREW
Facility person in charge of call *(name and phone)* _____

_____

	Number	Hour In	Show Call	Hour Out
Performer's contract	_____	_____	_____	_____
Sound company	_____	_____	_____	_____
Light/design or company	_____	_____	_____	_____
Stage manager	_____	_____	_____	_____
Union steward	_____	_____	_____	_____

Minimum call per union steward _____

Final call confirmed with *(name/date/date in writing)* _____
_____

Category crew call time for *load-in*

_____ hrs @ $ _____ plus _____ = total
_____ hrs @ $ _____ plus _____ = total
_____ hrs @ $ _____ plus _____ = total
_____ hrs @ $ _____ plus _____ = total

Category crew *show call*

_____ hrs @ $ _____ plus _____ = total
_____ hrs @ $ _____ plus _____ = total
_____ hrs @ $ _____ plus _____ = total
_____ hrs @ $ _____ plus _____ = total

Category crew time *load-out*

_____ hrs @ $ _____ plus _____ = total
_____ hrs @ $ _____ plus _____ = total
_____ hrs @ $ _____ plus _____ = total
_____ hrs @ $ _____ plus _____ = total

Loaders
        Check details of call/minimum and usage. Check that loaders can enter trucks.

TECHNICAL INFORMATION AVAILABLE
Sound rider _____
Stage diagram _____
Lighting plot _____
Lighting rider _____
Hall lighting information _____
Sound information _____
        (sent to) _____
Hall contact person for artists' representative to contact *(name and phone)*_____
_____

Technical riders are to be sent to *(check that received)*

    Facility manager handling contract ————————————————————————

    Union steward ————————————————————————————————

    Sound company ————————————————————————————————

    House sound technician ——————————————————————————

    Light company ——————————————————————————————

    House sound person ————————————————————————————

    Stage manager ——————————————————————————————

    Co-producer ——————————————————————————————

When possible, send a record or cassette to persons not familiar with the act.

PLAN OF WORK FOR TECHNICIANS

Lights

    In charge of crew ————————————————————————————

    In charge of design ————————————————————————————

    In charge of gels ——————————————————————————————

    Paid for by ——————————————————————————————————

    Crew in call time *(and number)* ——————————————————————

    Position of board ——————————————————————————————

    Board operated by ——————————————————————————————

    Position of spots ——————————————————————————————

    Spots operated by ——————————————————————————————

If equipment is not provided by the facility, list companies providing and time of arrival/person in charge, phone number for day of show).

    Estimated time to hang and focus *(time per __)* ——————————————

    Time loading crew free to assist sound ————————————————————

    Person responsible to spike stage for focus ——————————————

    Artists' representative to give final okay ——————————————————

    Time for approval ——————————————————————————————

    Light cues called by ————————————————————————————

    Headsets needed *(number)* ——————————————————————————

    Position of headsets ————————————————————————————

    Lighting technical check to consist of ——————————————————

——

Sound

    In charge of crew ————————————————————————————

    In charge of mixing sound ——————————————————————————

    Separate monitor mix ————————————————————————————

    Mixer ——————————————————————————————————————

    Position of house board ——————————————————————————

    Position of monitor board ——————————————————————————

    Load-in time ——————————————————————————————————

Crew contracted for with sound company _____

Facility crew to assist sound company *(number and time)* _____

Name of sound company _____

Contact person _____

Day of show phone _____

Sound check time _____

(Allow one hour — if artists request rehearsal time, arrange advance.)

Technical check to be finished by latest _____

> *Stage manager to confirm crew call day before show, have day of show staffing sheet and confirm work hours.*

Details of opening act, technical requirements, and schedule check

_____

_____

_____

Facility crew method of payment
    Check _____ Cash _____ Facility _____ Individual or group _____
Additional crew committed by producer _____

Requirements Regarding Crews
Facility stage hands
    Meals provided _____
    Break times _____
    Overtime starts _____
    Fees for recording _____
    Fees for taping _____

Light company
    Meals provided _____
    Break times _____
    Overtime starts _____
    Fees for recording _____
    Fees for taping _____

Sound company
    Meals provided _____
    Break times _____
    Overtime starts _____
    Fees for recording _____
    Fees for taping _____

RECORDING AND VIDEOTAPING
Organization ——————————————————————————————
Address ——————————————————————————————

——————————————————————————————
Phone ——————————————————————————————
Contact person ——————————————————————————————
Day of show phone ——————————————————————————————
Waivers signed ——————————————————————————————

——————————————————————————————
Equipment set up *(time and location)* ——————————————————————————————

——————————————————————————————
Seats required (?) ——————————————————————————————

——————————————————————————————
Light/sound check ——————————————————————————————

——————————————————————————————
Tape required for:
     Artists ——————————————————————————————
     Received ——————————————————————————————
     Producer ——————————————————————————————
     Received ——————————————————————————————

HOUSE STAFF (Production manager to utilize staffing sheet)
Facility provides ——————————————————————————————
Person in charge *(name and phone)* ——————————————————————————————

Ticket Takers
     Number *(and position)* ——————————————————————————————
     Time arrive ——————————————————————————————
     Positions during show ——————————————————————————————
     Time off ——————————————————————————————
     How paid ——————————————————————————————
     Rate of pay ——————————————————————————————
     Overtime starts ——————————————————————————————
     Will do drop count ——————————————————————————————

Ushers
     Number *(and position)* ——————————————————————————————
     Time arrive ——————————————————————————————
     Positions during show ——————————————————————————————
     Will hand out programs ——————————————————————————————
     Time off ——————————————————————————————
     How paid ——————————————————————————————
     Rate of pay ——————————————————————————————
     Overtime starts ——————————————————————————————

BOX OFFICE FEE
Facility charges for selling tickets ⎯⎯⎯⎯⎯⎯⎯⎯⎯⎯⎯⎯⎯⎯⎯⎯⎯⎯⎯⎯⎯⎯⎯⎯⎯⎯⎯
Number of weeks on sale through facility ⎯⎯⎯⎯⎯⎯⎯⎯⎯⎯⎯⎯⎯⎯⎯⎯⎯⎯⎯⎯⎯⎯
Charge for more additional weeks of sales ⎯⎯⎯⎯⎯⎯⎯⎯⎯⎯⎯⎯⎯⎯⎯⎯⎯⎯⎯⎯
Ticket agencies utilized by facility ⎯⎯⎯⎯⎯⎯⎯⎯⎯⎯⎯⎯⎯⎯⎯⎯⎯⎯⎯⎯⎯⎯⎯⎯⎯
Location of outlets ⎯⎯⎯⎯⎯⎯⎯⎯⎯⎯⎯⎯⎯⎯⎯⎯⎯⎯⎯⎯⎯⎯⎯⎯⎯⎯⎯⎯⎯⎯⎯⎯⎯⎯
Information for press release/flyers ⎯⎯⎯⎯⎯⎯⎯⎯⎯⎯⎯⎯⎯⎯⎯⎯⎯⎯⎯⎯⎯⎯⎯⎯
⎯⎯⎯

Box office phone number ⎯⎯⎯⎯⎯⎯⎯⎯⎯⎯⎯⎯⎯⎯⎯⎯⎯⎯⎯⎯⎯⎯⎯⎯⎯⎯⎯⎯⎯⎯⎯
Hours of operation ⎯⎯⎯⎯⎯⎯⎯⎯⎯⎯⎯⎯⎯⎯⎯⎯⎯⎯⎯⎯⎯⎯⎯⎯⎯⎯⎯⎯⎯⎯⎯⎯⎯⎯
Charge by phone number ⎯⎯⎯⎯⎯⎯⎯⎯⎯⎯⎯⎯⎯⎯⎯⎯⎯⎯⎯⎯⎯⎯⎯⎯⎯⎯⎯⎯⎯⎯⎯
Mail order ⎯⎯
Will facility pull tickets for producer sales ⎯⎯⎯⎯⎯⎯⎯⎯⎯⎯⎯⎯⎯⎯⎯⎯⎯⎯⎯
Procedure ⎯⎯
⎯⎯⎯

Box office manager *(name and phone)* ⎯⎯⎯⎯⎯⎯⎯⎯⎯⎯⎯⎯⎯⎯⎯⎯⎯⎯⎯⎯⎯
Day of show contact *(name and phone)* ⎯⎯⎯⎯⎯⎯⎯⎯⎯⎯⎯⎯⎯⎯⎯⎯⎯⎯⎯⎯⎯
Fee structure minimum ⎯⎯⎯⎯⎯⎯⎯ % ⎯⎯⎯⎯⎯⎯
Charge for pulled tickets ⎯⎯⎯⎯⎯⎯⎯⎯⎯⎯⎯⎯⎯⎯⎯⎯⎯⎯⎯⎯⎯⎯⎯⎯⎯⎯⎯⎯⎯⎯
Procedure for settlement ⎯⎯⎯⎯⎯⎯⎯⎯⎯⎯⎯⎯⎯⎯⎯⎯⎯⎯⎯⎯⎯⎯⎯⎯⎯⎯⎯⎯⎯⎯
⎯⎯⎯

Sample settlement form requested in advance ⎯⎯⎯⎯⎯⎯⎯⎯⎯⎯⎯⎯⎯⎯⎯⎯⎯⎯

Ticket Commissions
Facility charges beyond box office fee ⎯⎯⎯⎯⎯⎯⎯⎯⎯⎯⎯⎯⎯⎯⎯⎯⎯⎯⎯⎯⎯⎯
Agency charges passed on ⎯⎯⎯⎯⎯⎯⎯⎯⎯⎯⎯⎯⎯⎯⎯⎯⎯⎯⎯⎯⎯⎯⎯⎯⎯⎯⎯⎯⎯
Contract with agency through facility ⎯⎯⎯⎯⎯⎯⎯⎯⎯⎯⎯⎯⎯⎯⎯⎯⎯⎯⎯⎯⎯⎯⎯
Contract with agency through producer ⎯⎯⎯⎯⎯⎯⎯⎯⎯⎯⎯⎯⎯⎯⎯⎯⎯⎯⎯⎯⎯
Alternative commissions ⎯⎯⎯⎯⎯⎯⎯⎯⎯⎯⎯⎯⎯⎯⎯⎯⎯⎯⎯⎯⎯⎯⎯⎯⎯⎯⎯⎯⎯⎯
Group sales ⎯⎯⎯⎯⎯⎯⎯⎯⎯⎯⎯⎯⎯⎯⎯⎯⎯⎯⎯⎯⎯⎯⎯⎯⎯⎯⎯⎯⎯⎯

Ticket Printing
Person responsible ⎯⎯⎯⎯⎯⎯⎯⎯⎯⎯⎯⎯⎯⎯⎯⎯⎯⎯⎯⎯⎯⎯⎯⎯⎯⎯⎯⎯⎯⎯⎯⎯⎯⎯
Charge ⎯⎯

Production manager to check ticket "copy."

Box Office Day of the Show
Facility box office *(person in charge and phone)* ⎯⎯⎯⎯⎯⎯⎯⎯⎯⎯⎯⎯⎯⎯⎯
⎯⎯⎯

Number of persons provided by facility *(number and hours)* ⎯⎯⎯⎯⎯⎯⎯
⎯⎯⎯

Producer representative in box office ⎯⎯⎯⎯⎯⎯⎯⎯⎯⎯⎯⎯⎯⎯⎯⎯⎯⎯⎯⎯⎯⎯⎯
⎯⎯⎯

Procedure for handling complimentry/will calls, etc. ⎯⎯⎯⎯⎯⎯⎯⎯⎯⎯⎯⎯⎯

Facility charge _____
Location of box office _____
Access to box office by _____

Security (provided by facility)
Minimum facility requirement _____
Person in charge _____
Person in charge day of the show _____
Number ordered by producer *(number and location)* _____
_____

Rate of pay _____
Number of hours _____
Overtime starts _____
Information on procedures utilized by house security.

Custodial
Minimum _____
Facility required _____
Charge _____

House Sound
       Note if utilizing only house or enhancement from sound company.
Charge for usage _____
Acoustic shell available _____
Charge for shell _____
Technical information available _____
Contact *(name and phone)* _____

House Lights
       Request detailed information from house light technician.
Contact *(name and phone)* _____
Charge for usage _____
Charge per instrument _____
Charge per gels _____

Spot Lights
Kind available _____
Number _____
Charge _____
Facility arrange for rental _____
Crew cost to deliver and retrieve from facility _____

Piano
Kind available at facility _____
Permission to use required _____
Charge _____

How to confirm condition of piano ——————————————————
Tuner available through facility ——————————————————
Facility piano tuner *(name and number)* ——————————————
Fee ——————————————————————————————
Scheduled times of tunings *(times and charges)*
        Before load-in ————————————————————————
        After sound check ———————————————————————
        Before concert ————————————————————————
        At intermission ————————————————————————
        Full standby ——————————————————————————
Outside piano rental required ——————————————————
Company *(name and phone)* ——————————————————
Contact person *(name and phone)* ——————————————————
Day of phone contact *(name and phone)* ————————————————
Delivery time ——————————————————————————
Day of show contact delivery *(name and phone)* ——————————————

Facility Advertising
Advance mailer or program advertising available ——————————
Cost ——————————————————————————————
Spot rate with local radio ——————————————————————
Details of deadlines, copy requirements, rates, etc. ——————————
        ——————————————————————————
        ——————————————————————————
        ——————————————————————————

Other Facility Expenses
Nurse ——————————————————————————————
Dressing rooms ————————————————————————————
Phones ————————————————————————————————
Marquee —————————————————————————————
Child care ————————————————————————————
Rental tables/chairs lobby ——————————————————————
Concessionaire percentage for record sales ——————————————
Concessionaire contact *(name and phone)* ——————————————

PRODUCER EXPENSES
Advertising

        *Review plans for advertising with artists' representative. Contact artists'
        record company for promotion plan and solicit cooperation with print and
        radio ad buys.*

Record company contact *(name and phone)* ——————————————

Insurance
Hall requirements _____

_____

Contract from hall to agent _____
Sound and light company requirements _____

_____

Artists' contract requirements _____

_____

Insurance confirmed _____
Certificate sent _____
Cost for budget _____
Child care insurance _____
Cost of child care insurance _____
Requirements _____

_____

Programs
Hall requirements _____
Artists' requirements _____
Person in charge *(name and phone)* _____

Detail timelines, ad selling strategy, copy, etc.

_____

_____

_____

Hospitality
Person in charge *(name and phone)* _____

Catering Company	Phone Number	Cost Bid	Number of Persons
1. _____			
2. _____			
3. _____			

Contract agreed on _____
Day of show contact *(name and phone)* _____
Load-in hospitality *(time)* _____
Meal for performers/crew *(time)* _____
Notes on set up, etc. _____

_____

Special requirements artists/check rider/attachment _____

_____

Equipment Rental

Rider requirements _____

Rental company _____

Address _____

_____

Contact *(name and phone)* _____

Day of show contact *(name and phone)* _____

Equipment _____

Arrival time _____

Pick up _____

Cost _____

Billing _____

Sound Expense (use of outside sound company)

Company   **Dollar Amount**

1. _____

2. _____

3. _____

Contract agreed to *(attach)* _____

Company name *(address)* _____

_____

_____

Contact *(name and phone)* _____

Day of show contact *(name and phone)* _____

Head of crew _____

Number of crew _____

Per sound company:

     Number of hours for in_____

     Number of hours for out _____

     Number of stagehands _____

     Number of loaders _____

Artists' road person or technician to contact *(name and phone)* _____

_____

Artists' recording/technical rider sent *(date)* _____

Stage diagram sent _____

Notes _____

_____

_____

Light Expense (use of outside light company)
Artists' lighting designer *(name and phone)* _____
Artists' lighting plot _____
Artists' lighting rider _____

Company   **Dollar Amount**

1. _____
2. _____
3. _____

Contract agreed to *(attach)* _____
Company name *(address)* _____
_____
_____

Contact *(name and phone)* _____
Day of show contact *(name and phone)* _____
Head of crew _____
Number of crew _____
Number of stagehands _____
Number of loaders _____
Estimate of set up time _____
Estimate of strike time _____
Notes _____
_____

Stage Manager
House requirements _____
_____
Production stage manager *(name and phone)* _____
Fee _____
Advance work _____
Day of show call _____
Detail responsibilities _____
_____

Day of show schedule reviewed *(attach)* _____

Additional Box Office
House policy on producer box office participation _____
_____
Person representing producer *(name and phone)* _____
_____
Box office hours *(opens/closes)* _____

ASCAP/BMI
Hall contract with _____
ASCAP fee _____
BMI fee _____

If artist exclusive on one, arrange for waiver.

Transportation
Artists _____
Detail arrival time, drivers, etc. _____
_____
_____

Backstage Security (in addition to hall provided, based on backstage set up)
Person in charge *(name and position)* _____
Hours *(load-in to strike)* _____
Cost _____

Additional Loaders/Runners

	Name	Phone	Hours
1.			
2.			
3.			
4.			
5.			

SAMPLE ARTISTS' SCHEDULE

November 15

11:00 a.m.	Jesse picks artists up at airport, takes them either to lunch or to Leslie's house (4444 44th Avenue) where they will be staying.
2:00 p.m.	Band driven to hall for load-in.
2:45 p.m.	Spokesperson picked up from Leslie's for interview with KWIK radio.
3:45 p.m.	Jesse takes artists to hall for sound check.
4:00 p.m.	Sound check.
6:00 p.m.	Dinner. (Try to have dinner catered at venue or at restaurant within walking distance. Include amount of money per musician covered by producer.)
7:00 p.m.	Doors open.
7:15 p.m.	Return to the hall for the concert.
8:00 p.m.	Emcee announcements, introduce band.
9:00 p.m.	Intermission.
9:20 p.m.	Second set.
10:30 p.m.	Be off stage.
10:35 p.m.	Melanie escorts artists to lobby to sign autographs.

Producer Information

Hall _____

   Producer's Name _____

   Address _____

   Box office phone _____

   Back stage phone _____

Addresses and Phone Numbers

Leslie: Production Coordinator, housing _____

_____

Melanie: Stage Manager _____

_____

Jesse: Publicity _____

_____

Joan: Lobby Manager _____

_____

SAMPLE ARTIST'S CONTRACT
(Simple)

Live Performance Agreement

This contract for the personal services of *(artist's name)* on the engagement described below, made this _____ day of _____, 19 ___, between the undersigned purchaser of music *(employer)* and _____ *(artist).*
The artist is engaged on the terms and conditions on the face hereof. The artist represents that the members of artist's group designated have agreed to be bound by said terms and conditions. Each member of the artist's group yet to be chosen, upon acceptance, shall be bound by said terms and conditions. The members of artist's group severally agree to render services under the undersigned leader.

1.   Billing for artist _____

2.   Name and address of place of engagement _____
_____

     Print name of band or group _____

3.   Date of engagement _____

4.   Starting and finishing time of engagement _____

5.   Type of engagement (*specify concert, dance, stage show, banquet, etc.*) _____

6.   Wage agreed upon $_____
_____

_____

     This wage includes expenses agreed to be reimbursed by the employer in accordance with the attached schedule, or a schedule to be furnished by the employer on or before the date of engagement.

7.   Employer will make payments as follows: _____

_____

     Upon request by the artist, employer either shall make advance payment hereunder or shall post an appropriate bond.

8. Special provisions: _____

_____

_____

9. The employer shall at all times have complete supervision, direction, and control over the services of the artists on this engagement as agreed to in Number 5.

10. The parties will submit any claim, dispute, controversy, or difference involving the services arising out of or connected with this contract and the engagement covered thereby for determination by the American Arbitration Society or a similar board and such determination shall be conclusive, final, and binding upon the parties.

_____
Print employer's name

_____
Print artist's name

_____
Signature of employer

_____
Signature of artist
(or representative)

_____
Street address

_____
Artist's address

_____
City   State   Zip Code

_____
City   State   Zip Code

_____
Telephone

_____
Booking agent   Telephone

SAMPLE ARTIST'S PUBLIC APPEARANCE AGREEMENT
(Complex)

Agreement made this _____ day of _____, 19___, by and between
_____ (hereinafter referred to as producer) and
_____ (hereinafter referred to as artist).

IT IS MUTUALLY AGREED BETWEEN PARTIES AS FOLLOWS:

The producer agrees to engage the artist for performances, terms and conditions being hereafter set forth.

1. **Producer** *(Person in charge of production)*

   _____   _____
   _____   _____
   _____   _____
                                             Phone numbers
                                             Day _____
                                             Night _____

2. **Sponsor(s)** name, address, and phone numbers

   _____   _____
   _____   _____
   _____   _____

3. **Place** of engagement

   _____   Hall office number _____
   _____   Backstage number _____
   _____   Wheelchair entrance _____

4. **Date(s)** and **Time(s)** of performance(s) _____
   The performance is scheduled to begin at _____ and every effort will be made to begin on time. No performance will begin more than 10 minutes past the designated time, without approval of the artist.

5. **Artist** agrees to provide the following services _____ .
   Each performance shall be at least _____ sets of _____ minutes in duration. In the event that there is an intermission, the intermission shall not exceed 20 minutes.

165

6. **Performance fee** agreed upon $_____.

    6.1 Producer agrees to make payment as follows: $_____ as a non-refundable deposit to reserve the date, due with return of the signed contract no later than _____. The balance of the guarantee, $_____, shall be personally delivered to the artist or the artist's representative no later than immediately following the performance.

    6.2 All guaranteed payments by the producer for the services of the artist and all applicable percentage provided herein shall be made payable to artist *(social security number)* and delivered to the artist or artist's representative in the form of cash, money order, or cashier's check, or in the case of performance at and for a recognized college or university, by check of such institution.

    6.3 In an engagement where artist's fee is contracted in part based on producer's production costs and/or where artist is to receive a percentage of the gross ticket sales, the attached CONTRACT/BUDGET must be signed by producer and is incorporated into this Public Appearance Agreement. It may be amended only with written approval of the artist or artist's representative. Producer is to provide complete itemized receipts of actual expenditures with settlement for percentages above projected expenses of $_____ due artist. If the expenditures are less than $_____, as stated in the attached CONTRACT/BUDGET, and if this results in an increase in the amount of the split, the difference will be allocated with the artist receiving _____ and the producer receiving _____. Producer's actual costs will be limited to those which itemized receipts can be produced. Producer agrees to make payment within _____ days.

7. **Tickets**

    7.1 Price and scaling: Producer warrants that the tickets for each performance will be priced as follows:

    _____ seats @ $_____
    _____ seats @ $_____
    _____ seats @ $_____

    7.2 Producer agrees that advance sale of tickets will be provided and will commence at ticket outlets at least _____ weeks prior to the performance.

    7.3 Complimentary tickets: Producer agrees to provide

    _____   for producers
    _____   for members of the press
    _____   for distributors and record store personnel
    _____   for artist *comps* to be held at box office until released by artist or artist's representative.

8. **Billing**
   8.1   Unless otherwise advised by artist because of personnel changes, producer agrees to comply with the following requirements in all manner and form of advertising in connection with the performance, including but not limited to, tickets, paid newspaper advertising, publicity releases, programs, flyers, posters, signs and billboards. Billing as follows: ARTIST'S NAME with (name(s) of others following).

   8.2   The producer understands that artist is on a regional tour and that said performance is not an exclusive engagement and will not be billed as such unless otherwise agreed to in writing prior to performance.

   8.3   Producer will not use the word "benefit," either in fact or by implication, in any promotional materials for said performance, unless artist is being paid NO performance fee and has agreed, in writing, that the performance is a benefit. The words, "sponsored by," "produced by," or "part of the proceeds will go to. . ." may be used when appropriate.

   8.4   Artist reserves the right to approve or deny any other persons appearing on the same bill, to determine the length of such person's performance and to approve amount of compensation for such performance prior to hiring, and to the release of any publicity. Additional performers and set lengths:
   Name _____ Set length _____
   Name _____ Set length _____
   Name _____ Set length _____

   8.5   Artist reserves the right to invite on stage any unscheduled guest performers, at her or his discretion, provided that it does not impose technical or economic burden on the producer.

9. **Promotion and publicity**
   9.1   Producer agrees to assume the responsibility of organizing and promoting said performance(s) and will use best efforts to publicize the events and to appeal to a broad definition of general audience, including, for example, the feminist, peace, environmentalist, human rights and social justice organizations and committees, and _____ as well as general music-appreciating audiences.

   9.2   Producer will typeset, print, distribute, and post flyers and/or posters to publicize the event to above referenced, at least six weeks prior to the performance date. Producer will place at least one ad in local leading newspapers and/or agreed upon alternative papers at least <u>six weeks</u> prior to the date of engagement.

   9.3   Producer agrees to send promotion materials including press releases, press kits, flyers, and/or records to local press, including, but not limited to, newspapers and periodicals, television and radio stations, and to make personal contact with such media contacts to insure maximum coverage by performance or record reviews of artist's work.

9.4 Producer agrees to coordinate local promotion with artist's representative and to provide artist with sample copies of all local promotional materials, and with original copies of all newspaper coverage, articles, or reviews of the performance or recordings of artist, with publication masthead.

9.5 Producer agrees specifically to obtain prior approval from artist's representative for any and all scheduled activities or appointments proposed for artist or anyone in artist's tour group.

9.6 If producer provides a printed program for the audience, a half-page ad provided by (*record company*) _____ will be included at no charge. (In some cases, the record distributor will supply this ad.)

9.7 Producer will use only promotional and/or biographical material provided by (*record company*) _____ in regard to the artist in such a printed program.

9.8 Producer agrees that all photographs, biographical information, promotional albums and other materials furnished shall be and remain the property of the artist, and shall be used only in connection with the promotion and publicity of the performance.

9.9 Artist agrees to provide producer with up to five press kits. Producer may request additional press kits, photographs, and promotional recordings, if necessary.

10. **Facility requirements**

10.1 Producer agrees that there will be no banner, sign, slogans, etc., on stage without prior approval from the artist.

10.2 Producer agrees that the introduction and all announcements to be made from the stage must be approved by artist or artist's representative prior to the concert.

10.3 All important information, technical problems, and/or disputes relevant to the concert must be brought to the artist's attention prior to the beginning of the concert, and as soon as producer is aware of such problems (e.g., at sound check).

10.4 Every reasonable effort must be made to provide a performance space that is wheelchair-accessible as defined by International Accessibility Standards (see Form 4:2:5). If the facility meets accessibility standards, the wheelchair symbol should appear on all promotional material. If accessibility is limited, producer must notify artist's representative prior to signing this contract to arrange alternative means of accessibility and to include a brief description of such limitations and alternatives on all detailed promotion for said performance.

10.5 Producer agrees to provide comfortable and private dressing rooms. Each room shall be secured with adequate lock and must be clean, dry, well-lighted, and heated or air conditioned, and shall be within easy access to clean, private lavatories which are supplied with soap, toilet tissue, and cloth towels. These lavatories shall be closed to the general public.

10.6 Producer agrees to provide a comfortable temperature, at least 65 degrees Fahrenheit, in the performance space for the sound check as well as the actual performance when using an indoor facility.

10.7 Producer agrees that there will be no alcoholic beverages offered or sold on the premises before, during, or after the performance without prior written consent from the artist.

10.8 Producer agrees to prohibit smoking in the performance space, on stage, or in the dressing rooms during technical set-ups, rehearsal, sound and light checks, and the performance.

10.9 Producer agrees to provide a table in the entrance or lobby area of the performance space for the sale of records, tapes, songbooks, etc. (*Record company*) _____ shall have exclusive right to designate a representative to engage in sales of (*record company*) _____ records and other related products on the premises at reasonable times before and/or after the artist's performance, without charge by producer.

11. **General provisions**
    11.1 In the event that labor at the hall is on strike, at any time following the signing of this agreement and through the day of the performance, producer agrees to notify artist immediately, and agrees that the performance date may be rescheduled. Producer agrees to hold artist harmless in such event, and any expenses incurred to hall labor-management disputes will be included in the budget for said performance(s), if rescheduled.

    11.2 If any term, provision, covenant, or condition in this agreement is held by a court of competent jurisdiction to be invalid, void, or unenforceable, the rest of the agreement shall remain in full force and effect, and shall in no way be affected, impaired, or invalid.

    11.3 Producer hereby agrees to pay, discharge, and indemnify artist and her or his agents and employees against and hold them harmless from all expenses, costs, claims obligation, losses, damages, liabilities, and injuries to persons or property in any manner arising out of or incident to the performance of this agreement, including without limitations all consequential damages, whether or not resulting from the negligence of producer or its agents.

11.4 This instrument including Riders I, II, III, IV, and V contains the entire agreement of the parties relating to the rights granted and obligations assumed in this instrument. Any oral representation or modifications concerning this instrument shall be of no force or effect unless contained in a subsequent written modification signed by the party to be charged.

11.5 This agreement shall be interpreted in accordance with and in all respects governed by the laws of the State of California, and the laws of that state shall govern its interpretation and effect.

11.6 Any controversy or claim arising out of or relating to the agreement, or of the breach thereof, which cannot be settled out of court, shall be settled by binding arbitration within the State of California and in accordance with the California Civil Code Procedure 1280-1294.2 from time to time amended, and the judgment upon the award rendered by the arbitrator(s) may be entered in any court having jurisdiction. Attorney's fees and costs will be awarded to prevailing party.

IN WITNESS THEREOF, the parties have executed this agreement on the respective dates shown by their signatures, but effective as of the day and year first above written.

_____   _____
Producer   Artist or Artist's Representative

by _____   by _____

Date _____   Date _____

Return to: Artist's Representative _____

                  Address _____

                  Phone number _____

FORM 4:2:1

Sample Rider 1: TECHNICAL REQUIREMENTS FOR VOCALIST WITH PIANIST

1. **Production requirements**

   1.1   Personnel: Producer agrees to provide personnel to staff performance space for security, door monitors, ticket takers/sellers, backstage security, etc.

   1.2   Producer will provide experienced lighting and sound technicians and necessary stage management personnel working from set-up, performance, and through the strike (dismantling equipment).

   1.3   Technical Check: Producer will ensure that the light and sound equipment will be set up, tested, and ready (the lights ready for focus after artist and pianist check for stage placement) for the artist's technical check by the designated time: _____.

   1.4   On stage props, etc.: Producer will provide the following items on stage for the technical check and the performance: _____ glass(es) (not plastic or styrofoam) and pitcher of room-temperature water for each performer, one small table to hold artist's water, notes, flowers, etc.

   1.5   Walk-in music: If producer chooses to play appropriate recorded music through the sound system, it will be played only before the beginning of the performance, and not during intermission or after the performance. Artist's own recorded music will not be played through the sound system at any time.

2. **Keyboards**

   2.1   Producer agrees to provide an acoustic grand piano (preference #1 Yamaha, #2 Steinway, #3 Baldwin), in good working condition with all pedals and keys functioning property (no pedal squeaks).

   2.2   Producer agrees to provide an "artist bench" with adjustable height control. If producer is unable to provide such a bench, the piano bench must be of a height appropriate to the piano, and a cushion should be available for adjustment.

   2.3   Producer agrees to provide a small rug at least 2' x 3' for placement underneath the pedals of the piano. All edges of the rug must be taped down prior to technical check.

   2.4   Producer agrees to have the piano tuned to pitch A-440 on the day of the performance. The piano must be in good enough condition that it can be tuned to A-440 without damaging the strings or sounding board. Piano tuner must be available if needed for retuning immediately following sound check.

2.5   Piano position: Producer agrees that piano will be positioned on the stage by the artist or a member of the artist's tour group, if at all possible. If a member of the artist's tour group is not available to position the piano, it should be set according to the instruction and stage plan attached to this contract; the artist may make adjustment upon arrival at the hall. The piano should not be moved after the final tuning before the performance, except by the artist.

3.   **Sound Requirements**: Producer agrees to provide a high-quality sound system in good working condition, sufficient to provide good quality sound amplification throughout the entire performance space.

Sound equipment must include:

A.   A 12- or 16-channel mixing board with capacity for two monitor mixes or a separate monitor mixing board for same number of mixes. Smaller boards don't have this capacity. Suggested boards are:

     Yamaha PM-1000 or 917   Biamp 1624 or 1629
     Soundcraft 1S or Series 400 boards

B.   Two or three one-half or one-third octave equalizers, one of which is for the house mix, two or three of which are for the monitor mixes. Suggested boards are:

     UREI   SAE   Yamaha

C.   Two or three piano microphones with boom stands. Suggested brands are:
     AKG 414 or 452   Shure SM-57's
     Sennheiser 421's   ***PLEASE: NO PZM mics***

D.   One vocal microphone on an upright stand with a clip for easy pull-off of mic (Beyer makes one) and 15 feet of cable for on-stage movement. Suggested brands:
     Shure SM-87   Electro-Voice BK1   Beyer M-500

One vocal mic on a boom stand for pianist. Suggested brand:
     Shure SM-58

E.   At least one good-quality monitor speaker with clear sound for each on-stage performer (see Forms 4:2 and 4:2:4 (Rider IV) for additional technical requirements). Monitor speakers should have both bass speaker and tweeter enclosed in each cabinet and should be loaded with high-quality components. Suggested brands:
     JBL   Altec
     Gauss   Electro-Voice

F.   Monitor power amplifiers with sufficient power to drive monitor speakers cleanly and without distortion. *Please note:* The monitor system is extremely important in determining the quality of the performance. We need two separate monitor mixes.

G.   House speakers
    i.   Small Halls (200- to 500-capacity)
        -   House speakers should be equivalent of a biamped system consisting of: two (one per side) JBL bass cabinets with power requirement of 150 watts each.

        -   Two (one per side) JBL 90 degree radial horns with power requirements of 100 watts each.

        -   House power amplifiers with sufficient power to drive house speakers cleanly and without distortion. Suggested brands:
            Crown   Yamaha   BGW Crest

    ii. Medium Halls (500- to 1,200-capacity)
         Double the system described in Section A.

    iii. Large Halls (1,200- to 3,000-capacity)
         Coverage of halls ranging from 1,200- to 1,500-capacity and greater becomes much more critical depending on the shape and size of the hall. Proper splaying and stacking of the house speaker components is crucial, and requirements vary drastically from hall to hall. A good sound company with quality equipment to drive the speakers cleanly and without distortion, and past experience in doing similar acts is recommended. References are advised. To make sure you have adequate coverage for balconies and corners in the hall, the system should be biamped or triamped, if possible, and the components should be equivalent in quality to the manufacturers suggested in Section A.

    iv. Halls with built-in sound systems: Concert halls that have sound systems that are permanent installations often are not sufficient to reproduce adequately a high-quality concert.

4.   **Lighting requirements**
4.1 Producer agrees to provide lighting equipment and instruments adequate to provide ample focused light on the artist and other on-stage performers during the performance.

A.   Front and back lighting on the artist, other on-stage performers, and sign-language interpreter (if there is one) must be bright enough to illuminate each person's face to be seen easily from the most distant point in the performance space at all times.

B. Lighting from two directions simultaneously (cross-lighting) is preferable to provide dimension to the artists' faces.

C. One follow-spot to be provided for artist.

4.2 Artist's lighting

A. At least two settings with bright, widely-focused front lights.

B. Preferably a third setting with tighter, more intimate front lighting.

C. Suggested washes in:
     blue — Roscolux 79 or 80
     magenta — Roscolux 26 or 27
     light magenta — Roscolux 44
     lavender — Roscolux 58
     light blue — Roscolux 68
     lavender — Roscolux 54
     light pink — Roscolux 35

D. Pink Roscolux 35, lavender Roscolux 51, or straw Roscolux 17 on the front lights and in the follow-spots.

4.3 **Interpreter's lighting** (when an interpreter is included)

A. Lights must be focused on the interpreter to illuminate clearly her or his face, hands (outstretched to side and over head), and upper body to the most distant spot in the performance space. Front and back lighting are necessary to accomplish this.

B. Lights on the interpreter must not be taken down at any time during the performance, unless requested by the artist.

4.4 Focusing

A. Stage placement must be approved by at least one performer before the final focusing of the lights.

B. Stand-ins should be used for all persons who will appear on stage. (Note that the artist is 5'8" in shoes. Pianist is 6'2" and at the piano.)

C. Lights must be focused with the piano lid open at the high stick position in such a manner as not to cast a shadow across face and torso of the pianist. The special on the pianist must have the capacity to be as bright as the light on the interpreter.

    D.   Lights must be focused without light being spilled offstage or in the audience.

    E.   House lights must be out for level setting and final light check.

    F.   All lights must be focused and ready for final focusing by the beginning of technical check.

    G.   Lighting personnel must be available to make necessary focusing adjustment during or following the technical check.

4.5   Artist will provide producer with a set list and simple lighting notations on the day of the performance. Producer will use best efforts to incorporate artist's lighting requirements.

5. Broadcasting/Reporting

5.1   No portion of stated performance shall be filmed, video-taped, or audio-recorded without prior written authorization of artist/artist's representative.

5.2   If artist or artist's representative grants prior written permission for tape-recording which will be connected in any way to the sound system or for video-taping or filming, such equipment must be set up and operating by the time of the technical check, and artist shall receive a copy of video-tape, in VHS 1/2" format, or film or audio tape, at no charge to artist.

5.3   No cassette recording shall be made of the performance without permission from artist.

5.4   Still photographs taken by members of the audience for personal non-commercial use are permitted unless they constitute a distraction to the audience or the performers. Producer shall not, in any way, publicize this allowance.

This technical rider is hereby incorporated as if fully set forth in the attached artist Public Appearance Agreement between artist and producer.

_____   _____

Producer   Artist/Artist's Representative

_____   _____

Date   Date

Sample Rider 2: HOSPITALITY

As per our contract agreement, producer will provide one hot meal per person, day of show, served in a restaurant, catered to backstage, or catered to housing at the convenience of the artist.

Good food on the road is often difficult to find; we appreciate your attention to the artist(s)' food needs.

Backstage: Please be sure the following items are available to the artist(s) before, during, and after their performance.

> Spring water
> Apple juice (not cider)
> Cranberry juice (no sugar)
> Fresh fruits, uncut
>
> Black tea (Earl Grey or English Breakfast)
> Peppermint tea (herbal, no caffeine)
> Half and half, sugar
>
> **NO GRAPES** (due to United Farm Workers boycott and dangerous pesticides)

Also, please provide eating utensils, including sharp knives, and napkins. Please, no styrofoam or plastic cups.

On stage: Two or three glasses of water (please, no styrofoam cups) on a small table center-up stage for water and notes.

Concert meal: Please include meals featuring vegetables. Chicken or fish (not fried or breaded), steamed or sauteed vegetables, vegetable salads with dressing on the side. No cream or cheese sauce would be greatly appreciated, due to their negative side effects for vocalists.

Additionally, *please provide an iron and ironing board at the hall*, and if showers are available, provide soap and towels for everyone.

Hospitality expenses are not to exceed $100 without permission from artist's representative.

This rider is hereby incorporated as if fully set forth in the attached Artist Public Appearance Agreement.

_____   _____
Producer   Artist/Artist's Representative

_____   _____
Date   Date

FORM 4:2:3

Sample Rider 3: HOUSING

Private hotel accommodations for each person in the tour party is preferable. Alternative housing as described below is also acceptable. Producer will provide warm, clean housing including two separate beds in two separate rooms.

The artist(s) may be allergic to cats and, therefore, must be housed in a cat-free house. In general, animal-free housing is preferred.

It is important that there be little activity and a lot of quiet in the house when artists are there, so they may practice, sleep, and relax. They do little socializing while touring, and when they do, it is not usually in the house where they are staying.

Do not plan any parties in artist's housing.

In all housing, producer will provide (in quantities appropriate to the number of people and duration of stay):

* Spring water
  Cranberry juice or cranapple (no sugar)
  Drip coffee and container to brew in (Melitta-type filter, cone, and pot)
  Half and half, sugar

* Apples, bananas (uncut)
  Peppermint tea
  Black tea (English breakfast, Earl Grey)
  Seltzer or mineral water

* If artists are staying in a hotel, only the starred items are necessary.

Fresh clean linens and towels should be provided. An ironing board should be provided in each house.

During the period that artist or artist's tour party is locally available to the producer for promotion and performance purposes related to this contact, producer will provide at least one hot meal per person per day.

Hospitality expenses are not to exceed $200. This amount includes day-of-show dinner and all items required in artist's housing.

This rider is hereby incorporated as if fully set forth in the attached Artist's Public Appearance Agreement.

_____   _____
Producer   Artist/Artist's Representative

_____   _____
Date   Date

179

FORM 4:2:4

Sample Rider 4: SIGN LANGUAGE INTERPRETING
(optional)

In the event there is a hearing-impaired audience in your community, it will be your responsibility to provide a sign language interpreter/artist who signs ASL and is experienced in signing music. (Refer to Chapter 15 — Accessibility for more information.)

Placement
The interpreter placement is approximately as far stage left of the artist as the pianist is stage right (see stage diagram). She or he should be one foot upstage of the artist. The interpreter will move in a 5' x 5' area. Her or his lighting spike will be placed toward the stage left margin of this area. If a rug is used on the stage, it should not extend into this 5' x 5' area.

Lighting
Instruments with sufficient wattage will be used so that people sitting in the back row can see the interpreter clearly. She or he will be front-lit and back-lit as well as cross-lit so as not to create shadows, which make the sign language impossible to read. Regardless of light changes during the concert, the interpreter must always remain bright enough to be seen clearly by the hearing-impaired audience. The only exception is in the case of blackouts between songs.

Monitors
If three monitor mixes are used, the interpreter will have a separate mix. With two monitor mixes, the interpreter would like two speaker cabinets. One cabinet will have the same monitor mix as the artist uses; the second will have the mix used by the pianist. On a smaller stage with two monitor mixes, one speaker cabinet with the artist's monitor mix will be sufficient. However, two monitors are always preferable if there is room on the stage.

Hearing-impaired audience seating (see seating map, Form 6:3)
The best location for seating the hearing-impaired audience is between the center of the house and the house right. Seating the hearing-impaired audience to the extreme house right makes it difficult for them to see well and forces the interpreter to play to the corner of the house rather than to the whole audience. This creates an uncomfortable separation on the stage and among the performing group.

The hearing-impaired audience seating will begin about 15 to 20 feet away from the interpreter and move back into the house; the front rows are usually too close. The first few rows of the balcony are also ideal if a railing does not block the view.

Ticket prices will be adjusted for the hearing-impaired so they are not forced to pay only the highest ticket price because of seating location.

Billing
In the event that there is an interpreter, the interpreter's name will be included on the promotion and in the program whenever possible. The billing will be in this order: "Artist with (*pianist*) _____ and (*interpreter*) _____." Information about the accessibility of the event and the interpreter will be included in all promotional materials and media.

The enclosed logo (Form 15:1) means "this event will be interpreted in sign language" and will be used in all print media with the interpreter's name.

181

Suggested Guidelines for Community Liaison
The community liaison to the hearing-impaired community should be responsible for the following outreach activities:

-   Send out a mailing to deaf, hearing-impaired, and signers' community groups, organizations, media, and interested individuals who are on your own or the producer's list, or other relevant lists with information about the concert.

    A concert flyer provided by the producer could be included for them to post or include in newsletters along with additional information about the concert.

    The producer will pay $_____ for the mailing (cover letter, concert flyer, postage) for _____ pieces unless other arrangements are mutually agreed to.

-   Be available to answer questions regarding ticket information, the artists, signers, etc.

-   Do interviews with representatives of media doing outreach to the deaf community.

-   Be the "out front" person for the concert to the deaf community.

-   Arrange for a TDD or TTY machine for phone calls.

Additional Needs
A glass of water on a small table or stand should be provided on stage.

This rider is hereby incorporated as if fully set forth in the attached Artist's Public Appearance Agreement.

_____   _____
Producer   Artist/Artist's Representative

_____   _____
Date   Date

Sample Rider 5: ACCESSIBILITY

Producer will make every effort to find a hall that is wheelchair-accessible.

To determine if a hall is accessible, use these specifications:

- A standard adult wheelchair is 25" to 27" wide.
- Doorways into and around the hall should be 30" to 32" wide.
- Bathroom and tight corners must have a 5' turning radius.

The best way to determine accessibility is to have someone sit in a standard size wheelchair and make her or his way through the hall from outside to the seating area to the bathrooms and back.

Seating Arrangements
It is best to have some of the seats in the hall removed, if possible, and a special section set up for wheelchairs. If the hall does not have removable seats, the next-best arrangement is to reserve aisle seats for wheelchair users and have them transfer into those seats. Their chairs should be able to be kept close by, and seats also should be reserved for their friends. Should neither of these arrangements be possible, flat seating at the top or back of the hall should be reserved and folding chairs set up for friends. (In most halls there are enough exits to allow wheelchairs in one or two of the aisles.)

Promotion
The accessibility symbol (Form 15:1) should be used on all promotional material if the hall is completely accessible. (Complete accessibility is defined when at least one entrance, the first floor of the hall, the lobby, and the bathrooms are accessible.) If the hall is partially accessible, describe on all promotional material exactly what the situation is for wheelchair-users. Examples of statements used to explain partial accessibility.

- Entrance to hall is accessible. However, there are two steps inside; assistance will be available.

- Concert hall is completely accessible; there are bathrooms next door which are accessible.

- Flat seating will be available at back of hall with folding chairs for friends; first-floor bathrooms accessible.

- The hall is accessible but bathrooms are not.

ALSO: If there is specific handicapped parking, this should be noted on all
promotion. If the wheelchair entrance is different from the main entrance, this,
too, should be noted.

This rider is hereby incorporated as if fully set forth in the attached Artist's
Public Appearance Agreement.

_____   _____
        Producer   Artist/Artist's Representative

_____   _____
        Date   Date

FORM 5:1

HALL RESEARCH DATA

Date _____

Name of Hall _____

Location _____

_____

Contact Person (name and phone) _____

Telephones (box office, stage door, etc.) _____

_____

Suitability (details) _____

_____

Capacity _____

   Main Floor _____

   Balcony _____

Dates Available _____

Dates on Hold (details) _____

_____

Price _____

Union Hall (details) _____

_____

Contract (get sample; details) _____

_____

Transportation _____

Parking _____

Accessibility _____

Services _____

Lobby Space _____

Food Sales Permitted (details) _____

_____

Room for Record/Promotional Sales _____

Child Care Space _____

Dressing Room Space _____

Acoustics _____

Lights _____

Ticket Sellers _____

Box Office _____

Insurance _____

Security _____

NOTES: _____

FACILITY CHECKLIST

Name _____

Address _____

Contact persons _____

Phone _____

Capacity _____

Ticket scale *(reserved seating)*

1. _____ 3. _____

2. _____ 4. _____

HALL

Confirmed date *(include date confirmed and by whom)* _____

_____

Dates available _____

Dates on hold _____

Dates on second hold _____

Preferred dates _____

Facility expenses

   Hall rental _____

   Flat _____

   Percentage _____

Includes _____

_____

Disabled access _____

Insurance

   Amount _____ Due _____

Deposits

   Amount _____ Due _____

MANAGEMENT ATTITUDE _____

_____

TICKETS

Box office _____

Tickets sold via _____

Box office hours _____

Ticket information number _____

Contacts _____

Box office fee _____

Includes _____

Box office day of show _____

Counts available _____

Contact day of show *(name and phone)*_____

ENVIRONMENT
Ground transportation *(airport location)* _____

_____

Hotels _____
Location _____
Parking _____
Lobby Sales _____
Catering requirements _____
Restaurants *(open late, vegetarian, cheap, nice)* _____

_____

CHILD CARE _____

STAFFING
Union crews _____

_____

Box office _____
Ushers _____
Ticket takers _____
House manager _____
Security _____
Piano tuner _____

PRODUCTION
Adequate power _____
House sound _____
Equipment available _____
House lights _____
Equipment available _____
Dressing rooms _____
Stage space _____
Other equipment _____

HALL NOTES
Location _____
Transportation _____
Parking _____
Lobby sales _____
Catering requirements _____
Disabled access _____

DAY OF THE SHOW
Show time _____ Doors Open _____
Show call _____
Out _____

SAMPLE HALL RENTAL CONTRACT

This Sample Hall Rental Contract is provided as a guideline. Several provisions, particularly those concerning stage crews, technical assistance, and concession sales, may be negotiable, depending upon the particular hall.

License Agreement
Contract No. _____

THIS LICENSE AGREEMENT is made and entered into this _____ day of _____, 19_____, by and between the _____ Convention Center, hereinafter referred to as "CC," a non-profit corporation, acting by and through its General Manager, and (*name and address of show*) ____

_____

_____

Telephone _____
hereinafter referred to as "LICENSEE."

RECITALS

1. CC operates the Convention Center located at _____, hereinafter referred to as the "CENTER";

2. The Center is owned by the City of _____ ("CITY"); and

3. LICENSEE desires to hire the premises in the Center as described below.

NOW, THEREFORE, FOR AND IN CONSIDERATION OF THE FOLLOWING PROMISES, COVENANTS AND CONDITIONS, THE PARTIES AGREE AS FOLLOWS:

PRINCIPAL TERMS

LICENSED PREMISES

CC hereby grants LICENSEE a license to enter into and use the following areas of the Center (the Premises) at the times set forth below for the purpose of (*title of show*) _____

_____

and for no other purpose.

Facilities used: [   ] CC

Date of Use	Time Period	Area	Activity	License Fees
_____	_____	_____	_____	_____
_____	_____	_____	_____	_____
_____	_____	_____	_____	_____
_____	_____	_____	_____	_____
_____	_____	_____	_____	_____
_____	_____	_____	_____	_____
_____	_____	_____	_____	_____
_____	_____	_____	_____	_____
_____	_____	_____	_____	_____
			License Fees	_____

Estimated Other Fees: _____

_____

_____   _____

                                        Total Fees $_____

1. LICENSEE has paid CC $_____ on (*date*) _____,
   and the balance of $_____ is due no later than (*date*)
   _____.

The License Fee stated above shall be the minimum fee for use of the facility. LICENSEE agrees that the actual fee shall be the greater of this deposit or, if exhibit space is used, the exhibit space charges assessed at .10/net sq. ft. per day of exhibit space or, in the case of paid admission events, 10% of gross ticket sales. Overtime rates (see rates) are applied to facility usage in excess of the time period specified herein. Estimated reimbursables are not fixed and may change depending on the needs of the LICENSEE. All funds due to CC must be settled 30 days prior to the event closing.

2. LICENSEE shall provide CC a Certificate of Insurance naming the City of
   _____, its Council, CC and its board of directors,
   officers, representatives, agents, and employees as additional insured with the
   same coverage and limits of liabilities shown on Attachment "A," no later than
   30 days prior to first day of event.

3. LICENSEE agrees to abide by rules, regulations, standard terms, and
   conditions as adopted by the City of _____ and CC and shall, at its
   own expense, obtain all permits required for the conduct of each event.

4. The LICENSEE shall indemnify and hold CC and its board of directors, the
   City of _____ and its council, and the officers,
   representatives, agents, and employees of CC and the City free and harmless
   from and against all claims, losses, damages, and liabilities of any kind arising
   directly or indirectly out of this license or its performance.

5. Execution of the license is evidence of the fact that the signatory is authorized
   to sign on behalf of LICENSEE and the official purpose stated above is
   correct.

6. This license shall be returned to CC within _____ days, otherwise it
   shall be considered null and void.

7. CC retains the right to enter upon and inspect the premises at any time.

FEES: All fees must be paid at least 30 days prior to date of use, unless prior
agreement is reached with CC. Failure to pay fees when due may result in
cancellation of the event. If an event is booked less than 30 days in advance, all
fees are due immediately upon booking.

**Cancellation by Licensee: should Licensee cancel the event covered by this
agreement within the _____ period prior to the event, no deposit
refund shall be made and the entire fees shall be payable by the Licensee to the
Center as liquidated damages and not as a penalty.**
Initials: _____ (CC)   _____ (Licensee)

LICENSEE also agrees to pay any reimbursable expenses incurred by CC in
connection with the event covered by this Agreement.

FACILITY SET-UPS: All set-up information must be presented to the
Convention Center a minimum of two weeks prior to the event. Set-up revisions
accepted within 72 hours of the event will be billed on a time-and-material basis.
If the event is booked less than two weeks in advance, the set-up information is
due immediately upon booking.

This license may not be assigned without the prior written consent of Convention Center.

LICENSEE _____   CONVENTION CENTER

By: _____   By: _____
    (name)   *(name)*

ATTACHMENT A
Comprehensive General Liability Insurance

The Comprehensive General Liability Insurance obtained by the Licensee shall protect the City, CC, and the Licensee from contingent liability which may arise from the use of the facility. The overall limit for General Liability has to be $1,000,000. This limit can be obtained by having it all under the Primary policy or split out between the Primary (a) and the Excess of Umbrella (b) policies. Also, the Licensee shall secure Certificates of Insurance naming the City and its Council and the Board of Directors, representatives, agents, and employees of the City and CC as additional insured with respect to work or operations for the Licensee and providing that such insurance is primary insurance with respect to the interests of the Licensee, the City, and CC.

The following endorsements and Indemnification Agreement shall be a provision of any insurance coverage required to be obtained by the Licensee and shall be endorsed on the reverse sides of all certificates of insurance:

"The City of _____, the Convention Center, and the employees, officers, agents, contractors, and invitees of both are hereby added as additional insureds.

"This policy shall be primary insurance. Any other valid and collectible insurance or insurance reserves the Convention Center possesses shall be considered excess insurance only.

"This insurance shall act for each insured and additional insured as though a separate policy had been written for each. This, however, will not act to increase the limit of liability of the insuring company.

"The Licensee agrees to protect, defend, indemnify and hold the City of _____ and its Council, Convention Center (CC), and its board of directors, and the officers, representatives, agents, and employees of the City and CC free and harmless from and against any and all losses, penalties, damages, settlements, costs, charges, professional fees, or other expenses or liabilities of every kind and character in connection with or arising directly or indirectly out of this Agreement and/or the performance hereof. Without limiting the generality of the foregoing, any and all such claims, etc., relating to personal injury, death, damage to property, defects in materials or workmanship, actual or alleged infringement of any patent, trademark, copyright (or application of any thereof), or of any other tangible or intangible personal or property right, or any actual or alleged violation of any applicable statue, ordinance, administrative order, rule, or regulation, or decree of any court, shall be included in the indemnity hereunder. The Licensee further agrees to investigate, handle, respond to, provide defense for, and defend any such claim, etc., at her or his sole expense and agrees to bear all other costs and expenses related thereto, even if it (claim, etc.) is groundless, false, or fraudulent."

MASTER TICKET ACCOUNTING CHART

This master ticket accounting form can be used to keep track of all your advance ticket sales through community and alternative outlets. As you distribute tickets to various outlets and organizations, note the ticket information listed on the form below. Use this to keep accurate records of all your outlets. Later, this will help you identify the best outlets so you can plan to use them again, and eliminate the non-producing outlets. The completed form should be attached to your final budget sheet as a form of documentation.

Name of Seller/ Organization	Phone	Ticket numbers	Quantity sent	Date	Quantity returned	Date	Quantity sold	@ Price	Total due

FORM 6:2

SAMPLE TICKET SELLERS' CONTRACT

AGREEMENT BETWEEN *(producer)* _____ and *(seller)* _____ for the sale of tickets to a concert by *(artists)* _____ on *(date)* _____ at *(time)* _____ at *(place)* _____. Child care and ASL interpretation provided. Wheelchair accessible.

1. Ticket price is $ _____ .

2. People 16 and under, 60 and over, or persons with disabilities may buy tickets for $ _____ . Such tickets shall be marked by Producer. Seller shall sell only those tickets so marked as $ _____ tickets.

3. Seller may charge a service fee to customer of _____ percent of ticket price (or $ _____ per ticket) in cash for the service of selling tickets.

4. Seller will be responsible for the number of tickets given to sell. In the event of a discrepancy between the amount of money collected by Seller and the amount due Producer for the number of tickets sold, Seller will be responsible for the difference.

5. In the event Seller runs money through her or his books, Producer will be responsible for bad checks, provided that Seller obtained proper identification from ticket buyer (including name, address, phone number, driver's license number). Seller will receive no service fee on bad checks.

6. In the event Seller does not run ticket money through her or his books, Seller will have ticket buyers make checks payable to _____. Seller will get proper identification.

7. *No tickets will be sold after (time)* _____ on *(date)* _____ . Approximately four hours before the show on *(date)* _____ (or the preceding day if Seller is not open on *(date)* _____). Producer will call Seller and get final count of tickets sold and tickets remaining.

8. Seller shall provide Producer with all unsold tickets, upon completion of concert.

I have received _____ **tickets, numbers** _____ **date** _____ **initials** _____

_____   _____
Producer   Ticket Seller

_____   _____
Address/Phone   Contact Person

Total tickets sold _____ at $_____ = $_____   _____
                                                                                    Address

Total tickets sold _____ at $_____ = $_____   _____
                                                                                    Phone

Total received by Producer $_____   Total fee received by Seller $_____ .

FORM 6:3

SAMPLE HALL SEATING MAP

Every hall manager should have a seating map of the facility. Use it to acquaint yourself with the theater and to identify various seating options for different ticket pricing; to select appropriate seating areas for sponsors or benefactors; to plan where a control board could be placed, if necessary, etc. Study the plan, and make copies for your ticket sellers. However, don't forget to visit the facility personally to check for accessibility, locations for concessionaires, any seats where visibility is poor, etc. Your personal review of the facility will help you satisfy your audience as well as run a much smoother event.

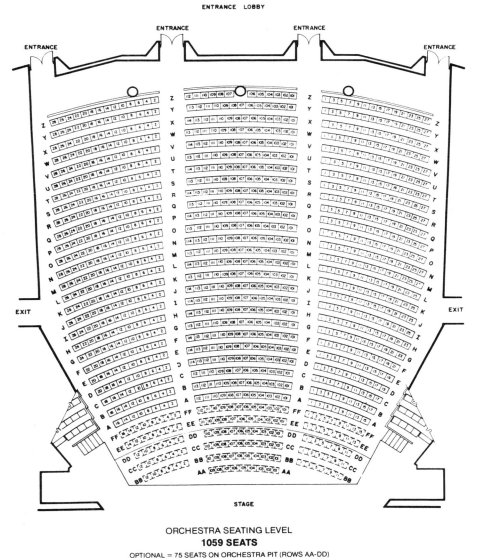

ORCHESTRA SEATING LEVEL
1059 SEATS
OPTIONAL = 75 SEATS ON ORCHESTRA PIT (ROWS AA-DD)
30 STANDEES AT REAR

Partial view. Tiers, mezzanine, and balcony levels not shown.

Total Theatre
Capacity: 2978 Seats

Main Floor   1557 Seats

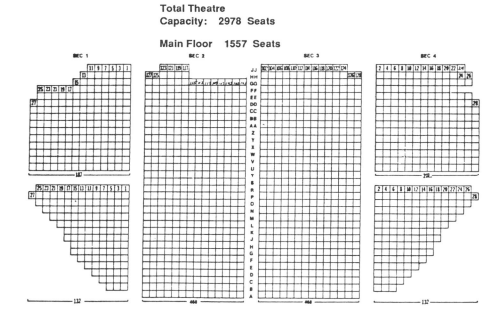

Second Level   1421 Seats

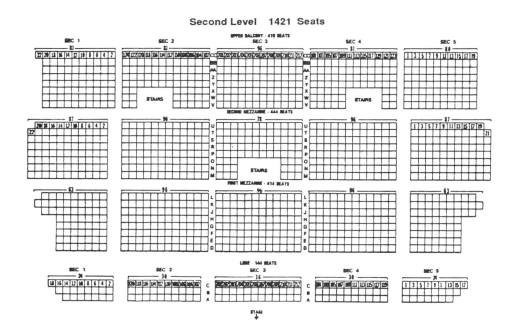

FORM 6:4

SAMPLE BOX OFFICE STATEMENT

SHOW: _____   DATE: _____

FACILITY: _____   TIME: _____

PROMOTER: _____   WEATHER: _____

Ticket price	Quantity printed	Disc.	Comps.	Dead-wood	Quantity sold	Adm. tax	Gross Taxes	Gross Net	Gross Sales

This is a true and correct statement.

_____
Box Office

_____
Promoter

Deadwood counted, verified,
and approved for destruction.

TOTAL EVENT GROSS .... $ _____

ADMISSION TAX .... $ _____

CITY TAX .... $ _____

STATE TAX .... $ _____

TOTAL GROSS NET .... $ _____

SAMPLE NOTIFICATION TO OTHER PRODUCERS

(Double-space all press releases)

Get out your calendars and red pens, here's a date you'll want to remember.

FRIDAY, JANUARY 19, CATHY FINK

is performing a benefit concert for Community Music and *(your organization)*. Please don't schedule any events to conflict with this date, and please DO plan on spending the evening with us!

We anticipate having the concert in the Herbert Hoover Auditorium (Commerce Building at the Federal Triangle Metro stop) at 8 p.m. There will be sign language interpretation for hearing-impaired, child care, and good accessibility for persons with disabilities.

If you have any questions or want to help call Sheila Kahn at (301) 270-3873.

Watch for more information to come.

FORM 7:2

SAMPLE PRESS RELEASE

(Double-space all press releases)

FOR IMMEDIATE RELEASE   Contact: Sheila Kahn
                                                                                301-270-3873

CATHY FINK and PATSY MONTANA

Together again in an old-time radio barn dance.

On Wednesday, January 9, Cathy Fink and Patsy Montana will be reunited in a special concert dedicated to women in country music and to the days of live, old-time radio. In fact, the stage of the Birchmere Restaurant in Alexandria, Virginia, will look much like the stage of the WLS Barn Dance where Patsy Montana first sang her million selling song, "I Wanna Be a Cowboy's Sweetheart" (1935) and where she performed for more than 20 years.

Cathy and Patsy will be joined by Washington's finest country and swing musicians: Pete Kennedy, Marcy Marxer, Mike Stein, and Bryan Smith. The evening's emcee will be Lee Demsey of WAMU-FM, introducing songs and remind us of the entertaining commercials from the days of old-time radio. You can expect hot harmony, singing, twin yodeling, fancy picking and plenty of good music and entertainment.

Cathy and Patsy's last show together received excellent comments from Mike Joyce of the Washington Post. He said, "Fink's show was engagingly buoyant," and Ms. Montana, "sang of the American west with such warm affection that the vigorous applause she received from the packed house seemed inevitable from the start."

The show is on Wednesday, January 9, 1988, at the Birchmere Restaurant, 3901 Mt. Vernon Avenue in Alexandria, Virginia. It will start at 8:30 p.m., and tickets are $8 at the door. For more information, call the Birchmere at (703) 549-5919.

# # #

SAMPLE ISSUES-RELATED PRESS RELEASE

(Double-space all press releases)

This is a sample of incorporating issues into press release, although this is probably longer than preferred by most editors.

FOR IMMEDIATE RELEASE   Contact: Sheila Kahn
                                                                                    (301) 270-3873 (day)
                                                                                    (703) 573-4716 (eve)

Si Kahn and Cathy Fink will perform together on Friday, February 17, 1988 at the kick-off concert of the National Toxics Concert Tour. This performance (their third annual in Washington) will begin at 8 p.m. at the Hoover Auditorium, Commerce Building. The concert benefits Clean Water Action Project and the National Toxics Campaign, which seeks far-reaching changes in federal programs dealing with dangerous wastes in America's water, workplaces, and communities.

Si Kahn is a full-time grassroots and community organizer as well as one of the nation's best known topical songwriters. His song, "Aragon Mill," has been recorded by more than 20 groups in the U.S. and Great Britain. Cathy Fink is a spectacular banjo-picker and singer with exquisite voice; she sings traditional and contemporary folk music.

The goal of the national campaign against toxics is to accomplish reforms that will require greater disclosure of dangers, expanded cleanup of existing toxics problems, tighter restrictions on the disposal of presently generated toxic wastes, and alternative industry practices for reducing and preventing waste at its source. Clean Water Action Project's partner in this national campaign is Citizen Action. Citizen Action has successfully campaigned for policy changes on local, state, and national levels.

-more-

The National Clean Water Action Project office will undertake several tasks in this national campaign.

- Coordinating research identifying the extent and source of toxic contamination on a state-by-state basis.

- Channelling widespread public concern to national legislative efforts.

- Offering technical assistance in clean-up efforts.

- Drafting protective legislation.

The performance will be in the Herbert C. Hoover Auditorium of the Commerce Building on 14th Street N.W. between Pennsylvania and Constitution. The Metro's Federal Triangle stop is nearby, and street and lot parking is available. The auditorium is accessible to disabled persons, and the concert will be interpreted for the hearing-impaired. Child care will be available with advance registration.

Tickets are $6 in advance and $7 at the door. For information about child care and volunteer opportunities call Clean Water at (202) 638-7574. Tickets are available at the Bethesda Coop, Common Bookstores, Lammas Bookstore, The House of Musical Traditions, or on MasterCard and Visa by calling (202) 638-7574.

# # #

Clean Water Action Project is a nonprofit national citizens' organization working for clean and safe water at an affordable cost, control of toxic chemicals, and preservation of our nation's natural resources.

Photos and interviews available.

FORM 7:4

SAMPLE MEDIA CONTACT SHEET

Name of publication/station _____

_____

Type of media _____

(___) Newspaper; (___) Radio; (___) T.V.; (___) Magazine

Contact person _____

Address _____

_____

Phone _____

Community/Public Affairs Director _____

Phone _____

Referred by _____

References to others _____

Circulation/broadcast audience _____

Deadlines/lead time required (10th of preceding month, one week, etc.)

_____

Locally-produced programs/feature columns _____

_____

Promotions/special events coordinator _____

Phone _____

Preferred copy form (live, notes, recorded, length: 20/30/or 60 seconds)

_____

Complimentary tickets (how many offered) _____

_____

Packet mailed (date)_____ Follow-up: _____

Comments _____

SAMPLE PUBLIC SERVICE ANNOUNCEMENT (PSA)

Start: January 2, 1988.

Discontinue: January 20, 1988.

Contact: Sheila Kahn (301) 270-3873

20 SECONDS

On Saturday, January 19, at 8 p.m., a benefit concert of original topical folk songs by Si Kahn will take place in the Herbert Hoover Auditorium in the Commerce Department Building.

Proceeds will benefit Grassroots Leadership, Inc. For more information, call *(your organization)* at *(your phone number)*.

_____

_____

_____

30 SECONDS

On Saturday, January 19, at 8 p.m. a benefit performance by Si Kahn of original topical folk songs will take place in the Herbert Hoover Auditorium (in the Commerce Building). Tickets are $7 at the door or $6 in advance by calling *(ticket outlet or your phone)*.

_____

_____

The proceeds from the concert will benefit Grassroots Leadership, Inc. and *(your organization)*. For more information on the concert and on *(your issue or organization)*, call *(your organization's phone number)*.

FORM 7:6

SAMPLE VIDEO/AUDIO RECORDING RELEASE

Director _____   Program _____

Address (City/State/Zip Code/Telephone) _____
_____

Artists grant permission to the above video/audio group to record _____
_____

on _____. The program director agrees that the rights of the artists will be fully protected and the following stipulations will be met:

1. All recording equipment will be set up and operational at the time of the Artists' soundcheck.
   Time: _____

2. Artists will be provided with a high-quality tape of the rough recording. The tape will be mailed to: _____
_____

   Attn: _____
   within 30 days of the recording. A copy of the *final edited version* of this program will be mailed to the above address *as soon as possible upon completion of final editing.*

3. Artists reserve editing rights over the recorded material in both image and/or audio form.

4. Permission from artists or artists' representative is required for all future broadcasts or sales. In addition, a fee must be negotiated between *(recording organization)* _____ and artists or artists' representative prior to the sale of this video/audio recording.

5. Programmer agrees that this recording of _____
   will *not* be broadcast simultaneously with the performance.

6. Credit will be given as follows:
_____

_____   _____
Program Representative   for Artists

Date _____   Date _____

Please return signed contract copy to: _____
_____
_____

SAMPLE VIDEO/AUDIO STATION BROADCAST RELEASE

Station _____

Street Address _____

City/State/Zip _____

_____

Telephone _____

_____ grants permission to the above station to broadcast the following tapes:

_____

_____

_____

on *(date)* _____

The station agrees that no commercial use or distribution to other commercial or non-commercial stations, individuals, etc., will be made of these tapes. The station further agrees that the rights of the artists will be fully protected, and the following stipulations will be met:

1. Permission is granted for broadcasting four (4) times per year for a period not to exceed two (2) years. Permission for artist or artists' representative is required for all future broadcasts.

2. Credit will be given as follows:

_____

_____

_____

_____   _____
Station Representative   For Artist

Date: _____   Date: _____

Please return signed contract copy to: _____

_____

_____

FORM 7:8

SAMPLE CLIP LICENSE AGREEMENT

AGREEMENT made and entered into as of the ____ day of _____, 19__, by and between the network and artists (licensee). Licensee's use of video tape recordings of the network programming shall be governed by the following terms and conditions.

SCOPE
The videotape recording (clip) which licensee is licensed to use hereunder is the following song(s) or segment(s): *(list artists and program)*

_____

_____

Licensee is granted a limited, non-exclusive license to use the clip, in connection with the following event or program:

_____

_____

Use of the clip by licensee or others for any other purpose or in connection with any other event or program is expressly prohibited.

COSTS
Duplication of the clip referenced herein shall be performed by the network. All expenses incurred by the network in connection with duplication, shipping, handling, or otherwise, together with a license fee of $_____, shall be paid by licensee upon presentation of an invoice to licensee at the following address:

_____

_____

_____

CREDITS
Licensee agrees to exhibit any and all visual credits inserted in the clip by the network during each exhibition of the clip, and to include any audio or visual credit requested by the network in each program in which the clip appears.

INDEMNITY
Licensee agrees to defend, indemnify, and hold harmless the network from and against any and all claims, demands, damages, actions, or other expenses, otherwise arising out of the acts or omissions of licensee or its agents, employees, affiliates, or contractors. Licensee acknowledges that it is responsible for any and all fees payable to any artist, musician, union, or guild, or to the copyright owner of any music contained in the clip, arising out of the use of the clip. Licensee agrees that it shall obtain prior consent to use the clip from any featured artist appearing in the clip. Licensee specifically recognizes that, in the case of a clip containing musical performances, any promotional use of the clip in excess of one minute and 15 seconds or news/magazine show use in excess of two minutes (as well as any use for any other purposes), will generate additional fees, payable to the American Federation of Musicians, which shall be the responsibility of licensee.

IN WITNESS WHEREOF, the parties have set their hands by their duly authorized representatives as of the day and year first above written.

_____   _____
Program Representative for artists   Network

By: _____   By: _____

Please return signed contract copy to: _____

                        _____

                        _____

ADVERTISEMENT SIZE CHART

Below is a sample of the kind of information you should send to potential advertisers so they can evaluate the opportunity, placement, and cost of advertising in your program. While the format below is set up to show dimensions for an 8-1/2" x 11" program, the sample cleary indicates what is required for any format. Just change the dimensions if your program size is different.

Once you have determined pricing for different size ads, you may add a price column to the format.

Special dimensions are available, including spreads, gatefolds, and inserts.

A special section is available for ads displaying business cards call for details.

Dimensions (Non-bleed)	Width	Height
Double Page Spread	15"	10"
Full Page (Live Area)	7"	10"
Full Page (Teim Size)	8-1/8"	10-7/8"
2/3 Page Vertical	4-5/8"	10"
1.2 Page Vertical	4-5/8"	7-3/8"
1/2 Page Horizontal	7"	4-7/8"
1/3 Page Vertical	2-1/4"	10"
1/3 Page Square	4-5/8"	4-7/8"
1/6 Page Vertical	2-1/4"	4-7/8"
1/6 Page Horizontal	4-5/8"	2-3/8"

Unit Size (Bleed)	Width	Height
Double Page Spread	16-3/4"	11-1/4"
Full Page	8-3/8"	11-1/4"
2/3 Page Vertical	5-1/2"	11-1/4"
1/2 Page Horizontal	8-3/8"	5-1/2"

PROGRAM AD SOLICITATION CONTACT FORM

Keep track of your potential advertisers with a form of this kind. Use one per business. Even if you talk to several people in one organization, put them all on the same sheet. If you have more than one person doing sales for you this is very important. Don't end up soliciting two ads from different departments of the same business.

Name of Firm _____

_____

Address _____

_____

_____

Contact person *(title)* _____

Phone number _____

Initial contact *(letter, phone, visit)* _____

_____

Date of contact _____

Response _____

Follow up _____

Size of ad *(full, vertical 1/2, horizontal 1/2, vertical 1/4, horizontal 1/4, 1/3 horizontal, sponsor)*

_____

Space reservation made: *(date)* _____ *(by whom)* _____

Fee received *(amount, date)* _____

Artwork received *(date, notes)* _____

_____

Source of lead _____

_____

Comments _____

_____

_____

_____

_____

FORM 10:1

SAMPLE "VOLUNTEERS WANTED" ANNOUNCEMENT

FOR IMMEDIATE RELEASE
(date)

Contact: Sheila Kahn
(301) 270-3873

CATHY FINK CONCERT ON *(date)*

Volunteers are needed to help with the Cathy Fink benefit concert for *(your organization)*. We are looking for house manager, lobby manager, child care workers, house doctor, and people who can help with mailings, concessions, ticket taking, ushering, postering, and silkscreening (tee shirts).

If you can help, please call *(your organization)* at (301) 270-3873 and ask for Sheila Kahn.

SAMPLE SIGN-UP ROSTER FOR VOLUNTEERS

*If you have a clear idea of what is happening when, it will be easier to find people willing to help with the task. It is easiest for a volunteer to commit to do a specific task at a specific time. A simple list will be a great help. Have this all figured out before you call a meeting of your volunteers. Keep your meetings with them fun but organized (**do not waste their time**). List all the tasks, how many hours you need on each, and all the times you need their help with that task. Fill in their names as you go.*

Who can help with:

Telephones (to follow up press mailings) *(date, time, name)*

_____
_____
_____
_____

Telephones (to develop list of potential block sales) *(date, time, name)*

_____
_____
_____
_____

Telephones (to enlist other volunteers) *(date, time, name)*

_____
_____
_____
_____

Number tickets *(date, time, name)*

_____
_____
_____
_____

Prepare mailings (probably more than one date) *(date, time, name)*

_____
_____
_____
_____

Copying *(date, time, name)*

_____
_____
_____
_____

Assembly *(date, time, name)*

_____
_____
_____
_____

Envelope preparation *(date, time, name)*

_____
_____
_____
_____

Typing address labels *(date, time, name)*

_____
_____
_____
_____

Stuffing/sealing *(date, time, name)*

_____
_____
_____
_____

Postering *(date, time, name)*

_____
_____
_____
_____

Silkscreening tee shirts (if you are doing this) *(date, time, name)*

_____
_____
_____
_____

Contacting groups about lobby tables *(date, time, name)*

_____
_____
_____
_____

Taking tickets to outlets *(date, time, name)*

_____
_____
_____
_____

Plan concessions *(date, time, name)*

_____
_____
_____
_____

Baking *(date, time, name)*

_____
_____
_____
_____

Helping at reception *(date, time, name)*

_____
_____
_____
_____

Finding donated doorprizes *(date, time, name)*

_____
_____
_____
_____

Add others as you identify them

_____
_____
_____
_____

Day of the show availability and skills *(name, working hours)*

_____
_____
_____
_____
_____
_____
_____

SOUND SYSTEM WORKSHEET

Artists _____

Producer _____

Contact _____

Address _____

_____

_____

Phone (day) _____ Phone (evening) _____

Contractor _____
Contact _____
Address _____

Phone (day) _____ Phone (evening) _____

Hall _____
Address _____

Backstage phone _____
Load-in time _____
Hall size _____
Concert starting time _____
Stage dimensions _____
Sound check time _____

Equipment artists require _____

_____

_____

_____

_____

_____

_____

Equipment available from contractor _____

_____

_____

_____

_____

_____

_____

	Artists' Requirements	Available from Contractor
Mixer		
Number of channels		
Separate monitor mix		
EQ stages		
Microphones		
Number of vocal		
Suggested model		
Number of instrumental		
Suggested model		
Direct boxes		
Microphone stands		
Number of straight stands		
Number of boom stands		
Number of goosenecks		
Equalizer		
House		
Monitor		
Other signal		
processing equipment		
Amplifiers		
House		
Monitor		
Speakers		
House		
Monitor		
Other equipment		
Other requirements		

SAMPLE LIGHTING PLOT

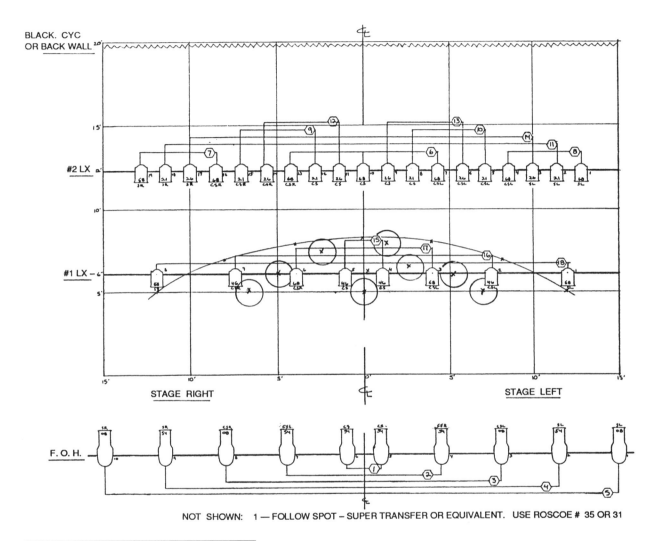

BLACK. CYC
OR BACK WALL

#2 LX

#1 LX

STAGE RIGHT   STAGE LEFT

F.O.H.

NOT SHOWN: 1 — FOLLOW SPOT – SUPER TRANSFER OR EQUIVALENT. USE ROSCOE # 35 OR 31

ELECTRICIAN'S SCHEDULE

DIMMER	CIRCUIT	PIPE / INST		FOCUS	COLOR
1		F.O.M.	5, 6	CS	2 X 54
2			4, 7	SL, SR	2 X 54
3			3, 8	CSL, CSR	2 X 08
4			2, 9	SL, SR	2 X 54
5			1, 10	SL, SR	2 X 08
6		2nd LX	7, 10, 13	CS BLUE	3 X 68
7			16, 19	SR BLUE	2 X 68
8			1, 4	SL BLUE	2 X 68
9			12, 15	CS, CSR AMB	2 X 21
10			5, 8	CSL, SL AMB	2 X 21
11			2, 18	SL, SR AMB	2 X 21
12			11, 14	CS, CSR RED	2 X 26
13			6, 9	CSL, CS RED	2 X 26
14			3, 17	SL, SR RED	2 X 26
15		1st LX	4, 5	CS MAG	2 X 46
16			2, 7	CSL, CSR MAG	2 X 46
17			3, 6	CSL, CSR BLUE	2 X 68
18			1, 8	SL, SR BLUE	2 X 68

NOTES

— CHOOSE HOUSE PIPES CLOSEST TO MEASUREMENT GIVEN.

— X – REPRESENTS PLACEMENT OF MUSICIAN.
THIS VARIES WITH SIZE OF STAGE
PLACE ON 4' CENTER WHEN POSSIBLE

— GELS LISTED ARE ROSCOE

— K E Y —

PAR 64 MFL 1K
— IF PARS NOT AVAILABLE.
USE 8" FRESNEL 1K

6 X 16 LEXO 1K

DIMMER #

INST. #

COLOR

FOCUS

— TOURING PLOT —

DESIGNED BY:	**KIM LAFONE**
REVISED BY:	

REVISION	NOTES

SCALE 1/8" = 1'0"

SAMPLE DAY OF SHOW SCHEDULE

It's important to remember that this schedule can vary widely, depending on the event's size and complexity, the technical requirements, how early the hall is available, the artists' arrival time, whether they have interviews, what other activities you've arranged with the artists (receptions, dinners, interviews, etc.), and generally what type of scheduling the artists prefer. For example, some artists like to arrive in town, do a sound check in mid-afternoon, then go home, and relax until just prior to the show. Others will wish to have the sound check as close to show time as possible.

Allow enough time to set up and have a full sound and light check, give the artists time to relax before the concert (assign someone to drive the artists or run errands as needed), and have enough advance time for ticket sales and seating so the concert can start on time. The tasks involved can be hired out to experienced professionals, or you can use responsible staff members or trained volunteers. Whatever you decide, the final scheduling requires cooperation and goodwill from all sides, as well as flexibility around last-minute changes (delayed plane arrivals, etc.).

1:00 p.m.   Piano tuning.

1:30 p.m.   Lighting crew hangs lights and gels and aims — keeping interpreter and all stage placements in mind.

2:00 p.m.   Pick up artists at airport, take to radio interviews, or to lodging.

2:30 p.m.   Sound crew unloads and sets up sound equipment.

3:30 p.m.   First volunteers or staff arrive at hall; set up for reception; set up artists' dressing room; alphabetize all press, complimentary, and will- call tickets for box office.

4:30 p.m.   Sound is set up and tested, ready for artists' technical check. Bring artists to hall for sound check and final setting lights.

5:00 p.m.   More volunteers or staff arrive for lobby set-up and reception help.
Bring all materials to hall for evening: box office and administrative supplies, raffle/auction materials, records, programs, tables, literature, concessions, signmaking materials, etc.
Set up lobby for all activities.
Make and post signs (bathrooms, prices of items for sale, box office, etc.).

6:00 p.m.   Sound check completed.
Dinner or reception.
Prepare box office for opening.

6:30 p.m.   Ticket takers, ticket sellers, ushers, child care people arrive.
Food for concession sale arrives.
Box office opens.

7:00 p.m.   Doors open.
             (Reception clean up.)
             All talent in hall — artists, interpreter, emcee.

8:00 p.m.   Concert begins.

9:00 p.m.   Intermission.
             Lobby activities (door prizes, raffles, sales, records, etc.).

9:20 p.m.   Begin second set.
             Pack up box office and finish lobby activities.
             Account for ticket sales. Prepare bank deposits.
             Settle with hall.

10:30 p.m.   Concert ends.
             Final lobby sales, album signing.
             Strike sound, chairs, lights.
             Thank all involved in show.

11:00 p.m.   Clean up hall.
             Strike lobby tables and set ups.
             Prepare account of record sales; package unsold albums for return.
             Settle with and pay artists. Take artists to lodging.

12:00 p.m.   Cleaning finished; vacate hall.

STAFFING SCHEDULE

Event _____
Date _____
Facility _____
Producers _____
Assistant _____
House manager *(name, hours)* _____
Stage manager *(name, hours)* _____
Sound company _____
Arrival _____
Light company _____
Arrival _____
Piano tuner *(name, scheduled tuning)* _____
House electrician _____
Arrival _____
Stage hands *(hours)* _____
_____
_____

Loaders *(hours)* _____
_____
_____

House sound crew _____
_____

House light crew _____
_____

Hospitality coordinator _____
Caterer _____
Arrival _____
Meal schedules _____
_____
_____

Backstage security *(hours)* _____
_____

Box office manager *(hours)* _____
Box office staff _____
_____

Head usher _____
Ushers _____
_____
_____
_____

Ticket takers _____

_____

_____

_____

_____

Front security _____

_____

_____

_____

_____

Child care coordinator *(hours)* _____
Workers _____

_____

_____

_____

_____

Others _____

_____

_____

_____

_____

_____

_____

_____

SAMPLE STAGE DIAGRAMS

Below and on the following page are sample stage diagrams for two different kinds of performances. Artists frequently send a stage diagram with their signed contracts. If they do not, the following layouts may give you some ideas. Final positioning of mics, instruments, and other required pieces of furniture will be done during the technical check.

WORKING AREA
APPROX 20' x 25'

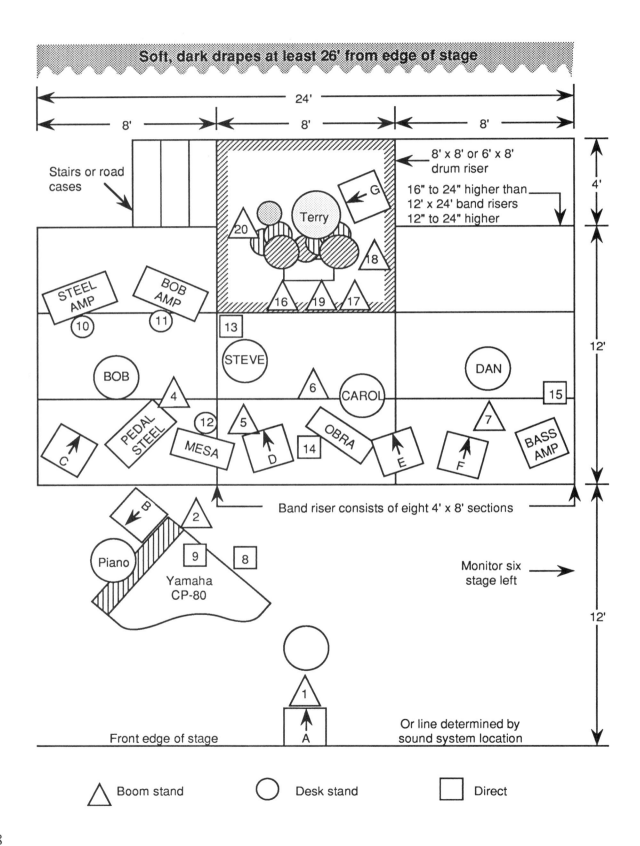

CHECKLIST OF THINGS TO TAKE TO THE HALL ON THE DAY OF THE SHOW

Unless the hall or vendors handle it, get plenty of change for the box office and sales tables. For a large concert at which you plan to sell many tickets at the door, you might have to give your bank advance notice for them to provide you with enough small bills. For weekend shows, remember to go to the bank on Thursday or Friday.

Here is a list that will begin to jog your imagination:

- ___ Programs, national and local
- ___ Records
- ___ Door prizes
- ___ Box to pick winners from
- ___ Pens and pencils, mailing list forms
- ___ Tickets on hold, alphabetized
- ___ Envelopes for tickets
- ___ Tickets for sale
- ___ Cash boxes, for box office and concessions
- ___ Bank bags
- ___ Deposit slips
- ___ Bank stamp — *FOR DEPOSIT ONLY*
- ___ Stamp with your organization name (save time at ticket sellers' window when people write checks)
- ___ Check book, SIGNED checks for artists, technicians, whoever else gets paid. (Sign them ahead of time or be sure a signator is there to do it on the spot.)
- ___ Receipt book
- ___ MasterCard/Visa machine and forms
- ___ Sign-making material and tape, staples, string, scissors. Signs you may need include a menu/price list for concessions, *No Food In Auditorium, Box Office, Records Available Here, All Profits After Expenses Go To . . . , Restrooms, No Smoking, Child Care, Wheelchair Entrance, Press,* etc.
- ___ Tee shirts
- ___ Literature
- ___ Tables
- ___ Cash in small bills and enough change for food concession
- ___ List of volunteers and name tags
- ___ Inventory forms for records, tee shirts, etc.
- ___ Refreshments for crew, artists
- ___ Refreshments, supplies for child care
- ___ Articles for artists' dressing room (ironing board and iron, flowers, etc.)
- ___ Additional stage equipment/props (stool, rug, straight-backed chair, water glasses and pitcher, guitar stands, music stands, plants, flowers)
- ___ Budget settlement form and receipt copies

SAMPLE EVENT EVALUATION

To: Production Crew, Area Coordinators, and Volunteers of Concert
From: Production Coordinator

Please take a few minutes to comment on the items listed below. We would like this feedback to help us sharpen our production skills and be able to identify areas where we did well, as well as areas where there is room for improvement. These evaluation forms will become part of the permanent files of this event and serve as a tool to complete our own assessment of this event. Thanks for taking the time to complete the evaluation. And, especially, thanks for helping to make this a successful event.

Name _____   Date _____

Responsibility _____   Concert _____

1.   What is your evaluation of your particular job/responsibility? _____
_____
_____
_____

What did you do well/what worked well for you? _____
_____
_____
_____

What did not go well/what would you do differently next time? _____
_____
_____
_____

2.   What is your feedback/evaluation of how things went in your area the day of the event?
Note changes or improvements you would make _____
_____
_____
_____

3.   What is your feedback/evaluation of how things went in general the day of the concert?
Note changes or improvements _____
_____
_____
_____

4.   What support did you get to do your job? Note lack of support or specific areas of
support which helped you _____
_____
_____
_____

5. Please comment/evaluate the following areas to the best of your ability recognizing that not all of us know what was involved in each area.

a. Ticket sales _____
_____
_____
_____

b. Publicity _____
_____
_____
_____

c. Door _____
_____
_____
_____

d. Lobby _____
_____
_____
_____

e. Lobby hall display tables _____
_____
_____
_____

f. Program book _____
_____
_____
_____

g. Hospitality/back stage _____
_____
_____
_____

h. Stage _____
_____
_____
_____

i. Sound _____
_____
_____
_____

j. Lights _____
_____
_____
_____

k. Performer friends _____

_____

_____

_____

l. Artists *(et al.)* _____

_____

_____

_____

m. Set-up/take down _____

_____

_____

_____

n. Interpreters _____

_____

_____

_____

o. The actual event _____

_____

_____

_____

p. Emcee/announcements _____

_____

_____

_____

q. Technical crew _____

_____

_____

_____

r. Work-exchange/volunteers _____

_____

_____

_____

s. Security _____

_____

_____

_____

t. The reception _____

_____

_____

_____

u. Overall production _____

_____

_____

_____

v. The hall/dressing areas/hospitality area _____

_____

_____

_____

w. Accessibility/outreach _____

_____

_____

_____

x. Should we do a production on this scale ever again? Why or why not? When?_____

_____

_____

_____

y. Budget _____

_____

_____

_____

Other comments _____

_____

_____

_____

Many, many thanks!!

ACCESSIBILITY

Here are copies of the logos being used to indicate that a concert is being interpreted for the hearing-impaired and that the facility is wheelchair-accessible.

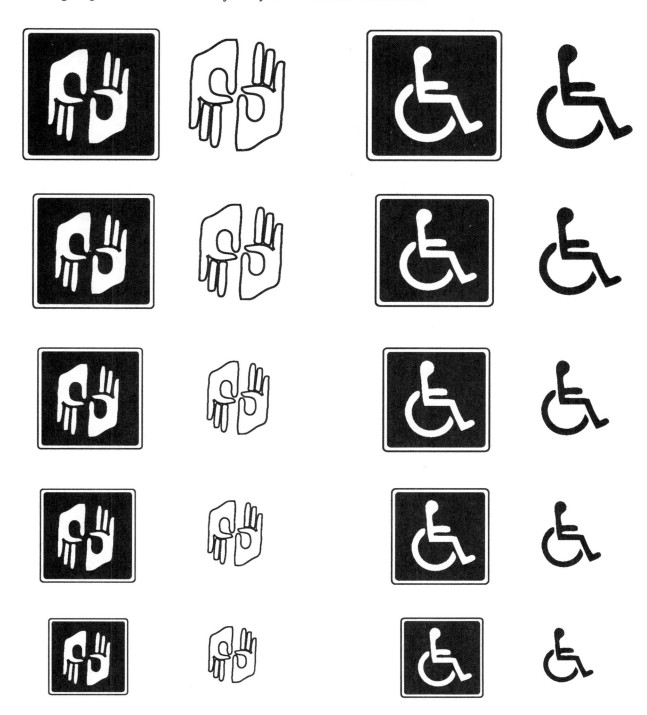

SAMPLE EVENT CHILD CARE INFORMATION

All ages

The following is a sample of an information sheet usually given to parents of children who attend child care.

Dear Parents,

Welcome to our concert child care. We hope your child enjoys the program and you feel comfortable and secure about leaving your child with us. To ensure a successful and safe child care situation, we ask you to read these instructions, *fill out the appropriate accompanying form(s),* and follow the suggested procedures about leaving your children. If you have any questions, please ask the staff. Our child care coordinator is _____.
She or he will be happy to talk with you about any of your concerns.

Address of Care _____ Phone _____

1. Please complete the registration process before leaving. We will not accept children whose parents have not filled out all forms and signed children in on the sign-in sheet.

2. Please use the adhesive tape and markers at the registration desk *to label all clothing and other belongings.* We will try our best to keep track of your child's clothes, toys, etc. However, we cannot be responsible for lost belongings, so please do not leave items of value (monetary or sentimental) such as jewelry or "special" clothes.

3. We will serve _____ snacks during the concert. *Children with special dietary needs should have food provided by the parents* — please make these arrangements with the coordinator. Also please make the staff aware of any *children with food allergies.*

4. We are sorry, but we will only take children who have advance reservations for child care. If you *do not* have reservations, please see the coordinator to place your child on a waiting list. You will be contacted *if and when* openings occur. We are placing this limit on the care to be sure of having the space and staff to do a good job.

5. We will try to make sure all children are happy in child care. However, if your child becomes ill or is too upset to participate, we will ask you to take your child out of care. If your child is in the older group, and cannot conform to the safety and behavior rules for that group, the staff will contact you.

6. If for any reason we must contact you, a staff member will first check for you in the concert hall area you indicated on your intake form. If we cannot find you, the conference coordinator will page you, or a security person will try to locate you. Please indicate on the intake form where you will be. It is important in cases of emergencies to be able to find parents quickly.

7. Please *read the medical release form carefully and sign it*. If your child is injured we will make every effort to contact you but we must have a signed medical release form so hospital personnel can treat your child if you cannot be located.

8. Child care is open from _____ to _____ p.m. *There will be a late charge of $5.00* for every half hour after _____ p.m.

9. If you have any questions, please contact the coordinator. Enjoy the concert.

SAMPLE EVENT CHILD CARE REGISTRATION FORM

Over 2-1/2 Years

Please *print* and answer all questions.

Child's name _____

Parent/responsible adult _____

Home address _____ Home phone _____

1.   Child's allergies (if any) _____

_____

2.   What should we know about your child? Please list any special needs, fears, likes, or dislikes your child has. We would like to know as much as possible about your child to help her or him enjoy child care.

_____

_____

_____

3.   Does your child need to nap? When? Any special ritual before or after sleeping (e.g., go to the bathroom, read a story, have a back rub, etc.)?

_____

_____

_____

4.   Please state where you will be while your child is in child care during the concert (row and seat number, if possible).

_____

_____

5.   What adults other than you have permission to pick up your child? We will not release children to any adults other than you or those listed below.

    Name _____ Relationship _____

    Name _____ Relationship _____

    Name _____ Relationship _____

6.   What belongings did your child bring to child care? Please label them before leaving them with us. Please describe them below (e.g., "blue & white sweater," "Raggedy Ann doll," etc.).

    _____

    _____

7.   Child care closes promptly at _____ p.m. There is a late fee of $5.00 for every half hour after that time. Please contact the coordinator if you know you will be late.

8.   What time do you plan to pick up your child? _____

I have answered all questions and will follow all the rules for this event child care.

_____   _____
Date   Signature of parent or responsible adult

Please return this completed form to a staff member.

SAMPLE EVENT CHILD CARE REGISTRATION FORM

Infant or Toddler

Dear Parents of Infants or Toddlers,

Please read the information sheet for parents and take it with you. We ask you to fill out this form in detail to make child care as pleasant and safe as possible for your young child. Please be assured that our child care staff is qualified and experienced. The staff ratio is one adult to every three infants, and your baby will be with the same staff member during the entire concert except for _____ 15-minute breaks. Another staff member will see to your child's needs during those times. It is extremely important that you also fill in the medical consent form.

Please do not return to care until it is time to pick up your child unless we contact you (nursing mothers excepted, of course). We have found from experience that young children are easily upset if parents reappear before it is time to leave. Be sure to ask any questions you have of the staff before you say good-bye.

1. Child's name _____

2. Parent/responsible adult _____

3. Where you will be during the concert (*seat and row number, if possible*)

   _____

4. Child's allergies (if any) _____

   _____

5. Is this the first time your child has been left in group care?   [ ] Yes   [ ] No

6. If not, what kind of care is she or he used to (a play group, child care center, family day care, full-time, part-time, etc.)? _____

   _____

   _____

7. We will do our best to help your child become comfortable in the care center. However, if she or he is crying or otherwise upset, how long do you think we should wait before contacting you? _____

8. Did you bring your own food? If so, do you want your child fed anything besides the food you brought? For example, may your child have whole milk if she or he runs out of the formula you brought for her or him? *(Label all bottles and food containers with your child's full name.)*

    _____

    _____

    If you want us to feed your child, what kinds of food does she or he like to eat?

    _____

    _____

9. If you are a nursing mother, at approximately what times will you return to nurse?

    _____

10. When does your child nap and for how long? _____

    _____

    In what position does your child go to sleep best? _____

    Please tell us what routine you use in putting your child to sleep and in awakening her or him.

    _____

    _____

    Does your child cry when going to sleep or when awakening?   [ ] Yes   [ ] No

11. How does your child respond to diapering? Is this typically a fun or a difficult time? What routine do you use and is there a toy you use to distract your baby while diapering? Did you bring the toy with you? If so, please describe it below, and label it with your baby's full name.

    _____

    _____

Do you use any powders or ointments in diapering, and did you bring them along? If so, please label them with your baby's full name.

_____

_____

Did you bring a diaper bag with you? If so, please describe it below and label it.

_____

_____

12. If your child is in the toilet-training process, please tell us how you remind her or him to go to the bathroom. Do you have a set schedule?

_____

_____

_____

13. Does your child need diapers at nap time?   [ ] Yes   [ ] No

14. What words does your family use for urination and defecation? _____

_____

_____

15. Please tell us about any special fears or anxieties your child has and how you comfort her or him.

_____

_____

16. What activities does your child enjoy? _____

_____

17. How does your child let you know when she or he wants or needs something?

_____

_____

18. Is there anything else we should know about your child? _____

_____

19. What adults other than you have permission to pick up your child? We will not release children to any adults other than you or those listed below.

    Name _____ Relationship _____

    Name _____ Relationship _____

    Name _____ Relationship _____

20. What belongings did your child bring to child care? *Please label them before leaving them with us.* Please describe them (e.g., "blue and white sweater," "Raggedy Ann doll," etc).

_____

_____

21. Child care closes at _____ p.m. There is a late fee $5.00 for every half hour after that time. Please contact the coordinator if you know you will be late.

    What time do you plan to pick up your child? _____

22. I have answered all questions and will follow all the rules for this event child care.

_____   _____

Date   Parent's signature

Please return this completed form to a staff member.

SAMPLE EMERGENCY INFORMATION
AND MEDICAL RELEASE FORMS

(All ages)

EMERGENCY INFORMATION (Please print)

Child's name _____

Address _____ Home phone _____

Parent or other adult responsible for child during this event

Name _____ Relationship _____

Name _____ Relationship _____

Name _____ Relationship _____

Please list two friends or relatives who can be called if parent or responsible adult cannot be reached. Please list people who are not at this concert and who can be reached.

Name _____ Home phone _____ Work phone _____

Address _____ Relationship to child _____

Name _____ Home phone _____ Work phone _____

Address _____ Relationship to child _____

Child's doctor _____ Phone _____

Child's medical number, if any _____

Any known allergies to medication? _____

255

Medical Release

Please read, date, and sign.

I give my child permission to participate in the event child care provided for this concert. I understand that participation is purely voluntary and that the sponsor and staff do not assume liability in case of injury.

I hereby authorize _____ *(name of coordinator and/or her or his delegate)* and staff into whose care the minor listed below has been entrusted as agents for the undersigned to consent to x-ray examinations, anesthetic, medical or surgical diagnosis, or treatment and hospital care which is deemed advisable by, and is to be rendered under the general or special supervision of any physician and surgeon licensed under the provisions of the Medical Practice Act.

It is understood that this authorization is given in advance of any specific diagnosis treatment or hospital care being required but is given to provide authority and power on the part of my aforesaid agents to give specific consent to any and all such diagnoses, treatment, or hospital care which the aforementioned physician in the exercise of her/his best judgment may deem advisable.

_____

Child's name

_____   _____

Date   Signature of parent or responsible adult

SAMPLE IMMIGRATION DOCUMENTATION LETTERS

Following are sample letters written by individuals in the performing arts illustrating the kind of affidavit required to encourage the United States Immigration and Naturalization Services to issue an entry visa to a non-U.S.-citizen performer. Remember, the following letters are just samples of successful letters used in the past. You need to solicit letters from appropriate people in your community or from those acknowledged experts in the performing art of the individuals you are trying to bring into the United States. All letters of this nature should be sent on the professional or personal letterhead of the author.

DECLARATION OF *(AUTHOR OF LETTER)*

SECTION 1

I am a musician and actress with 35 years of professional experience. My work is included on more than 20 records. I have appeared in dozens of plays in the United States and abroad as well as in several films. I am a member of the Actors' Equity of America, the American Federation of Television and Radio Artists, and BMI (Broadcast Music, Inc.).

SECTION 2

I am familiar with the work of *(artists' names)* from *(country)*, having heard their recordings. *(Artists' names)* have created music that is both original and yet an excellent example of the folkloric tradition of their country.

SECTION 3

As a professional expert in the field, I can state without hesitation that *(artists' names)* are leading contributors in the field of music and that they are of distinguished merit and ability. I feel strongly that it is important to allow international artists entrance to this country, since most U.S. citizens will not otherwise be able to enjoy their special skills and art, as we cannot all travel to their countries.

* * * * *

I hereby state under penalty of perjury under the laws of the United States that the above statement is true and correct.

Executed this _____ day of _____, 19_____, in the City of
_____, State of _____.

_____
Signature

DECLARATION OF *(AUTHOR OF LETTER)*

SECTION 1

I am the President of *(company name)*, a very well-respected independent record production and distribution company formed in 1972. I have had a leadership role in the company for the past seven years, and am a member of the Board of Directors of the National Association of Recording Arts and Sciences. We have a catalog of more than 40 titles, have sold more than one million records, and distribute the works of a number of Latin American musicians.

SECTION 2

I have heard *(artists' names)* perform, both in *(country)* and in the USA. They are a very gifted team, and thrill the crowds with their beautiful original compositions in the folkloric tradition. They are eloquent and extraordinary representatives of the people of their country and are often asked for by concert-goers in the USA. I am sure a return trip by all would be well-received.

SECTION 3

As a professional expert in the field, I can state without hesitation that *(artists' names)* are leading contributors in the field of music and that they are of distinguished merit and ability. As with many international artists, unless they are allowed entrance into this country, most U.S. citizens will be deprived of their special skills and art, as we cannot all travel to their countries. It will enrich the cultural life of our communities to sponsor them here.

* * * * *

I hereby state under penalty of perjury under the laws of the United States that the above statement is true and correct.

Executed this _____ day of _____, 19_____, in the City of _____, State of _____.

_____
Signature

READER FEEDBACK

Please complete and mail to Redwood Cultural Work, P.O. Box 10408, Oakland, CA 94610. Thanks for taking the time!

1. How many concerts have you previously produced?

    [ ] 0   [ ] 1   [ ] 2-10   [ ] 10-50   [ ] 50 or more   [ ] more than 50 per year

2. Are you a commercial producer, non-profit presenter, or benefitting organization? _____

    _____

3. Did you attend a workshop or course where *Note by Note, A Guide to Concert Production* was used as a text or resource? _____

    _____

4. What chapters or sections were most useful to you? _____

    _____

    _____

    _____

5. What chapters or sections were least useful to you? _____

    _____

    _____

6. Are there glossary terms you wish we had defined? _____

    _____

    _____

7. Did you reproduce sections for other crew members? Which ones? _____

_____

_____

_____

8. What recommendations do you have for our next edition? _____

_____

_____

9. Will you recommend this book for others to use? Why or why not? _____

_____

_____

_____

Thank you for completing this feedback form. It will be useful to us in planning for the next edition to more specifically answer your questions. Would you like to be on the Redwood mailing list to receive notice of future editions and artist/record information?

Name _____

Address _____

City _____

260

Appendix B: GLOSSARY

Accessibility. Making sure your event is available to community members with special needs and physical abilities, i.e., hearing- and visually-impaired, using wheelchairs, etc.

Acoustics. The sound-transmitting qualities of a concert hall.

Advance sales. Making tickets available to the general public through specified ticket outlets and/or the hall box office prior to the actual performance.

Advancing the show. Means making personal contact with the artists' representative in charge of that particular aspect of the show and to review carefully the technical rider, as well as other details including lights, dressing room, hospitality, accessibility, etc.

Agency discount. Discount given by the publication to the ad agency that sells most of its advertising space.

Alternative outlets. The use of local merchants and organizations to help sell tickets, usually to reach a special audience.

Amplifiers. Sound equipment to boost the signals fed from the stage to the speakers.

American Sign Language (ASL). The language used by most deaf and hearing-impaired people in the United States.

Artist guarantee. The minimum guaranteed amount you agree to pay the artist.

Artist's representative. The person responsible for acting on the artist's behalf with producers, technicians, etc.

Author's alterations or *Author's correc-*

tions. In typesetting or printing, changes and additions in copy after it has been set in type. Often called *AAs* or *ACs*.

Billing. How the names of the artists, producer, venue, and sponsors appear on promotional materials, including the size, typestyles, treatment, and placement of names and logos.

Binding. Converting single printed sheets into booklets, books, or magazines.

Bleed. Anything that goes over the edge of the paper. It means printing on over-sized paper and trimming it to create a *going off the page* effect. It adds to the cost of the project.

Block ticket sales. Tickets offered at a slight discount to groups, usually of at least five people.

Blueline. A proof to check position and quality of finished products before printing. The varying shades of blue in this proofing method indicate the various colors in the printed piece. This is the last possible time for any changes or corrections before a job is completed.

Booking. The process of securing the necessary elements for a performance, including the artists, the venue, the sound and light systems, etc.

Booking agent. Hired by the artist to secure bookings. Her or his functions are usually limited to booking only.

Broadcast media. Radio and television, including public, commercial, and cable.

Calendar listing. The simplest form of publicity. A calendar listing states the bare facts about your event: time, date, location, artists; usually included in a regular feature or section of the paper or broadcast with other events happening in your community.

Camera-ready copy. Written or designed material for an ad or brochure which has been set up for the printer with all stats, type, and halftones in position.

Cancellation clause. Provision in the artists' contract that specifies procedures to follow if the event is cancelled for any reason. Often contracts require percentages of the agreed-upon artists' fees depending on the reason for the cancellation and its proximity to the actual performance date.

Cash discount. Many publications give a small discount if you pay the cost of the ad when you deliver the copy.

Complimentary tickets. Tickets given to individuals free of charge. Most artists' contracts specify a certain number of *comps.* Tickets often are also given away for publicity purposes, to media representatives, volunteers, or others who donate their time and expertise to your production.

Concessions. Any product offered for sale at your event, such as tapes, records, tee shirts, candy, beverages, buttons, etc.

Co-op advertising. Sharing the cost of paid ads with the local distributor of your artists' records, the local record store, buying space in the regular ad your venue runs or a similar arrangement.

Copy deadline. The time at which all written information for your program is due to be typeset.

Cue sheet. List of when the lighting changes are to take place during the performance.

Cues. Agreed-upon signals or actions to alert the artists and technical staff to begin the production or to make needed changes in the set, sound, or lighting.

Cropping. Indicating which part of a photo/illustration you do *not* want to show in the printed piece.

Deadwood. Tickets left unsold.

Desktop publishing. Using the more sophisticated software and portable computers available today to do the layout and design of your promotional and publicity materials.

Direct box. Matches the signal level of the musical instruments to the level needed by the microphone inputs of the mixer.

Direct mail. Sending promotional materials directly to potential concert goers, using a specialized mailing list.

Distortion. Different microphones having varying tolerances for sound levels and ranges.

Door sales. Tickets that are sold only on the day of the performance, at the concert hall box office or door, before the performance begins.

Drop count. Special count of ticket stubs *dropped* by the ticket takers into a special container to determine actual attendance at the performance.

Dummy. Copies of camera-ready art pasted together and trimmed to show size folding, what is on front, what is on back, etc. It is helpful to send a dummy to the printer with your camera-ready art.

Electronic crossover. Used to divide the sound into separate low-, mid- and high-frequency bands and route them to separate speakers designed to handle that frequency.

Enlargement. Making the size of the original piece of art or type larger.

Equalizer (EQ). Divides the audio spectrum into different frequency bands and provides control over those frequencies to eliminate distortion and feedback.

Feedback. The howling regeneration of sound caused by the microphones picking up sound coming out of the speakers then reamplifying it.

Flat fee. Agreement by artists or producer to work on an event solely for a specified amount of money.

Frequency discount. A reduced rate often available if an advertisement is run more than once in a publication within a specified timeframe.

Front money. Money needed to cover initial costs before any ticket revenues are received, e.g., hall rental, sound system costs, publicity.

Gaffers tape. Also known as duct tape. Used to bind and place the cords and cables so that people don't trip over them.

Galley proofs. Sheets of typeset copy from the type shop which is then pasted up in the right order by the layout artist or graphic designer.

Gatefolds. Oversize pages in a program or brochure which are specially folded to fit the final published piece.

Gel. Special cellophane covers to change the colors of the lights.

General admission. Also known as unreserved seating, allowing each patron to choose her or his own seat, usually on a first-come, first-served basis.

Gross potential. The total amount of money you can theoretically make from a production, including ticket revenues, ad book income, concessions, sponsors, etc.

Gross revenues. Total amount of money made from all aspects of a production. See gross potential.

Gutter. White space between columns of type or between two pages of facing copy.

Halftone. The reproduction of a photograph or continuous tone artwork which converts images into dots of various sizes so the images can be printed.

Headliner. The main performer at your event.

Honorarium. A payment given for services rendered in lieu of the standard fee.

Initial hold. Informal agreement with the management of a concert hall to hold a certain date for your event. The hall manager then will call and give you the first chance to make a more formal agreement and perhaps make a deposit to keep the hall if another group expresses interest in your date.

INS. The Immigration and Naturalization Service, a federal agency that makes decisions about who may visit the United States and/or become a permanent resident.

Laser printer. Sophisticated printer that works by a heat process (lasers), putting dots together to create letters.

Layout. A drawing of your ideas for a final printed piece indicating the position of type and/or photos/artwork on the page.

Leading. In typesetting, the spacing between lines of type.

Letter of agreement. Written agreement between a producer and artists specifying the details of the production.

Liability insurance. Insurance to cover any potential accidents or injuries to anyone involved in your event, including technical crew, artists, the hall staff, and the audience. Liability insurance is often required by law and/or the artists' contract.

Light board. The console that controls the stage lights.

Lighting design. How the stage and set are lit during the production.

Local distributor. The person or business in your area that sells recordings by your artist to wholesale and retail businesses.

Market survey. Polling the concert goers about how they learned about the concert to evaluate your promotional efforts.

Masthead. A newspaper, newsletter, or magazine's name as it appears in their

specific typeface, also called logotype.

Mechanical. Camera-ready artwork with all elements (type and artwork) in position. Used to print the final piece.

Microphones. Convert sound waves (from instruments or vocals) into electrical energy which is transmitted to the audience through the sound system.

Mixer. Takes signals from two or more sources (microphones, for example) and blends them together at levels set by the sound technician.

Monitor mix. Separate set of controls to adjust the sounds coming out of the monitors on stage, does not affect the sound the audience hears.

Monitors. Special speakers pointed toward the performers so that they can hear themselves.

Multiple entry visa. Authorization to travel in and out of the country repeatedly within a specified timeframe and for a specified purpose.

Natural market. The audience you can easily draw, familiar with your organization and the types of events you produce, the club or venue itself, or the artists performing.

Net income/revenue. Income from the event after total costs are covered.

Networking. Letting other organizations and clubs in your area know about your event in hopes they will support it and encourage their members to attend.

Opening act. A short performance designed to open the show and welcome the audience, usually by a local artist, before the major act begins.

Opportunity cost. The cost of choosing between two activities or alternatives because of scarce labor or materials.

Outreach. Special efforts to involve certain segments of the community or to reach a new and different, more diversified, audience.

Performer friend/liaison. Special persons whose responsibilities are to escort the artists and take care of any needs they may have from the time the artists arrive until the time the artists leave. This duty may be shared by more than one person if the artists will be in town for more than a couple of days or if a large party is involved.

Phonebanking or telemarketing. An organized effort to inform people about the concert by telephone. This is very labor-intensive work.

Pica. In typesetting, this is a unit of measurement of 12 points which is equivalent to approximately 1/6 of an inch. Picas are often used to indicate widths.

Plot. The plan for the lighting changes throughout the production.

Point. This is a unit of type measurement whereby 12 points equals one pica. 72 points equal approximately one inch. Type is measured in height by points.

Press clippings. A compilation of any articles or reviews on the production or the performers.

Press kit. This contains all the information anyone interested in your event will need. It should include a photograph,

biography, and credit list for each artist performing, and recent reviews of their work, if possible. It also should contain information about the date, time, and location of your event. If possible, advance press kits should include an album or tape of the artists' work, especially if the media contact is unfamiliar with it.

Press list. The formal comprehensive list of media contacts you believe should be informed about your event. This list should include print, broadcast, and electronic media, both local and national.

Press release. A special announcement of your event, targeted directly to inform the media. It contains all the pertinent information about the location, time, and artists performing.

Print media. Newspapers and magazines primarily (both local and national), although newsletters for sympathetic organizations should be included on your print media contact list.

Printer's error or PE. In typesetting, this refers to mistakes made by the typesetter and should be fixed at no charge.

Program book or adbook. The written program you offer to the people attending your event.

Promotion. Any and all activities you engage in to make the public aware of your event; activities designed to sell tickets to your event.

Promotional materials. Anything used to make the general public aware of your event, including press releases, publicity kits and photos, postcards, flyers, posters, PSAs, etc.

Proof or type galley. See galley proofs.

Public Service Announcements (PSAs). Used by broadcast media for nonprofit or charity organizations and for events that are open to the public without charge. As they are legally required to broadcast a certain number of PSAs, it is a good way to reach a large audience with information about your event.

Rap sheet. Simple script with the pertinent data about your event to be used by volunteers when answering information calls or marketing.

Reduction. Making a piece of art or type smaller than its original size.

Release form. A formal agreement by the artists to tape a copy of their performance to be used in a later broadcast. The release form should state the purpose of the taping, specify how it may be used, how often, and how long it may be used.

Reproduction proof or type galley or galley proof. The actual type that will be pasted up to create your camera-ready art. Copies of the type galley are what you will proofread and mark for corrections/changes.

Reserved seats. Assigning each patron a specific seat location, usually printed on their tickets.

Road manager. A professional employed by the artist to ensure that all technical and logistical details involved with the performance go smoothly.

Rush work. Last-minute changes after the agreed-upon deadline with the printer or graphic designer. Most printer and designers charge extra for this last-minute work.

Sans serif. In typesetting these are letter without serifs. See serif.

Scaled ticket prices. Offering different ticket prices for different hall sections, based upon the quality of the seats; reserved seating is used.

Screen. Used to make a halftone from a photograph/illustration. The screen creates a series of dots from tones. The dots allow the printer to print the image.

Serif. Any of the short lines stemming from and at an angle to the upper and lower ends of the strokes of a letter.

Set. The artists' actual performance time.

Settlement. The final tally and distribution of revenue from the event among production staff, artist, and venue.

Settling up. Paying the artist, the hall, the technical crew, and anyone else involved in putting together your event.

Sliding scale. Offering a percentage of the tickets to your event at reduced prices for people with lower incomes or special needs.

Snake. Used by the sound system, an extra-long cable that is really many cables, all bundled together.

Sound board. The console that controls the various components of the sound system.

Sound/light checks. Times set aside before the performance begins for tests to ensure that all equipment is functioning properly and the artists are comfortable with the stage set. This is also the time to work out and agree upon cues.

Sound displacement. The way sound reflects off various objects depending on the size and structure of your venue.

Space reservation deadline. The time by which you must reserve ad space for your event with your local newspaper.

Speakers. Converts the electrical energy sent from the microphones back into sound, which goes out into the audience.

Specifications. The exact sizes of the pages and ads to be included in the ad book.

Spikes. Markings on the stage to indicate where performers or instruments are to be placed.

Spillover. When the lighting from the stage area goes into the audience or the wings of the stage.

Split point. The net income (after expenses, artists', and producer fees) to be divided by producer and artist. The percentage is agreed upon prior to the event and specified in the performance contracts.

Sponsorship. An arrangement with a local business, nonprofit organization, radio station, or similar supporting organization to help with the costs of your concert in exchange for having their name on the publicity and promotional materials distributed.

Spreads. In advertising terms, information that reads across two pages.

Stock. Type of paper or other materials upon which to print.

Strike the set. The process of cleaning up the concert hall after the performance has concluded. Dressing rooms and the backstage area are included in striking the set.

Subscription tickets. A special agreement with the performance venue whereby tickets to your event are sold as part of a series of performances at the same venue.

Tag-along mailing. Using the newsletter of a sympathetic organization to publicize your concert with an announcement, calendar listing, or flyer.

Technical rider. The part of the artists' contract that specifies the exact type of instruments, staging, sound and light equipment required by the artists to perform, as well as a schedule for rehearsals and performances.

Ticket commission. A fee paid to your outlets for selling your tickets — usually a small percentage of the face value of the ticket above a certain minimum.

Ticket counts. Regular periodic checks with your ticket outlets to determine how ticket sales are going and whether extra publicity or promotional efforts are needed.

Ticket outlets. Any business that agrees to sell tickets to your event to the general public, including local businesses and/or professional computerized outlets.

Timeline. The actual written planning schedule and tasks to be accomplished before the event, including the day of the event.

TTY phone. A telephone specifically

designed for the deaf and hearing-impaired, it is connected to a keyboard and printer so that the caller can communicate in writing.

Type galley or proof. See galley proof.

Union crew. Members of the production staff who also are members of the local stage or musicians union.

Venue. The hall or auditorium where your event will take place.

Visa. An official authorization attached to a passport granted by the federal gov

ernment allowing entry and travel within the United States.

Windscreens. Covers added to the microphones to prevent popping sounds.

Work and turn. Pasting information in position head to head or foot to foot so that the sheets can be printed more economically. Ask the printer for details on how mechanicals should be prepared.

Work exchange. Agreement with certain individuals for preproduction work or professional services in exchange for complimentary tickets to the event.

Appendix C: RESOURCES

APPENDIX C: Resources

The following resources offer practical guidelines for planning, preparing, and promoting fundraising campaigns,as well as printing and production.

Allen, Herb. *The Bread Game*, Glide Publications, 1974.

Bakal, Carl. *An Investigation into the Hidden World of the Multi-billion Dollar Charity Industry*, Times Books, 1979.

Bayley, T.D. *The Fundraiser's Guide to Successful Campaigns*, McGraw-Hill, 1987.

Brace, Thomas E. *The Guide to Raising Money from Private Sources*, Oklahoma Press, 1979.

Brakeley, George A. *Tested Ways to Successful Fundraising*, Amacom, 1982.

Brown, Jeff. *How to Produce and Promote Small Concerts*, 135 West 2nd Street, Juneau, Alaska 99801, 1981.

Connors, Tracy D. *The Nonprofit Organization Handbook (practical guidelines on how to hold special events)*, McGraw-Hill, 1980.

DeSoto, Carole. *For Fun and Funds*, Prentice-Hall, 1984.

Dunn, Thomas G. *How to Shake the New Money Tree*, Penguin (Paper), 1988.

Flanagan, Joan. *The Grass Roots Fundraising Book*, Arlington, 1982.

Getting It Printed, Coast to Coast Books, Portland.

Green, Danielle. *Guidelines to the Making of a Successful Home Party Benefit*, Redwood Cultural Work, 1987.

Gurin, Maurice. *What Volunteers Should Know for Successful Fundraising*, Arlington, 1981.

Knowles, Helen. *How to Succeed in Fundraising Today*, Cumberland Press, 1975.

Nielsen, Waldemar A. *The Golden Donors*, E. P. Dutton, 1985.

Pocket Pal, International Paper Company, New York.

Schneiter, Paul H. & Nelson, Donald T. *The Thirteen Most Common Fundraising Mistakes and How to Avoid Them*, Taft Group (Paper), 1982.

Sheerin, Mira. *How to Raise Top Dollars from Special Events*, Public Service Materials, 1984.

Seymour, Harold J. *Design for Fundraising*, McGraw-Hill, 1960.